THE SPELL CASTER

Contents

Author's Note

This series contains subject matter that might be difficult for some readers: Mild to moderate fantasy violence (scenes of conflict with injuries/death, not described in graphic detail); high control groups (cults) and religious abuse; emotional abuse, manipulation, and gaslighting by parents and authority figures; depiction of war-related PTSD; open door, consensual love scenes.

This book contains a scene of a parent grabbing their adult child by the arm and causing injury.

Please take care of yourself and reach out if you would like more specific details.

For you, the one who believes in hope in the face of impossible odds.

THE UNITED STATES
OF AMERICA
THE NORTHERN
SEA CIRCLE
THE MOUNTAIN
CIRCLE
THE TIDEWATER
CIRCLE
THE HILLSONG
CIRCLE
THE SALTMARSH
CIRCLE
THE CYPRESS
CIRCLE

Chapter 1

LAYLA

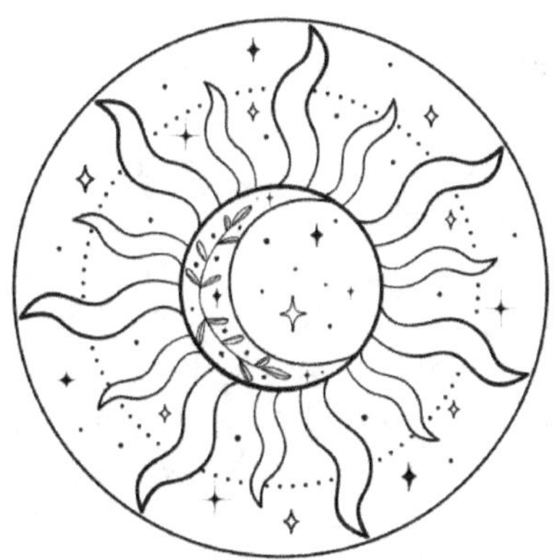

The summoning room was darkening, the arched stone windows flooded with gold as the sun set. I hadn't stood up to turn on the electric light. The scent of hot beeswax and herbs had faded in the hours since the candles burned down. I was freezing, curled small in the center of the imposing circular chamber.

My face had dried, and my hands were steady enough now to remove the evidence of my failed spell—the one last chance I had given myself.

My eyes ached as I drew myself up. It was time to face the truth—without a demon familiar, I could not be a spell caster.

I delayed, scraping the wax and buffing out the burn marks until the polished marble floor gleamed. Not a hint remained of the intricate spellwork I'd spent hours on my knees tracing.

Now all that was left was to deliver the news that would break the hearts of everyone I'd ever known. No witch of magical ability had ever failed at summoning before.

Numbly, I straightened my tea-colored skirt and smoothed a hand over my long dark hair. I cracked open the door of the summoning room and squinted into the hallway full of still-bright banks of windows. The council building was mostly empty this time of day, but I didn't want anyone to see me.

Keeping quiet on the stairs, I hurried out into a warm evening full of salty sea air and the droning of late-summer insects. Other witches moved along the crushed-shell walkways, thankfully too far away to pay me any mind.

My heart squeezed as I took in a tall figure. Costi Blackthorn was waiting for me.

My best friend had the look of a witch, the same as me—dark hair, tawny complexion, light eyes. I was surprised to see him wearing the black tactical uniform of the guardians. He had trimmed his hair short on the sides, leaving longer, messy strands at the top. The new look both suited him and made him look a little dangerous. He leaned against a wooden railing lining the walkway, using one massive black combat boot to prop himself up. He looked up as he noticed me.

"Where have you been?" I blurted. And how had he found me? It wasn't as if either of us hung out at the council building. At least, I never did until recently.

"Layla," he said, taking in my face, which must have still carried hints of my crying jag earlier. He pushed off the rail and stalked toward me. "What—"

"I-I have to tell you something." I swallowed, trying to ease the tightness in my throat.

"What's wrong?" He leaned closer to me, stretching out a hand to my shoulder, but his expression became wary and he straightened, his eyes shifting to someone behind me.

"Oh, Layla, there you are."

I froze at the sound of my mother's voice. Her high heels ground the shells into the path as she stepped beside me. I should have been more careful. She was always lurking around the Council.

"Hello, Constantine," she addressed Costi, who pulled his hand away from me slowly. "Do you have some business at the council building? It's after hours."

Costi's gray eyes churned like the nearby ocean as they cut to my mother. "Just passing by," he said, giving me a look that promised he'd talk to me later. I didn't watch him as he left.

My mother gave me a tight-lipped smile. She was a taller and willowier version of me—but her dark hair was smooth where mine was wild, and her blue eyes were critical where mine were sad.

My stomach sank. "He was only saying hello."

"I didn't know you were still hanging around with him."

"I'm not, really." I wrapped my arms around myself despite the warm evening. I was sick of this. She'd never approved of Costi as my friend. She couldn't see him as anything but *Troubled.*

My mother let her breath out in a sigh. "I'm trying to save you some heartache. You know that, right? Witches like him only become more unstable over time."

I said nothing, fixing my eyes on a tangle of moonflowers in the grass beside the walkway. We'd done this for years—Mother picking away at me as I tried to appease her. If I engaged, it would go on and on until I dissolved into incoherent tears. Then her smile would turn nasty. *Triumphant.*

I swallowed back bitterness. I was about to devastate the entire witch community, but it was her unpredictable reaction that I dreaded the most.

"Layla, I know you need to choose a guardian, and you may feel some loyalty to Constantine since you knew him as a child"—she scowled at the thought—"but there are those among the Troubled who are… less troubled. Ash Vervain would make an excellent choice."

"Maybe," I said. Costi had always been my choice, ever since we figured out that he would finish his training at the same time as I graduated.

Mother glanced at the council building, and her expression brightened. "Well? Is there some good news you'd like to share?"

I opened my mouth to tell her. I *had* to tell her. But nothing came out.

Her pouty lips turned downward as she examined me, and her hands came to her waist. "You *still* haven't done your summoning?"

"I… wasn't quite ready—" A sea breeze carried the sound of rustling leaves from the trees along the walkway.

Mother's frown deepened, emphasizing the line between her brows. She had sculpted her face with criticism. "You're twenty years old, and you graduated months ago. It's time to summon your familiar and join the coven of spell casters," she said. "I don't know what you think you're trying to pull by stalling, but you're embarrassing yourself."

Embarrassing *her*. That was the real thing she cared about.

She gave a sharp sigh when I didn't reply. "Fate help me, Layla. You need to stop acting like a child and take this seriously. Your future is at stake. Witches are starting to talk."

She had something to prove, and she was trying to do it through me. I didn't dare say it out loud, though.

With a frustrated sound, she turned to go. I trailed behind her as she strode along the walkways lined with cozy homes and gardens where solar path lights were beginning to blink on in the twilight. Since I hadn't joined the coven yet, I still lived with my parents in the heart of the Northern Sea Circle, our tiny seaside witch community hidden from the rest of humanity.

This place was all I'd ever known.

In moments I was trapped again in the house I grew up in. Our cottage was a typical witch dwelling—a blend of old and modern, handmade wooden fixtures next to technology borrowed from the outside world.

"Hi, Dad," I greeted my father, who responded by flicking his eyes to me for a moment. He was reclining in his usual chair in the living room. I looked him over, worried. The war had taken his peace from him years ago.

"Your father's not feeling well tonight, so it's just us for dinner," Mother called from the kitchen as she retrieved the food. "How was your day, sweetheart?" she asked as if our previous argument had been resolved, placing a baked dish that looked like a potato casserole on the dining room table.

"Mother—" I began. On top of everything, Dad was getting worse, and she was in some sort of denial.

"What were you doing all day?" There it was—the criticism had crept back into her voice.

What was I doing all day? The same thing I had been doing for months, in secret, over and over. I woke up before dawn to sneak out and work the summoning spell that should have opened a portal to Hell and bonded me to a demon familiar, as it had *every* spell caster for millennia. I was exhausted, physically and emotionally, from tracing the enormously complex magic circle again and again, six hours of my life gone each time.

I said nothing, blinking back tears. The worst part? I didn't know whether my mother would write me off as a failure or whether it would *please* her that I couldn't live up to the high expectations that had been with me from birth. She needed me to become a spell caster to prove her worthiness, but she also needed to be better than me. I didn't know which would win and what it would make out of me.

"Layla, what in fate's name is wrong with you lately?" Mother sighed.

I could never be what she wanted. I had tried and tried.

"Just go," she said from the sink, not turning around.

I went as quietly as I could, trying not to make any noise as I closed the door.

*　*　*

I thought I would break down, finally allowing the tears I had been holding back, but none came. I lay quietly on my childhood bed, watching the wavering shadows on the ceiling as branches swayed in the night outside.

I had prepared my whole life to become a spell caster and fight in the war against the angels.

I was a *blessing.* My father was—or had been—a powerful spell caster, but my mother was an ordinary witch—able to feel magic but not use it. They'd gone against society to be together. Fate had gifted me with this inheritance, and I'd grown up steeped in the sense of duty that came with it.

All witches could detect magic; it came naturally to us. A smaller number of witches, the circlewrights, could channel magic through traced circle spells. It was a slow and laborious process that didn't lend itself to battle.

But the ability to wield magic in high enough quantities to summon a familiar and become a caster was rare—I was one of only ten in the Northern Sea Circle. Together, a spell caster and their demon familiar could ignite magic strong enough to take down an angel—immediately and fatally.

It was the only weapon we had. My ability was *vital*.

The day after I graduated from school, I went into the summoning room at dawn, full of bright excitement for my rite of passage. With the completion of the circle spell, I would become a spell caster and finally, *finally*, have my own life.

I had stepped back from the huge, room-spanning circlework in satisfaction. I knew I had drawn every line and symbol perfectly. I felt it humming with resonance, ready to catch. I breathed magic into myself, swirling high and bright, and released it into the circle. The electric white blaze of it dazzled, my vision returning in flashing spots in the cool stone summoning room, my body languid with the relief of releasing so much power.

But no familiar appeared.

When I emerged, shaken, it was much later than it was supposed to be, and the crowd of witches waiting to congratulate me had dispersed. I told my mother I'd gotten stage fright and couldn't go through with it. I dodged concerned calls from my teachers and didn't show up for graduation parties. I tried again and again, pulling in stronger amounts of magic until there was so much it could hurt me.

And still nothing.

An unread text from Costi displayed on my phone: **Tell me what happened.**

Pushing myself from my bed, I pulled a half-packed shoulder bag from a large antique wardrobe. My life rattled around inside—folded clothing, small jars of cosmetics, toiletries. A collection of crystals, stones, and shells that represented twenty years' worth of memories.

At the bottom of the bag was an option I could only bear to touch lightly with my thoughts—a carefully hoarded bundle of paper money that was only useful among the non-magical. As a witch, I was only vaguely aware of the outside world. A frantic, competitive place full of strange beliefs, completely unaware of the angels that menaced them.

I didn't have a real plan. Without joining the coven of spell casters, I had nowhere else to go. But I had to get out of here for a while.

When I crept out into the hallway, there was no light from under my parents' bedroom door. Emboldened, I made my way silently down the stairs. The living room was lit dimly by the stove light from the kitchen.

"You're going?" Dad's quiet voice startled me. He was still in his recliner, awake despite the late hour. My mother had combed his long black hair, but the ends needed a trim.

"I'll... be back later," I said with a small smile for his benefit. I wasn't sure if it was true or not.

My hand paused on the door handle when he said, "This war... we're not going to win." His words were determined, like an ill prophecy.

An eerie chill washed over me as I turned back to him.

No one *won* the war against the angels—it wasn't even a real war. *War* was just an inspiring euphemism for a duty so timeless, it predated written records. Angels infested, witches destroyed them, and the rest of humanity continued on unaware. That was the way it was.

My thoughts moved quickly to deep concern. He'd never been prone to saying strange things like this before.

He didn't elaborate. His pills were still sitting in their tray with an undrunk glass of water next to them on the side table.

"Don't forget to take your meds," I told him.

He sighed, but his fingers strayed toward the pills and moved them around. "You're like me, Layla. You can see what others don't want to see. You have to make them understand."

My eyes pricked with tears even though I didn't really understand the advice. "I'll try," I said.

He nodded again, slowly, and I eased out the door without another word.

* * *

Out in the humid night, I finally took a deep breath, trying to shake the feeling of unease around my dad. Maybe I could talk to his doctors personally.

Stepping out onto a path paved with charming cobblestones set down hundreds of years ago, I made my way through the Northern Sea Circle. The little cottages that made up the bulk of our community were tucked in for the night, the pathways empty.

One particular window was still glowing with warm lamplight, and my heart clenched. I still considered Holly my friend, but lately she'd been... different. We'd drifted apart, and I didn't understand why. Just a year ago, I would have gone to her about this in a heartbeat. Now, though... I wasn't sure she'd welcome a visit.

There were some witches who disliked spell casters, jealous that they couldn't pull enough magic to summon a familiar. Holly had never been one of those. Two years older than me, she had graduated and gained a coveted position with the Council, working on administrative tasks. Her future was looking bright.

When I first noticed the shift, she had denied that anything was wrong. But it was never like it had been, and eventually we stopped talking altogether. Her childhood hadn't been a nice one—maybe I reminded her of that. I'd seen her around with her new friends. She looked happy.

Just before the bridge from our island to the outside world was a row of identical apartments, flanked by the old stone building that was our security office.

I hadn't visited Costi in his new place, but I knew which one it was. I pushed my bag into the branches of a short plum tree in front of the building. I hesitated, then knocked lightly, torn between not wanting to wake him, not wanting to face him, and needing to give him an explanation.

Before I could think better of this plan and escape, the door jerked open.

Costi stabbed at the porch light switch. "Layla."

My mind tripped over itself and spilled onto the steps. Gray sleeping shorts did very little to cover a body honed by four years of intense physical training. The dusky skin of his upper arms and chest was covered in a tangle of all-black tattoos—flowers, vines, script, an intricately shaded flying owl. When in fate's name had he gotten *those*? There were so *many*. His dark hair was messed up with sleep, long lashes sticking together over blinking storm-colored eyes, lips parted in surprise.

My words disappeared, and my cheeks flushed hot. Logically, I knew my childhood friend was a grown man. We'd been grown-ups for some time now. Adults. But this… this was…

We stared at each other until he glanced away, running a hand over the back of his neck.

"Come on," he said, his voice rough with sleep. His warm hand circled my entire upper arm as he guided me inside, stepping on the switch for a standing lamp. He glanced outside, checking behind me before shutting off the porch light. "Hang on a second," he said, then grabbed a handful of clothes from a drawer, disappearing into a bathroom.

So awkward. I put a chilled hand to my flaming face. Costi's tiny apartment was immaculately clean and without any decoration. Only the rumpled navy comforter gave any indication that someone lived here. It was a far cry from when we were kids and his room was a permanent mess that left his foster mom throwing her hands up. There was nowhere to sit except the bed, so I remained standing, losing my nerve.

As a spell caster, even an initiate, I wasn't supposed to be here. Spell casters were strictly off-limits to guardians. It wouldn't matter that we were just friends. Costi would get in trouble if anyone caught me here in the middle of the night.

Just as I decided to flee, Costi emerged. He had thrown on black tactical pants and a gray T-shirt that stretched over those muscles, the edges of his ink peeking out from the neckline. He hadn't even attempted to tame his wild hair.

"Sorry to wake you up," I said, wrapping my arms around myself.

"Don't be," he said as he bent to lace up a pair of tall black boots with some seriously thick soles. "Didn't think you'd come." He tilted his head at the door. I nodded.

I walked along beside him as he led us through a path in the field behind the apartments to the seawall. A salty, humid breeze kicked up from the ocean below. A few beacons blinked far out at sea, and the lights of the Northern Sea Circle glowed softly in the distance across the open space. The pathway along the wall was lit only by the waxing moon but was bright enough to walk by.

"You wanna tell me what's up?" Costi said after several silent minutes, pausing to turn and look at me. The sound of the sea hushed his voice.

"I haven't seen you in a while." I braced my hands on the seawall's protective metal railing, facing him.

He glanced away guiltily, and it struck me that *he'd* also been avoiding *me*. Why?

"How's—" I cleared my throat. This was ridiculous. I'd never felt nervous around Costi in my life. "How's guardian life?"

His expression lightened. "You saw my luxurious apartment."

I breathed out a laugh, then hesitated a moment. "I heard you haven't been assigned yet."

"Not yet," he said slowly, looking at me in a way I couldn't decipher.

Spell casters could create powerful bursts of witch fire, but our familiars were child-sized demons, and concentrating on casting made us physically vulnerable. A trained guardian was a necessity—we needed someone to defend us if the enemy got within range.

With four years' difference between us, he finished his guardian training at the same time I graduated from school. Ever since we realized the timing worked out perfectly, Costi and I had planned to pair up.

I was the only spell caster graduating in our Circle this year, but I hadn't come forward, and I was certain the guardians didn't appreciate him putting off his assignment for months like this. He was holding his career back, waiting for me, and hadn't even once questioned what was taking me so long.

He propped his arms on the railing, looking out into the dark distance as he waited for me to continue.

"You should let them assign you. I can't pair with you," I blurted. My voice was barely louder than the rushing waves, but he heard me. An unfamiliar feeling pricked at my awareness, a subtle brushing of something like magic. I shook my head to clear it.

For a moment, Costi was quiet, his gray eyes shadowed. "You changed your mind."

"No! Never."

He looked at me. "Tell me."

I took a steadying breath to tell him everything. "This morning—well, yesterday, at this point—I got up early and went to do my summoning circle." I scuffed my foot over the sand-strewn cement of the walkway.

Costi's solid presence drew the story from me.

"The spell worked perfectly, but—" I stopped in confusion as a wave of strange magic dumped over me, like being hit with a live wire. "What was *that*?"

He slammed a hand down over my mouth, staring into the sky behind me. His perfect stillness shot alarm through me, and I froze.

"Layla," he breathed into my ear. "I'm gonna need you to invoke your familiar. There are angels above us. They've already seen us. You need to hit them quickly."

What? Angels, *here*? I shook my head vehemently, pulling his hand from my face. "*I can't.*"

"I got you," he said as he whipped a dagger I hadn't noticed out of his boot, eyes on whatever was coming for us. He pushed me behind him. "I'll defend you."

"Costi, I don't have a familiar!" I whispered frantically.

Costi jolted as he realized just how screwed we were. He regained himself, though, tearing his phone out of his pocket and shoving it in my hands.

"Whatever happens, stay behind me. Do *not* run. Call Ash, tell them to get the guardians. *Now.*"

I couldn't look, just punched the phone on with shaking fingers. Costi didn't use a passcode.

Angels were *here*? At the Circle? *How were angels here?*

I found Ash at the top of the contacts and waited in agony while it rang through. *Please pick up.*

"Costi, what? It's late."

"Ash?" I gasped.

"Who's this?"

"Layla Rosen. Costi's with me. We're on the seawall. Get the other guardians *right now*. Angels are attacking us—"

"*What?*"

"Seven," Costi said grimly.

"S-Seven," I whispered into the phone.

There was a pause. Shock, I assumed.

"Stay where you are," Ash said. "Keep the phone connected."

Peeking behind Costi, I saw them. Human-shaped monsters of wing, claw, and sharp teeth silhouetted against the stars. Nothing like the adorable cherubs the non-magical painted in their cathedrals.

Costi moved viciously as the first angel spiraled close enough to hit. Feathers and talons tumbled through the air as the creature hissed and grabbed the metal railing, trying to haul itself up. Costi slammed his dagger into the angel's neck and kicked through the gap in the rails, sending it hurtling down into the sea.

There was a moment where all was silent except for Costi's heavy breathing.

In the distance, eerie sirens whirred to life, something I had never heard before. The guardians had sounded the alarm.

Background shouting came through the phone as Costi slashed at another incoming enemy, this one smart enough to dodge. Moonlight glinted off the eyes of the angels, hovering just out of reach.

"Backup ETA five minutes, Layla. Hold tight," Ash said through the phone.

Five minutes? We wouldn't survive that long. Without a spell caster, angels were unkillable. "Please hurry," I begged.

Two of the angels swooped in tandem, and I yelped, ducking low. The phone flew from my hand and clattered to the pavement. Costi hit one wing with his dagger, severed feathers flying, but he roared as the other angel ripped into his arm with its talons.

I had no weapons, no experience fighting, nothing at all. Panicking, I began to breathe in magic, hauling in huge amounts of power until my bones ached with it. The magic was like the waves battering the seawall. Relentless. Without a way to channel it, it was only going to hurt me, but I couldn't stop. I was *designed* for this.

The angels were swarming now, Costi whirling like a dancer to keep them from hitting us. Five minutes was an eternity. One of the sharp talons slipped past his guard, sending his dagger spinning, catching a flash from the moonlight as it careened off the wall.

I screamed, throwing my arms over my head to protect myself as one of the angels sliced the back of my shoulder with a wicked shriek. Costi's voice carried over the fray as he continued to lash out with his boots and fists, but I couldn't understand what he was yelling.

The magic I had gathered pulsed in me alarmingly, a dizzying force that threatened to shut down my consciousness. I wanted to push it back out. I *needed* to push it back out—this was going to kill me before the angels even got to me. But I couldn't stop pulling, and there was nowhere for the energy to go—

Until there was.

The intricate, glowing lines of a spell curled together, burning my eyes even though they were clamped shut. My hands grew impossibly hot, and I flung them toward the sky.

The connection completed, as nature intended.

The magic burst from me, flowing into the spell and surging out, an ecstatic tsunami of power that brutalized the enemies in its path and left me starkly, blessedly empty.

I heard the roar of the ocean in the silence.

Chapter 2

LAYLA

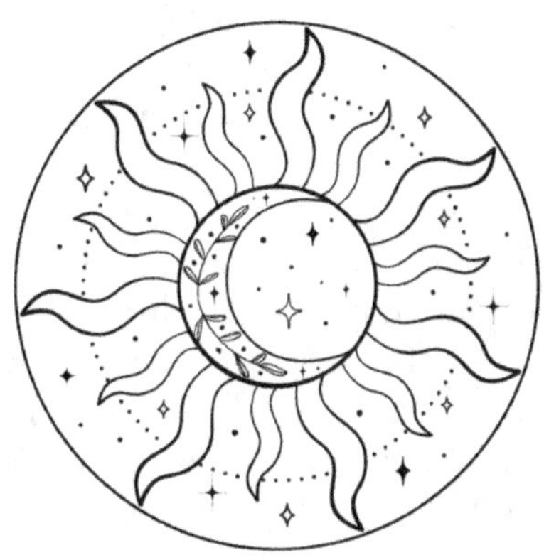

The world around me suddenly seemed bright and chaotic. Voices shouting in the distance, footsteps walking quickly, loud scraping and shuffling.

"Your spell caster is in good hands, guardian. She's going to be fine," someone was saying. "Can you let us take a look at that forehead?"

My eyes wouldn't focus properly. I blinked repeatedly, trying to clear the dark spots.

"Layla." I felt Costi's hand on mine. I was lying on a bed.

"What's going on?" I tried to say, my voice hovering far away from my body.

"Layla, you scared the *fuck* out of me."

I let my head fall to the side toward his voice, my vision clearing a bit as my consciousness strengthened. Costi was hunched over next to the bed on a too-small stool.

I gasped, taking him in. The right side of his forehead was marked with a wicked gash that had been barely cleaned, and his left arm was in a sling. His shirt was in tatters.

He ignored my reaction, holding my face in one hand and peering into my eyes, as if looking for signs of concussion. "You passed out and banged your skull."

I wiggled, trying to sit up, but Costi's hand on my arm kept me in place. "Don't," he said.

Something on my back burned, and I remembered. The attack. The angels. Those were *talon marks* all over Costi's body.

I was in the infirmary. An IV bag hooked above me was feeding fluid into the vein of my hand. Around me and outside, the Circle was pandemonium. It smelled like a mix of disinfectants and smoke. Something *very bad* was going on.

"Costi—"

An older medic in a blue uniform leaned over me. I'd seen him around in our tiny community but couldn't remember his name. He held up a pen in front of my eyes, moving it back and forth. As I followed it with my gaze, he grunted. I didn't know if that was good or bad. "I'll be back in a few minutes with the kit for your stitches, guardian," he said to Costi, pulling the partition curtain around the bed shut as he left.

Had Costi carried me here with his injured arm? My mouth tasted coppery, like I'd bitten my tongue. "What… happened?"

"What *happened*?" Costi shoved his good hand through his already messed-up hair. "You cast a spell big enough to knock satellites out of space and destroyed six angels at once. Ash was able to get our teams out just before the rest of the attack hit."

"*What?*" The *rest* of the attack?

Costi looked down at me seriously. "That was some kind of scouting squadron. It was sheer luck that we were out there and caught them at it, or we'd probably all be dead."

None of this made any sense. Angels didn't have *scouting squadrons*.

I jumped as a close boom rattled the infirmary. Costi placed a large hand over my blanket-covered arm.

"They have weapons," he said with grim eyes. "Some kind of staff that shoots light."

Weapons? My blood chilled as the full implications hit me. A large, organized attack, weapons that could hit at range, pinpointing the Circle's location. This was something *worse* than bad.

Something else didn't make sense. "Costi, I cast magic."

"*Yeah,* you did." His teeth flashed as he gave a half grin, wincing a little as it pulled the cut by his eye. "Never seen anything like it."

I licked my dry lips. "But I didn't. I mean, I couldn't have. It's… what I came to tell you. I don't have a familiar."

Costi frowned. "There wasn't anyone else close enough."

"It *was* me, though. I saw the spell form, and I pushed the magic into it. I felt it catch, just like a circle spell." It felt amazing—my body was still echoing with it, despite the stinging in my back as my bandages rubbed against the bed. "How could that be possible?"

Costi rubbed at the scruff growing on his face. "Shy demon?"

I stared at him.

He shrugged his uninjured shoulder. "Don't know anything about familiars. You've gotta have one, though, if you cast. Try invoking."

He was right. A flash of hope and excitement lit me, despite the dire situation. I gently took stock of my body and mind. Could I tell if there was a familiar bonded to me? Had that last spell worked after all? I was exhausted and hurting now, but before the attack, I hadn't felt any different.

Demon familiars were their own entities, our ancient allies from a realm called Hell. They couldn't speak or communicate beyond conveying their moods, and they came and went as they pleased. However, they could be called upon for battle, and they would respond.

Closing my eyes, I followed the mental sequence that we learned in school to invoke our familiars. I had tried it many times before, the first time my summoning failed, and again after the last one. The call echoed, seeming to move outside of me. I glanced around the bed. No demon. I sighed.

When I looked up at Costi, he was staring at me, his eyes moving around my face.

"I don't think it worked," I said. "What's wrong?"

"No, guess not. It's nothing. Just… are you okay? They got your shoulder pretty bad. Are you hurting anywhere else? You want some water?"

I looked down at my shoulder carefully, seeing the bandage peeking out from under a light fabric gown that was thankfully covered by the hospital blanket. "I think I'm all right. I'm tired, though. I didn't sleep before all this."

"Get some rest." He brushed some stray hair away from my face. The kind gesture made my throat tighten.

It was too bright in here, and the chaotic sounds around us were too nerve-racking to even consider sleeping. "What about you?"

"What *about* me?"

"Aren't you going to rest? You're hurt too."

"I am resting," he said, raising his eyebrows. He leaned back and crossed his arms. "This stool is real comfortable."

I breathed out a small laugh. I didn't have the will to tell him he didn't need to stay with me. Arguing with Costi was like trying to empty the sea with a cup. I had a feeling that if I didn't keep him here, he would charge back out into the battle. "At least let them look at your cut—"

We were interrupted by the curtain opening.

Jenny Luna, one of our elected councilors, strode in. She cut a dramatic figure with her black ceremonial robes fluttering behind her. She cleared her throat. "I came as soon as I could. I only have a moment, but I wanted to thank you on behalf of the Council and the Circle."

Costi and I shared a speechless look.

Councilor Luna was in her middle years, with bands of silver starting to creep into her short dark hair. Her blue eyes were tired. "You put on quite a show, Layla—the entire Circle felt the reverb from your spell. And Blackthorn, you managed to hold off a half dozen angels with just a dagger. Quite the team for a new guardian and a recent graduate." She nodded in acknowledgment and regarded us gravely. "Well done. You saved lives tonight."

"Thanks." I glanced away, plucking at my blanket with my free hand. Costi was silent. I desperately hoped that with all of this chaos, no one would put together the fact that we were out alone after dark on the seawall.

The councilor looked me over. "Are you badly injured? Can you go back out? We need all our spell casters on defense for the evacuation."

I blinked and opened my mouth, but nothing came out. *Evacuation?*

"Nope. She can't cast," Costi said. Relief washed through me.

"You burned yourself out? Cursed fate, that'll take days to heal." Councilor Luna swore, tugging a hand through her salt-and-pepper hair. Her phone dinged with a message, but she ignored it. "All right. I suppose that makes sense. That was a huge spell." She turned to face Costi. "And you?"

"I'm good."

What? He most definitely was not good. A line of fresh blood dribbled from the gash on his forehead. He looked exhausted.

"Then you need to get your spell caster out of here. We're regrouping at the Mountain Circle."

"What?" I said out loud this time. With my free hand, I pushed myself to a sitting position on the crinkling infirmary bed. Being careful of my IV, I pulled the thin blanket up to cover my chest.

"I'm sorry, Layla," she said, patting me on the arm. "We simply can't risk you. The Circle has been compromised. It's too dangerous to stay here. If you can't cast, you need to evacuate."

"Understood," Costi said.

"Good. I can't spare a vehicle for you—we have just enough to get the children and elders out. Don't call for a rideshare. I don't want non-magical humans anywhere near here. Walk out to town and rent a car." Councilor Luna's phone dinged again insistently. "I don't need to tell you to be extremely careful, especially on the bridge. Watch the skies."

Costi gave a single nod. "I got her."

The councilor returned his nod. "Fate go with you."

She was already picking up her phone and asking for updates from the witch on the line before she was even past the curtain.

Costi slid off his stool, not betraying any pain from his injuries. I stared at him in bewilderment.

The infirmary sounded less chaotic now—the shouts had quieted to snatches of conversations. The alarming bangs from outside the building had tapered off.

Had we beaten them?

Costi leaned over me, peering into my eyes. "How are you feeling?"

I swung my bare feet over the side of the bed. "I think I'm okay."

"Okay enough to walk out to town?"

"I can if you can," I said, but I wasn't entirely sure.

The corner of his lips twitched upward. It was an old joke between us from our childhood, me, younger and smaller, trying to keep up with him through countless adventures. He would tell me he wasn't going to slow down and then slow down anyway.

Costi called the medic over, and I shivered in the chilly air as he removed my IV.

"Normally, I'd never let you leave the infirmary this soon, but this situation…" The medic blew out a breath. "All right, guardian, your turn."

While the medic tended to Costi's forehead, I dragged myself into the nearby bathroom. Looking in the mirror was painful—my skin was sallow, and my eyes were wide and glassy. My hair was a tangled mess. The infirmary gown, as bad as I had thought, wasn't doing me any favors. It was a shame that witches couldn't just wiggle our noses and do healing spells like the outsiders showed on TV. We had to heal with time and medicine the way all humans did.

My clothes were ruined, but I found a cupboard that was stocked with a pile of folded nursing scrubs. My shower was awkward as I tried to wash my hair with one hand while not getting my shoulder bandage wet, but I emerged clean and dressed.

"Ready?" Costi's face had been wiped clean, his wound bound with neat stitches. "I gotta stop by my place and grab my gear and weapons." He looked me over, rubbing his chin. "You'll need some better clothes too."

"I… left a bag with some clothes in your tree. The tree in front of your apartment, that is."

Costi's gaze sharpened. "That was *before* the attack," he put together immediately.

I pulled in a breath.

"Were you—" He stopped speaking and glanced to the hall, pulling me protectively out of the doorway.

I heard the voices that had alerted him as two witches turned the corner. It was Aura, one of our older spell casters, and her guardian.

The two witches were still in sleeping clothes, the guardian with her sword strapped over flannel pants. They'd been pulled out of bed for the emergency.

Aura's demon familiar trailed behind her, a pale creature that looked like a child. Albeit a child with huge black eyes, sharp teeth, and pointed ears. The pair didn't notice us, but the little familiar turned and glared with a sulky hiss.

"You think someone in the community sold us out, you mean," Aura was saying.

"That has to be it," the guardian said. She was a tall witch with close-shaved hair who had been a few years above me in school.

"One of the mission teams could have led them here by mistake," Aura pointed out.

"This is just like what happened in Greece," the guardian insisted.

My eyes flitted to Costi in alarm.

He looked back at me steadily. If he had a reaction to their words, he kept it to himself. It wasn't something we talked a lot about as children, so I had no adult reference for his feelings about the Greek incident. It made my heart twist. I'd never considered it before.

How much of the attack on the Paralía Circle had he witnessed? Was history repeating itself?

Costi stepped out into the hallway, and I shuffled behind him. "Salix," he addressed the other guardian. "What's the situation outside?"

The pair stopped and turned to us. "Stable," the guardian answered. "For now. We haven't seen another wave of angels since we blasted back the third. Aura is cleared for duty, so we're heading back to the seawall. You coming?"

Costi shook his head. "She's injured. We're evacuating."

Aura looked me up and down dubiously but kept any thoughts to herself. I'd never gotten along very well with the coven.

"Good luck," the guardian bade us as Costi led me in the opposite direction with a gentle hand on my back. Our footsteps echoed through the quiet corridor of the medical center. The overhead lights were off, leaving only strips of emergency lights along the floor. At the end of the hall, Costi pushed open the wooden door with his good arm.

Outside, it was pitch-dark and silent. The outdoor lights had also been extinguished, and the sky was eerily muted and uniformly black.

Once the door was closed, I couldn't even see my hand in front of my face.

"The circlewrights," I whispered, feeling awed. This was witch work. To cover the entire sky with a cloak of darkness would have taken dozens of circle spells. All of our circlewrights must have contributed, tracing out spell after spell to make sure the angels couldn't see us from above.

Costi flicked on his phone, giving us just enough light so we wouldn't crash into things. The screen was cracked from where I had dropped it during the attack.

"My apartment," he said. "Walk quickly and close to walls wherever we can. Keep an eye out."

The Circle we had grown up in looked strange and menacing in the faint white phone light as we crept along the walkways, hugging the buildings. Not a single other witch made their presence known.

When we made it to his apartment, Costi didn't question me as I retrieved my bag from the tree.

* * *

After taking a few moments to duck into his apartment to change, I rejoined Costi, and we headed toward the road.

In minutes we reached the bridge. A small parking lot usually held the Circle's collection of vehicles that would be used in the evacuation effort.

The bridge itself was several miles long, spanning the tidal river and marsh that separated our island from the mainland, an American state called Massachusetts. The salty smell that rose from the marsh was just short of unpleasant, but it was the scent of home.

Walking out onto the bridge, we reached the edge of the shield spell. The moon and stars popped out, a faint tinge of dawn spreading above the line of distant trees. It was quiet. Costi scanned the sky. I looked up as well, trying to catch any hint of the electric feeling of angels I had come to recognize in the attack. After a moment, he motioned for me to follow.

Moving cautiously while watching the horizon, we made our way across. There was a gate at the far end of the bridge to keep tourists out, but we walked around it.

"How far is the Mountain Circle? It's in West Virginia, right?" I asked quietly as we passed onto the main road.

It was close to morning now, plenty of light to walk by. The air was cool and pleasant with the damp scent of the forest on either side of us. Nighttime insects began to hush with the approaching day.

"West Virginia, yeah. Takes a while to get there, more than twelve hours by car."

"Oh yeah, we're taking a vehicle." I brightened, bouncing a little on the dark pavement despite trying not to look too excited.

Costi gave me an amused look. "It'd take ages to walk that far," he said.

I had very rarely ridden in a vehicle. The Circle kept a fleet of them for teams to use on missions and procuring supplies from the outside, but I had no reason to leave the community most of the time. I'd only been outside a handful of times on field trips.

I supposed that, too, would change, if I really was a spell caster now.

The farther we walked, the freer I began to feel. My life was a giant question mark, and the only community I had ever known had just been tossed to the wind, so it probably wasn't right to feel this way. But I finally had room to breathe, equal parts terrifying and exhilarating.

More than an hour passed before Costi led us to a second street that looked larger. Here, the American streetlamp system began, little halos of yellow light dotting the way, and a traffic light glowed at the crossroads.

"If any cars come along, duck into the trees," he said. "The outsiders will get nervous if they see us walking on the road."

That was odd, but I believed him. He was well-versed in navigating the outside from the missions he'd gone on while in training.

It hit me again how far apart our lives had drifted in the past few years. As he advanced in training and I got busy with my schoolwork and preparing to graduate, we hadn't been able to see each other often. He would text me the names of places I'd never heard of that he was visiting, and I would dream of the day I joined him.

It was part of a guardian's job to track down angel nests. Teams with spell casters would then move in to exterminate them.

That was supposed to be my life too—burning angel nests to keep humanity safe.

Despite our grand mythology around them, in real life, angels were nothing more than mindless creatures. They infested abandoned buildings and lonely stretches at the edges of habitation, menacing the non-magical who stumbled upon them. There would start to be reports of missing hikers, strange sounds, monster sightings. In the winter, their hunts were lean, and they would creep out to snatch children from lonely farms. They were the nightmarish stuff of rural ghost stories.

Angels would go after a witch if one got near enough. We could sense each other to a certain extent, and witch magic enraged them. But they weren't sentient. They never went after us like we hunted them down. It had been seventeen years since an attack on a Circle—the one in Greece. It had never happened before or since.

We walked along the roads while the sun rose. At some point, Costi dropped his duffel to remove his more obvious weapons and stow them away. I wondered if we blended in as normal, non-magical humans.

Cars began to roar past, and the trees gave way to parking lots and shop buildings. He led us to a large building called a hotel—a sort of guesthouse that we could stay in.

I tried to look unimpressed as we walked in, but the amused smirk Costi gave me let me know I was failing.

"Good morning." The woman behind the counter gave us a wary, uncertain look. We didn't blend in that well after all.

"We need to book a room," Costi said.

"For tonight? Check-in isn't until three," she said suspiciously.

Costi argued with the woman, coming to some agreement so she would let us in now.

I looked around the hotel curiously. We witches brought in a lot of technology and supplies from the outside, but our cultures were far enough apart to make the differences stand out. The aesthetic here was far more minimalist than ours, with beige-colored walls and few decorative touches. It wasn't well cared for, with scuffs on the floors and worn, mass-produced furniture placed haphazardly. The vibe was simultaneously over sanitized and grungy.

"Don't we have to pay for everything here?" I asked Costi as we waited for the elevator.

"I did pay for it," he said, showing me a small metallic black card. "This thing keeps a tab. They send the bill to the Council later."

"Who's James Smith?" I asked, reading the name on the card.

"No idea. Some fake name," he said as another guest exiting the elevator gave us a weird look before hurrying away.

The guest room was a small affair with two identical beds and some sparse furniture, and it smelled strongly of cleaning chemicals. The air conditioning hummed quietly, making it chilly.

It suddenly felt small with just the two of us in here. I clutched my arms around myself. Sharing a room probably wasn't what Councilor Luna had in mind when she sent me with him.

"Take a shower if you want," Costi said. "I'll get some food ordered and see about a car." He pulled out his phone, plugging it into a charger, and started typing with one thumb.

I swallowed. It dawned on me how useless I was. Fate, I knew *nothing* about any of this. I didn't have a payment card. I didn't know how to order food. I'd never driven a car. Hadn't I had some vague notion of running away to the outside? I would have been lost if Costi hadn't come with me.

"Thank you," I murmured.

He gave me a half smile as if it was nothing, and I retreated into the bathroom. The heavy door and fan cut me off from the rest of the world.

Peeling off my top, I carefully pulled the bandage off my shoulder. It hurt, and my other shoulder was sore from carrying my bag on one side all night, but the jagged, angry-looking cut had scabbed over and wasn't bleeding, and it didn't look infected. I began shivering from more than the chilled air.

Only some blessing of fate had allowed us to survive, to somehow pull a spell out of me when I needed it most.

I went over every detail in my mind, but I hadn't seen my familiar then or any time before or since. There was only the swelling of magic inside me, the spell sigil, and the explosive release.

I showered, making the chemical-scented water as hot as it would go, then busied myself combing through my hair and trying to make myself look alive while considering my next move. What was going on at the Circle?

Costi showered after me, leaving me sitting on the edge of one of the two beds to munch on chips and a mix of foods rolled up in a thin flatbread. It was delicious, with beans and rice and different vegetables in some kind of spicy sauce.

My stomach churned with complicated feelings as I quickly typed out a text to my mother to let her know I had been evacuated.

Costi rejoined me dressed in a more comfortable-looking gray tee shirt and black cargo shorts, the longer strands of his damp dark hair curling a bit. He looked more like my childhood friend now that he'd shaved off his scruff and put away all the weapons and gear. He pushed a fabric-padded chair up so he was facing me and propped one bare foot insolently on my bed.

"I got us a car. We'll rest here today and pick it up tomorrow morning," he said. "Should be safe enough."

I nodded absently as he looked at me, his face not giving anything away.

"So," Costi said. "You wanna tell me why you were running away?"

Chapter 3

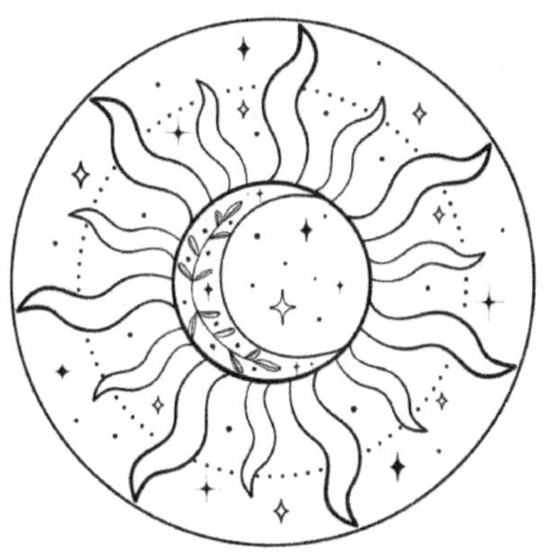

I blew out a breath.

"How are you feeling? Your arm got pretty banged up, and you haven't rested," I said.

"I'll live," Costi said dryly. "Tell me what's going on. Why were you trying so hard to get me in trouble?"

"You're always in trouble!"

His lips turned upward on one side, and I fought the urge to throw a pillow at his face. I'd save my revenge, biding my time until the cut on his forehead healed. "I'm a guardian now. I'm a changed man."

I scoffed. He looked at me intently from under languid eyelashes, waiting for my answer to his question.

"I'm… useless." I dropped my eyes from his as I confessed. "I can't fight." I touched the talon cut on my shoulder. I couldn't *believe* how helpless I was. It was an embarrassment. No training, no weapon, not even basic self-defense. Spell casters were sitting ducks.

Costi made a dismissive noise. "Fighting is *my* job."

"But they could have hurt you a lot worse. You could have *died*, and I couldn't do anything!"

Costi dropped his foot from my bed. He leaned forward to cradle my chin carefully with his calloused fingers, tilting my head up to look at him. "But you did. You got them."

My gaze drifted to his arm. The sleeve of his tee was rolled up, and he'd wound a fresh bandage around his injury. Inked lines of vines and flowers curled above the fabric.

"No," he said with finality. "It was your first time casting, and we were caught off guard. Don't you dare feel guilty. You were amazing." The last part came out in a rush of breath.

Still cupping my face, his gray eyes were warm, glowing with something. Fate, he was… he was *proud* of me. The knowledge lit up my insides before I was doused by another wave of self-loathing. I pulled away from him.

"But that's the thing. I shouldn't have been able to do that. I never summoned a familiar. I wouldn't even believe I cast at all if I hadn't felt the spell."

Costi frowned in thought. "Never heard of anything like this."

"Me neither."

"You said… the summoning didn't work."

I nodded slowly, nibbling at the inside of my cheek while I worked up the courage to admit how badly I had failed. I owed him an explanation.

"The day after I graduated, I had my summoning room reserved," I began. Costi nodded, leaning forward with his good arm propped up on his leg. "I learned how to do circle spells in school. They aren't too hard once you do the same one a few times, they just take forever to trace. So, that day, I traced the summoning circle and pushed the magic in. I felt it catch and burn up just like it's supposed to." I picked at a loose synthetic thread on the hotel blanket.

Costi watched me silently, with a serious expression.

I swallowed, my throat feeling tight. "I waited, but my familiar didn't appear… and then I didn't know what to do…" I'd been keeping this in so long.

I hadn't seen Costi in ages. Holly was pushing me out. I didn't have any other friends. I'd had no one to turn to, and I'd been so, so scared.

He made a small sound in the back of his throat and pulled me up off the bed into his arms before I realized I was crying.

Now that I'd opened the door, everything came tumbling out. "I tried over and over, and it never worked. And then suddenly I can cast spells without a familiar? There's something *wrong* with me." I shuddered miserably, the tears I had been holding back for months tracking down my cheeks.

Costi leaned his cheek on top of my head. He smelled good, like soap with a hint of sandalwood. "There's nothing wrong with you. We'll figure this out."

Something subtle shifted inside me, like a light being turned on in another room. I couldn't ever remember feeling *safe* like this, having someone *figure it out* with me. His body was solid against mine, this warrior who would fling angels over a railing with his bare hands to protect me. Fate, he saved my *life*.

He ran a hand over my head, stroking my hair gently.

I untangled myself from him in a hurry, my cheeks burning painfully. "S-Sorry," I mumbled, unable to look up at him, my mind caught in an awkward mess. I felt like a child, crying about my problems like this.

"Don't be."

I scrubbed at my eyes and cleared my throat, trying to push the sobs back down. "I decided I would try one last time, and if it didn't work, I would give it up. I didn't have much of a plan, I just wanted to get away from my mother for a while. She already hates me enough."

"No one could hate you," Costi murmured.

I didn't argue, but I knew the truth. "I'm sorry I let you down," I said, nearly a whisper.

"Me?" He looked genuinely shocked. "Why would you think that?"

"I ruined our plans to pair up. I know you were waiting for me, but you can't just go without a spell caster, especially with all of this going on." I wrapped my arms around myself, feeling chilled in the sterile hotel room.

Costi scrubbed a hand through his hair, then opened his lips and closed them again.

I blinked at him, my stomach twisting in alarm. It wasn't like him to be nervous.

"I thought… maybe you didn't want me. As a guardian."

My mouth popped open. "No, I—"

His ringtone sounded, and he cursed under his breath, grabbing the phone from his pocket. "Holly," he said, looking at the screen with a wince. "She's probably wondering what happened."

"Oh… you should, um…" My heart turned over painfully. Holly and Costi were still friends? Of course they were. It made sense. It was only me she had decided to ditch.

"Hey," he barked into the phone.

"Where *are* you? Everyone's saying you got hurt and left already. What's going on?"

I could hear Holly's reply clearly even though it wasn't meant for me. Her singsong voice carrying through the phone made me tear up all over again. I sat on the edge of the bed, ducking my head to examine the frantic pattern of the bedspread.

Costi turned, bringing a hand to the back of his neck. "In town. We're evacuating to the Mountain Circle."

"*We?*"

"Layla's with me," Costi rumbled.

Holly was quiet for a moment. "Is that a good idea?"

"Don't." Costi pushed a hand through his still-damp hair again, turning on his heel to pace away from me while he talked. He listened, agitated. "I know perfectly well," he said, turning his eyes on me.

Costi sighed and scrubbed a hand down his face once he had tapped the phone off. "You heard?"

"Yeah, a little." I fidgeted.

"Don't worry about it," he said.

But I'd been worried about it for more than a year.

The three of us spent our childhood together. From the outside, we looked like an unlikely group. I was a cherished young initiate spell caster, Holly an ordinary witch who was the daughter of a chef and a food server, and Costi… once they had slapped him with the label Troubled, people assumed all sorts of things about him.

But we understood each other in a way that other witches didn't. I never quite fit in—loved for my potential and not myself, hanging back shyly on the outskirts of every group. Holly didn't talk about her home life much, but she was eager to escape it. Costi's kindness and intelligence went overlooked because his English was bad and he didn't take direction well. We were the ones left behind by the rest of our society.

Until Holly pulled away without explanation, they were my closest friends—really my only friends. With Holly gone and Costi training as a guardian, my life became empty in a way I hadn't really recovered from.

"Why does she hate me?" I asked through a tight throat.

Costi rubbed at the back of his neck. "I don't know what her problem is these days," he said, looking away. "She's… got some ideas about how things should be."

Well, that cleared up exactly nothing. "What do you mean?"

Costi dropped onto the second bed, putting his elbow over his eyes. "Everyone's got all these ideas. They don't mean a damn thing."

He didn't explain further.

After a moment, I said, "Costi, thank you."

He let his arm fall and turned slightly so he could catch my gaze. "Hm?"

"You… you kept me alive. Fought for me. Stopped Councilor Luna from asking about my magic. Got me out of there. *Thank you.*"

He paused a moment. "You never treated me like I was Troubled. I'd fight angels for you any time."

* * *

I thought I wouldn't be able to sleep, but the stress and messed-up schedule caught up to me. I slept through the rest of the day, only waking to eat the pizza Costi had ordered, then slept through most of the night as well. We left early—as soon as the car was available.

I was feeling much better as Costi began to navigate the city streets like he was a born outsider. I vibrated with excitement in my seat, restrained by the safety belt. "Does it go faster?"

He gave a downright evil-sounding chuckle. "Just wait 'til we get on the highway," he promised ominously.

It turned out the car went a *lot* faster. Costi smirked as he punched the pedal all the way down and I shrieked in terrified delight.

I watched the scenery fly past as we drove. Forests, bridges, cities full of buildings—I hadn't ever really considered how people on the outside lived or just how many of them there were. Far more than witches, and almost none of them aware of us or the war. It was strange to think that the thing I had dedicated my whole life to just didn't exist to them. They just lived.

Out here, my problems felt distant.

We would be driving for quite a while, so I slipped off my shoes and drew my legs up onto the seat. "What's it like outside?"

Costi steered with his good arm, tapping his pointer finger on the wheel. "Different."

I turned my head to hide a smile at his very Costi-like short response. "You went all around during training." Guardians had an intense four-year course after they graduated from school.

"Yeah," he said. "Mostly following up on reports and tracking down nests. A few times I went out with teams to watch an extermination."

So that had been his first time fighting angels too. "How do you think they found us?"

"Don't know, but that was more than some random angels following a guardian team back to the Circle."

He was right. The attack had been coordinated. Deliberate.

"But how? They're just… creatures." Everything we had been taught suggested the angels were mindless, without thoughts or emotions. Incredibly dangerous and virtually indestructible, but more akin to animals than humans. Ancient witch myths about the war between good and evil were one thing, but in the real world, angels did not pick up weapons and mount an organized offensive.

"Don't know that either, but we better figure it out fast."

The world outside the car passed quietly.

"You've been okay?" Costi interrupted my churning thoughts. "After I graduated and went into training, I mean. You didn't mention anyone giving you trouble."

"I was fine, just… lonely." When we were younger, some of the witch kids would pick on me when Costi wasn't around. I tried to keep it from him—I knew he would confront them, and he was already marked as Troubled. But he always knew. "I missed you." *And Holly*, I thought with a pang.

"Me too," he said gruffly. Costi ran his hand along the steering wheel. "It's been hard to get away."

I frowned. "The guardians don't give you any free time?"

"Not a lot. They don't think it's good for us. The structure's supposed to help us focus."

"*What?* That's miserable."

Costi huffed out a laugh. "Fucking hate it."

The witch Circles prided ourselves on our peacefulness. Unlike the outside world, we strove for inner balance, allowing every witch the freedom to follow their bliss. But our harmonious life came with a price. Those with violent or antisocial traits were not welcome among us.

From childhood, Costi was marked as one of the Troubled. They were supposed to receive extra guidance and care, but it seemed like he'd only ever been ignored and outcast.

Once grown, the Troubled had few options. Costi's future had always been as set in stone as mine.

As we drove, he coached me through using the map on my phone for navigation.

Once I could no longer avoid it, I opened my messaging app.

Are you there? I hope everything is going well with your new job. That was my last text to Holly from over a year ago, unanswered.

Then her text from this morning. ***I don't know what you said to him, but you have to stop making Costi drop everything and come running every time you have a problem.***

Shame flooded me, and I thumbed my phone screen off, looking out the window. I hadn't *made* him come with me.

"You okay?"

I sighed. "I'm… sorry about all this. I know you have more important things than hauling me around."

He scoffed. "Don't start with that. And don't let anybody else give you shit about it either."

He always had an eerily accurate sense of what was going on with me, even when I didn't tell him the details.

"And me?" he went on. "I'll get a medal for protecting and escorting our new secret weapon."

"Some secret weapon." I rolled my eyes. "There's no way to turn me on."

Costi gave a dark laugh.

My face flushed hot once I realized what I'd said, and I wanted to hide. I'd walked right into that. But he'd picked it up and run with it. We never joked… like *that*. I wasn't sure how to continue.

"You wanna try Greek food with me?" he asked mildly, saving me from myself. "I saw a place last time I came through here."

"You haven't had it before?"

"I'm sure I did when I was little. I don't remember. I kinda want to try it."

"Let's do it," I said, smiling.

Costi gave me the name of the restaurant, and I set the phone to give us directions. It didn't seem too far off the highway before we came to yet another shopping center. The entire highway was lined from one end to the other with towns. There seemed to be an endless number of gas stations and shops.

He pushed the glass door open over my head and let me walk in before him. I was amused by the little chime that went off to announce our entrance. The delicious scent of spices filled the small space. A few outsiders were eating at the tables, but no one else was waiting, so we went straight to the counter.

An older man with a bushy mustache and tanned skin like ours greeted us warmly. "Hello, come on up. What can I get for you?"

I had been a little worried that everyone in the outside would distrust us like the hotel lady, but this man seemed nice.

"What's good?" Costi asked.

"Have you tried Greek food before?" We shook our heads as he continued. "No? Where are you from? You look like you could be my cousins."

"He was born in Greece, but not me," I said.

"Hey! Maybe you *are* my cousin." He looked Costi up and down with a chuckle. "Maybe not. My cousins are all short."

Costi gave a half grin at his antics.

"What part of Greece are you from?"

"Not sure, really." Costi shrugged. "I don't remember much. I left when I was seven, don't know my family."

"That's a sad thing. You don't speak any Greek?"

"I remember some prayers and songs and stuff. Can't speak it at all." Costi pushed up the hair at the back of his neck.

"Let's hear," the man said eagerly. "I can tell you north or south, maybe."

"It's probably awful," Costi muttered.

"Come on, give it a try,"

Shrugging, Costi sang a quick phrase, beautiful words tumbling from his lips that tugged at my soul. I didn't think I'd ever heard him sing before. That *voice*. Low and raw, like he'd been screaming.

Fate, he should be a singer.

He'd never mentioned that he remembered any Greek. It was a *travesty* that he didn't know more. It sounded like putting words to magic. I absolutely *loved* it.

"Ah? So bad I can't understand it," the man laughed. "Is that supposed to be Greek?"

Costi shrugged with a good-natured smirk. "Told you."

The man helped us order, and soon we were scooping foods from way too many dishes, each one more delicious than the last. I could get used to the food outside.

"Costi," I started as he finished the food I had given up on. All that muscle must have required a ridiculous amount of fuel. "Do you… I mean, when you were little, were you there? During the attack?"

He raised his eyes to me, putting down his spoon. "I must have been, but I don't remember anything. Maybe they hid me. I'm not traumatized."

"You spent our entire childhood mouthing off, fighting, and getting in trouble," I pointed out with a flat look.

Costi gave me a wicked half grin, and my heart tripped over itself. "Nah, that's not trauma. I'm like that naturally."

I quickly looked down at my plate, disturbed by my reaction. "What… what *do* you remember? If you want to tell me…"

He was thoughtful for a moment. Tinny pop music played softly in the background. "I think about it a lot, but there's not much. I remember my mom. She liked singing—she taught me a lot of little songs. We lived by the ocean, but the water was a lot bluer than back at the Northern Sea. Warmer, more sun."

I felt a twinge of sadness. It sounded like a happy life that had been stolen from him. "Do you remember coming to the Circle?"

Costi shook his head. "I remember you, though, in the park. You were so tiny. I just wanted to… I don't know… protect you or something. I think I had a little sister, and you reminded me of her."

My heart warmed. It was my earliest memory, playing in the park with Costi. I hadn't heard the full story until I was older—how the adults had realized that he wasn't anyone's child and couldn't speak English. At first, they thought he had wandered in from outside, but he had the look of witches with his dusky skin and light eyes, and he could sense magic.

The attack in Greece had happened only weeks before—it was all too clear what had occurred. Someone had abandoned him in the American Circle that was easiest to get to from Europe. We never found out who or why. They never came forward. As far as anyone knew, Costi was the only survivor of that tragedy.

Diana Blackthorn, an older witch who hadn't ever wanted a partner or her own children, fostered Costi until he was old enough to join the guardians.

"I never knew. I'm sorry you missed growing up with them. Your mom and little sister."

I wondered if anyone had gone back to investigate. What went so completely wrong that the angels were able to raze that Circle to the ground? Had it been the same as Northern Sea? Was there anything left? Records or something?

Costi shrugged. "I got to grow up with you."

After he had scraped every dish clean and been teased for it by the shopkeeper, we got back in the car. The highways turned to hills as the daylight turned gold and slipped away, and we finally passed the sign that declared "Welcome to West Virginia."

We arrived at the Mountain Circle well after dark.

Chapter 4

LAYLA

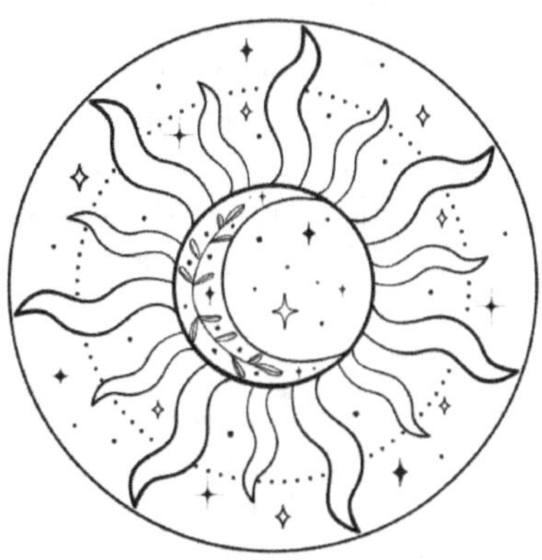

I had never visited another witch Circle before. A long dirt road led through a dense forest to an ornate metal gate, which had been left open. Our Circles were purposely in remote locations, both to keep the non-magical humans from discovering us and to be near the desolate places where angels were most likely to infest.

I gasped as I took in the scene before me. Beyond the gate, the Mountain Circle glowed with lights, hundreds of dwellings sprawling up into the silhouettes of the rounded hills behind it. It was easily three times the size of our Circle, maybe more. With the stars twinkling in the dark sky above, it was like something from a dream.

Floodlights had been set up, illuminating a wide field beside the road, where witches were busy setting up orange cones and tents. Costi parked the car in the grass, rolling his shoulder and trying to crack his neck as he got out. "No idea how I'm gonna get that thing back to the rental place."

"Will they be mad?" I hurried around the vehicle to catch up with him.

"They'll charge the Council a bunch of money, and I'll get yelled at."

Maybe we could find a way to fix the issue later, once we knew everyone was safe.

We approached a canopy that was coldly illuminated by a series of orb-like witch lights dangling from the frame.

"Another two arrivals. They're picking up. We'll probably see the influx soon," the witch sitting behind the table underneath the canopy said into a two-way radio. "Your names?" He looked at us expectantly.

"Layla Rosen. Constantine Blackthorn," Costi said.

The Mountain Circle witch looked at Costi's uniform. "Guardians stay in the barracks. Turn *left* and follow the signs." He shuffled through a stack of papers with a frustrated sigh. "Rosen, was it? You're with your coven in housing block F. Go *straight*, and look for the one labeled F."

"I… um…"

"Problem?" the witch growled at Costi and me when I didn't move.

"Did you say coven? I'm not in a coven."

He squinted at his papers. "Layla Rosen, Spell Caster, Mountain Thunder Coven." He shrugged angrily. "I don't handle the housing assignments. Just go there and figure it out later. Be happy you're not in the tents."

"What's that all about?" I whispered as we moved toward the path.

Costi scowled, the cut on his face making him look menacing in the orange glow of lamplight. "Stressed out, probably."

We stopped where the path split. I looked up at him. We'd been together ever since the attack, and now I wished I could keep him with me. I didn't want to be by myself in this new place, especially after that lackluster welcome. "I guess… I'll see you later."

Costi hesitated, and we stood awkwardly for a moment. He looked as lost as I felt. I swayed with the overwhelming urge to hug him, curling my hands against my thighs. It probably wasn't a good idea.

"Yeah. I'll find you soon," he said, then took the left path.

Adrift in the strange Circle, I moved along the lighted walkway that seemed to be a central path. Witches—all strangers—passed, not paying me any attention. The general mood seemed tense, everyone on edge after the attack.

I found housing block F, a square built around a courtyard with a dozen attached apartments. I swiveled my head helplessly. The coordinator at the gate hadn't told me which apartment I was in.

The sound of a door opening made me turn my head. A stoutly built witch a little older than me with a shaved head exited one of the apartments, hurrying down the steps.

"Excuse me," I said to catch their attention.

They stopped and looked at me. "Oh, hey. Are you one of the Northern Sea witches?"

"Yes. Do you know where the Mountain Thunder Coven stays?"

The witch looked horrified. "Fate bend me over, what for?"

"I'm supposed to stay with them. Is… is something wrong?"

They winced. "I'm sorry. No. Not really. They're just… you'll see. They're in the first apartment, right there. But I don't think anyone's home."

"Oh, um, thanks. See you around?"

"See you. Good luck," the witch said as they turned to go.

I knocked on the door, but as the witch had said, no one seemed to be home, and the lights were off inside. I sat down on the steps to wait, resting after my walk. If I was going to have to go up and down these hills every day, I'd be in great shape in no time.

An assortment of solar lamps lit the courtyard, two large oak trees standing over a blooming garden filling the night with the scent of blossoms. Crickets chirped in the quiet space.

Nature remained peaceful, the world humming along even during the worst human crises.

My fingers moved to my phone to text Costi… but I hesitated. Holly was right, even if it had hurt me to hear it. I needed to learn how to take care of my own problems.

Instead, I sent a text to my mother letting her know I had arrived at the Mountain Circle safely, trying not to read her messages above mine. I didn't mention where I was staying.

I sat for a few moments longer, conjuring up a plan to seek out something to eat, when a group of three witches around my age entered the courtyard, talking in hushed tones. They saw me sitting alone on their steps and halted.

I stood up to greet them.

"Is this her?" one of the witches asked, propping a hand on his hip. He was slender, with dark hair styled to perfection and looking purposely messy, with a pair of bright hazel eyes.

"You must be Layla," said another. She was a tall and willowy woman in a short dress, with gleaming black hair. She was carrying a fabric tote bag in both hands.

"I guess we can't get out of it now," said the third witch, all sulky lips and dark eyeliner. A mass of dark curls tumbled off her head and billowed around her curvy body.

"Hello, nice to meet you," I said with a smile, trying to look confident. They were all so well put together, and I felt like a mess. "I'm not sure what's going on. The witch at the gate said I would be staying with you. I hope it's all right."

The three of them burst out laughing at a joke I wasn't in on.

"Fate, she's super polite," the curly haired witch said.

"That won't last," the bright-eyed one said.

"I'm Sativa," said the tall witch, rolling her eyes. "This walking fashion show is Oliver, and somewhere under all these curls is Datura. Welcome to Mountain Thunder."

"I'm a little confused," I told Sativa as the others opened the door. The group tumbled inside and flicked on a light while we kicked off our shoes.

The main room of the apartment was spacious enough, with high windows shaded for the night.

The comfortable-looking couch set was strewn with clothes and bags. A tiny counter and island made up a small kitchen area with a mini refrigerator, toaster oven, sink, and a water boiler. It was piled with dishes and food containers. The place was a disaster.

Sativa pushed some of the mess aside, hoisted her bag up onto the counter, and began removing containers of food. I hoped they were in the mood to share or could at least tell me where to go get some.

"They said there was a new spell caster in Northern Sea who wasn't in a coven yet, so congratulations, you're in a coven now." She waved her hand at the messy apartment.

The Northern Sea Circle only had one coven of spell casters. How big *was* the Mountain Circle?

"Don't worry, you meet every qualification. You'll fit right in," Oliver said.

"We don't have any qualifications." Datura rolled her eyes, grabbing a plate and starting to fill it. "No one else would want to be in this coven."

"There's literally no one else *to* be in this coven." Oliver twiddled a spoon around in his fingers.

Sativa handed me a plate and a spoon. "Thanks," I murmured.

"Aw, she's all sweet and shy," said Oliver. "She can be our little baby caster, and we can teach her to be a vicious angel killer." He patted me on the head.

I was already a vicious angel killer. I had zapped a whole squadron of angels minus one. Even if I had no idea how.

"I appreciate you letting me stay with you, but you should know up front that there's a reason I'm not in a coven yet." I couldn't let this go on without being honest. My face flushed in embarrassment. "I can't invoke my familiar. It won't... come out."

"That's a new one," Sativa said, frowning. "Is it mad at you? They can be touchy if you mess with them."

"Hooray, another screwup for the screwup coven." Datura pushed a pile of glossy gossip magazines out of the way and plunked her plate down on the island to eat.

"Performance anxiety," Oliver declared, twirling his spoon around to point it at me.

"Maybe," I said. There wasn't anywhere to sit, so I balanced my plate, trying to eat while standing. My injured shoulder ached. I mindlessly filled my mouth with some sort of potato casserole.

"Who thinks we're going to get attacked next?" Datura sang with sarcastic glee.

Oliver raised his hand with a matching grin.

"Oh, here we go," Sativa said.

I cleared my throat. "Our teams were pretty thorough. I don't think there are any angels left to come attack here." I swallowed back a wave of tears. I was so tired.

Datura left her empty plate where it was, and Oliver stacked his on top of it. They retreated to the couch in the middle of the room, each pulling out a phone and sprawling out together.

"I heard one of the Northern Sea casters did some kind of super spell that killed a dozen angels at once," Datura said.

Oliver tapped his phone excitedly. "Ooh, is there video? Check the group chat."

"Did you see the super spell, Layla?" Datura called.

I cringed with a painful self-awareness that made me want to disappear into the floor. Both telling them and not telling them was awkward. But I would need to discuss it. At some point.

"I'm… I'm sorry, I'm just…"

"Cool it, you two. She's barely upright." Sativa took my empty plate and stacked it on the counter with the others. She gave me an apologetic look. "Come on, I'll show you your room."

The apartment had four bedrooms arranged with a bathroom on a short hallway. Sativa showed me to a small, plain room with two beds, not too unlike the hotel the night before, but much homier. A wide window was covered with a blind. "You'll have to share if we get any more members, but it's all yours for now."

I closed the door behind her and turned off the overhead light, leaving only the pretty glass side lamp on. I carefully sat down on the bed.

Aloneness and confusion pressed in on me.

Becoming a spell caster and joining the coven had been my life plan—really the only plan available. I never even considered anything else. I was supposed to team up with Costi, and we would venture around cleaning out angel infestations for a decade or so before I settled down with a nice, handsome spell caster from an exotic and far-off Circle.

My failure to summon a familiar, followed by the last two days, had delivered me into a nightmare and left me reeling. Would I ever see my home again? Were the angels somehow evolving to be deadlier? *Would* they come after us as Datura feared?

My phone blinked on as a message came through.

You okay?

One of the strings of tension in my body released.

I'm fine, I texted Costi back. *I found the coven. Are you okay?*

Fine.

I breathed out a silent laugh at his typically Costi reply.

I'd rather stay with you came the second message.

A wistful longing twisted through me, shocking me with its intensity and making my throat catch on a sob. I drew a shaking breath and forced myself to be calm. I could handle this. I *would* handle this. I just needed to rest and then do some thinking.

Determined, I pulled myself off the bed and crept out into the dim hallway, finding the bathroom to brush my teeth and clean myself up. The other bedrooms were closed, but I could see a strip of light under two of them. Oliver and one of the others chatted in the same scandalized tones that seemed to be their norm, but I didn't pause to listen.

I changed into sleeping clothes and inspected the bed nearest the door. It seemed to be clean and already made up, so I slipped under the covers.

I'd rather stay with you, my phone displayed mercilessly.

I stuffed my head into my pillow and pushed the phone as far away from myself as I could.

* * *

COSTI

Barracks, huh? My accommodations had just gone from bad to worse. At least Layla would be safe with her coven. The other witches from Northern Sea were out in tents.

My new home was a cot in a white-painted room, shared with eleven other guardians. A rack for equipment took up most of one wall, a row of dark square windows on the opposite side. It smelled like sweat covered up with herbal cleaning stuff. It was empty except for one guardian.

Ash sat up as I tossed my duffel onto the bed next to theirs. They were still in uniform, their black hair hanging straight to their shoulders. I couldn't see any injuries.

"Costi. Why don't you ever answer your phone?"

I pulled it out and showed them the cracked screen. "Got into a little fight. No big deal."

They smacked the phone out of my hand and sucked in a breath. "What in Hell's name happened? What were you doing out on the seawall in the middle of the night with that spell caster?"

"Talking. Good thing, too, or we would have all been burned to a crisp in our sleep." I sat on the creaky cot and pushed up my sleeve to examine the bandage on my bicep. The wound hadn't bled through too badly. "I got wrecked. You okay?"

"I'm fine. Mostly. After we cleaned up your mess, I drove all day with the first evacuation group."

"Did everyone… make it?"

They didn't answer right away. My heart dropped.

"Not everyone," they finally said. "Aspen, Myron, Kalmia. They… gave their lives. We didn't lose any casters, and the angels never got past the wall."

Shit. Three guardians dead. I used to sit with Aspen in the cafeteria. Myron was quiet, never saying much. Kalmia loved sunflower seeds and was always spitting the shells out everywhere. Three good lives ended—the first casualties in the war in a long time.

"Where did you end up?"

In a room alone with the spell caster I'm supposed to be avoiding. "One of the councilors had me evacuate Layla."

They raised their dark eyebrows.

I looked back steadily. There was no way they could see anything on my face. "Not important. I heard the angels had weapons."

"Yes. Some kind of lasers that could hit from the air about ten feet up. It was only thanks to fate that more of us didn't get toasted." They showed me a burn mark on their wrist.

I ran a hand through my hair. "What's the chance they won't follow us here?"

Ash barked a laugh. "Absolutely zero. We're screwed. We'd better stay ready."

The barracks door swung open, and black-clothed witches poured in. They were all Northern Sea guardians, about half of our twenty. *Seventeen now*, I remembered with a pang.

A giant of a witch named Bay plonked down on the cot next to mine. He gave an easy grin. "Blackthorn, Vervain. Glad to see you survived." He pointed at the gash on my forehead. "That's an improvement. Your face is too symmetrical."

"All right, guardians," called the middle-aged witch who followed the group in. Her hair was streaked with gray and pulled back in a severe bun. "I'm Tansy Daire, the security coordinator here at the Mountain Circle. I'll be helping you get settled. I'm reassigning all of you based on your skill level."

Ash caught my eye with a skeptical frown, and I saw others around me looking the same. Reassigning us without our input? That was… different.

"Our guidelines for guardians are similar to those of the Northern Sea Circle, designed to help you manage your Troubled natures and be a successful, contributing member of witch society."

I couldn't stop an eye roll, but Daire didn't seem to notice.

"One: stick to your routine. A scheduled bedtime helps you regulate your energy. Two: reach out to me or someone you trust if you're having difficulty. And three: keep your hands off the spell casters." Daire grinned.

The other guardians chuckled at the third guideline. I ground my teeth together against a flare of annoyance. Witches were all about freedom and choice until it came to their precious spell casters. Then it was *you better not contaminate that gene pool with your Troubled DNA* and *don't you dare distract our casters from their noble purpose.*

From the moment I got to the Northern Sea Circle, they told me to keep away from Layla. But I never could follow directions.

Daire continued, "I hope the Mountain Circle will be a new start for you. I'd hate to lose any of you."

The Troubled were too violent, too moody for polite witch society. For the ones who didn't respond to therapy, being a guardian was our last chance to prove ourselves. It didn't take much to get thrown out.

"All right." She clapped her hands. "I'll let you get some rest— you'll need it, we're about to put you on rotation. You'll get your updated assignments in the morning, and then there's an assembly."

When Daire had closed the barracks doors again, I picked up my shattered phone and tapped at the screen carefully, trying to text Layla to see if she was okay.

Ash scoffed, peeling off their boots. "That's it? No one's worried about another attack?"

But my mind was already on other things. "Ash. You know anything about familiars?"

Chapter 5

LAYLA

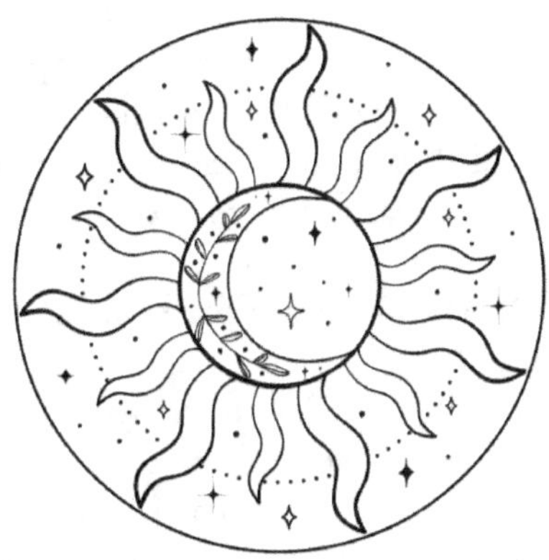

Harvest dawned clear and bright. In normal times, it would be a day for ritual and celebration. I didn't know what kind of holiday we would have with everything going on. I hadn't set an alarm, but I woke up to the sounds of people moving in the house and pulled on a linen summer dress to join them. It was a bit warmer here than back home.

"Hey, you don't have time for breakfast," Sativa said, looking me over. A crimson spell caster's robe clung to her lithe body and flared out around her legs. "But I brought you a fruit bar." She handed me the bar, wrapped in a cloth napkin.

"Thanks," I said with a small smile. We didn't seem that similar, but I liked her. "Are we in a hurry?"

"The Arcaenum is holding a general assembly this morning. We can go to the practice arena afterward. Datura and Oliver don't believe you about the familiar thing. They want to see."

"The Arcaenum?"

"It's our elected council."

Sativa led me out of the apartment and along the crowded walkways while I ate my fruit bar. Most everyone seemed to be going in the same direction. The fresh mountain air held a hint of a cool breeze.

"So, what's your story? Do you have a lover or anything?" Sativa asked.

"No, nothing like that," I said. I paused awkwardly before asking, "Do you?"

"Several," she preened.

I could see why. She was confident and beautiful. No one had ever shown me much interest in that department—spell casters were discouraged from dating other witches, and I had a reputation for hanging out with the Troubled. With only ten casters in the Circle and a few more still in school, there wasn't a large selection.

"I could hook you up," Sativa offered. "I know everyone in the Mountain Circle. Do you have any preferences? We have a few hot casters who are unattached."

I choked a little. "Thanks. I'm not really… looking right now." If I *could* invoke my familiar, I would have cast a spell directly into the ground in hopes that the blast would make a giant hole to swallow me.

But… was I really not looking? I was in a new Circle. One with hot, single spell casters. There was nothing stopping me. In the past, I'd sometimes imagined meeting someone—I'd thought about going on dates and finding a lover. But now my feelings were in knots.

"Let me know if you change your mind," Sativa said.

"Morning!" Oliver called brightly as he and Datura joined us. They were both dressed in athletic training clothes, but Oliver had styled his short dark hair into loose waves.

We walked into a large amphitheater with seats built into the hill above the stage area. It was already crowded with witches.

"Hey, Screwup," Datura said with a smirk.

Oliver gasped and smacked her arm. "D, be *nice*! She got attacked by like a hundred angels and fled for her life!"

"I heard they're switching up all the pairings now that Northern Sea got added." Datura changed the subject. "I saw Calamus Grey with a new guardian already."

The two continued to gossip while the amphitheater filled. I didn't see anyone I knew that well, but the crowd looked to be a mix of Northern Sea and Mountain witches. The evacuation must have been well underway.

There were far more Mountain witches. Our circle was—had been—the smallest in the eastern part of America, and the Mountain Circle was one of the larger ones, if not the largest. We were swallowed up by them.

A tall witch in the formal black robes of a councilor strode onto the stage below, and the witches began to settle. The councilor looked to be in his middle years, with neatly trimmed salt-and-pepper hair and beard. His face was lined with seriousness, and he walked with quick purpose, not pausing to greet the other councilors as he passed.

"Good morning," he said, his voice naturally projecting through the amphitheater. The crowd quieted.

"I'm Cedar Grey, elected councilor of the Mountain Circle Arcaenum and speaker for the assembly today." He folded his arms gracefully into his robes, moving restlessly as he addressed us. "The feast of Harvest is supposed to be a joyous time to celebrate the first harvest. But this year, we find ourselves in a state of distress."

Oliver whispered some reaction to Datura and then turned back to listen. Sativa was ignoring the speech, her thumbs flying over her phone. I imagined it look some effort to keep up with multiple lovers.

"Three days ago, the witches of the Northern Sea Circle suffered an unprecedented attack. Our ancient enemy discovered and menaced them in their very home, a Circle standing since the 1800s. The Northern Sea Circle battled bravely, and I would like to take a moment to acknowledge the three guardians who lost their lives defending their spell casters."

I felt numb as the witches bowed their heads in silence. *Three* guardians? Guardians fought angels all the time without a scratch.

A cold fear settled in me. Costi had mentioned weapons.

Fate, it could have been *us*.

I wondered who the guardians were—the councilor didn't mention their names. I scanned the crowd, trying to pick out Costi. He must have known them. My heart ached for him.

"Despite this tragic loss, fate was on the side of goodness that night. The Northern Sea caught the attack early enough to muster before the angels got to the Circle. They never made it past the line of defense, and the witches of the Circle remained safe, sheltered in their homes. Northern Sea was *victorious.*"

Councilor Grey nodded once and waited while thunderous applause swept the amphitheater. I breathed through the memory of the shrieking of angels and the feel of magic rushing through me.

"As of yet," he continued once it was quiet, "it is unclear how the angels were able to discover the location of Northern Sea. We do not know yet whether this tragedy was brought on by a mistake... or a betrayal."

A murmuring began in the crowd. I frowned at the implication—the same one the spell caster Aura's guardian had been muttering about in the infirmary. None of our witches would be that careless. And I couldn't even entertain the thought of a betrayal of that magnitude. Who would do such a thing? There were *children* in the Circle.

Councilor Grey held up his hand, and the chatter died down. "Know that the Arcaenum is taking this matter very seriously, and we will be leading a full investigation," he promised. "In the meantime, we are dealing with the influx of over four hundred refugees from the Northern Sea Circle, a large percentage of their number."

The rest of our witches must have scattered to other Circles, perhaps to extended family or friends.

"At this time, all witches have been evacuated from the settlement, aside from the monitoring teams. Angel scouts have been sighted several times, sweeping the area around the Northern Sea Circle."

Gasps and worried sounds rose from the crowd.

"We do not," said Councilor Grey over the din, "have any reason to believe angels tracked any of the escaping witches, or that they have discovered the location of the Mountain Circle. But we urge everyone to stay vigilant. In our lifetimes, we have had a reprieve, but we cannot forget that *we are at war.*" He punctuated his words, bringing his fist down into his palm.

"As for our new arrivals," he continued, "spell casters, guardians, and circlewrights have already been vetted and assigned—our top priority has always been and continues to be the protection of this Circle.

The rest of you are free to join in whatever endeavors you are called to. We have limited extra housing, so our second priority will be finding more long-term solutions and building new facilities."

Grey paced in front of the crowd of witches, catching eyes.

"Northern Sea witches may have noticed that we do things a bit differently here. We are a large Circle, and we rely on *organization* to keep us running smoothly. If you wish to stay on with us, I suggest you adapt."

I blinked, eyebrows raised. What in fate's name did *that* mean?

"The Arcaenum recognizes that the Northern Sea had their own council, but given the circumstances, that council has been dissolved."

My breath stuck in my throat as the Northern Sea witches erupted in confusion and outrage. "You can't *dissolve* our council!" shouted someone behind me. "There was no consensus!"

"You can't just take control. You're creating a hierarchy!"

"Order, please!" Grey boomed. "Accusations of Inperium are *extremely* out of line."

Mouths snapped closed in stunned silence. A chill went through me. Witches didn't just throw that word around casually.

"Our elections are held at Candle Day next year," Grey spoke up into the ringing quiet. "Until then, the *currently elected* Arcaenum of the Mountain Circle will continue to serve."

"What of the Northern Sea?" a witch shouted from the front.

Grey narrowed his eyes, focusing on them. "The destroyed Circle is welcome to reform and return to *their own* land. Any witches who choose to take up residence with the Mountain Circle are expected to become part of *this* Circle."

Voices picked up in anger as Grey strode from the stage in a flutter of robes into a knot of witches trying to get his attention. I saw our Northern Sea councilor—make that ex-councilor— Jenny Luna among the throng.

Around me, witches began standing to leave the amphitheater.

"Maybe we should head to Kentucky or the Carolinas," a Northern Sea witch behind me said to their companion. "I have a couple of cousins in the Saltmarsh Circle."

A wave of homesickness for a place that didn't even exist washed over me.

Maybe I could go too—start over somewhere else, away from my mother and the people I grew up with. I wondered how Costi was getting along with the guardians here, if he'd want to come with me.

"Let's try to get out of here quickly. Use your elbows," Sativa said, demonstrating. "We need some practice space, and if we don't grab ours first, it's going to be chaos."

"'Scuse us! Important coven business," Oliver called out as we pushed past witches, using the seats as stairs to avoid the slow lines.

Humiliated, I followed with my face down, hoping no one I knew would see me.

I didn't want to do this right now. I was exhausted and worried, and I just wanted to go somewhere quiet and try to make sense of all this. I needed to talk to Costi.

It turned out my coven's assertive exit technique did win us a space in the rapidly filling practice arena.

The arena seemed to be one of the largest buildings in the Circle. It had the look of a warehouse. The high ceiling was lined with rows of electric lights currently turned off while natural sunlight poured in from skylights. Stark yellow lines were painted onto the floor, designating practice spaces.

The open space was a far cry from the private practice areas back home, a riot of noise and movement as casters and their familiars blasted off spells into targets along the walls while guardians tussled in the center area. The sulfuric, burned-firework smell of spell casting mixed nauseatingly with sweat and breath.

Our coven's space was designed for spell casters—a long rectangle facing a reinforced wall with a target. We could cast small spells to practice our aim and control here. There was most likely an open space outside where casters could burn off larger spells safely.

"All right, whip them out," Sativa said with a cheeky grin, closing her eyes briefly as she summoned her familiar. Her demon companion appeared beside her with a rush of flame. Like all familiars, it was about the height and build of a human child and starkly pale, with large black eyes that lacked an iris. Wispy white-blond hair clung to its head around its sharply pointed ears. Its small bud-shaped mouth was closed around a jaw full of pointed teeth.

The familiars wore no clothing, but they had no sex to conceal and didn't seem to get cold or hot. They didn't speak, but it was a mistake to think they weren't intelligent and cunning. If they were displeased, their spell caster would know it.

Datura and Oliver followed suit, bringing out their familiars and leaving me standing awkwardly alone.

"This is Inky," Sativa said, patting hers on the head with a fond smirk.

I glanced at the little demon in alarm. They famously hated to be condescended to.

"I'm a natural summoner," Sativa continued. "Inky came to me when I was fourteen."

"Wow." That *was* surprising. I'd never met a natural summoner before; there weren't any in Northern Sea. Maybe it explained why Inky was so tolerant.

Most spell casters got their familiars by working a summoning circle when they graduated, but occasionally, an initiate would summon one early, without a circle. The reason and mechanism for this was completely unknown, but the leading theory was that demons were attracted to witches who could pull a lot of magic.

It didn't happen to every powerful witch, though, my case in point. I squelched a spark of envy for Sativa—she really was blessed in every area. This was hardly the screwup coven, as Datura had suggested.

"Our familiars don't have names, because we're *normal*." Oliver gestured between himself and Datura, who rolled her eyes. "We got them the normal way. A very normal summoning circle."

Sativa stuck her tongue out at him.

Datura shrugged. "We can still burn the fate out of things."

The conversation stalled. I rubbed my shoe along the sealed floor of the arena. "Are your guardians joining us? I should probably meet them."

The three covenmates glanced between themselves in a silent conversation.

Oliver chewed his lip, hedging. "We haven't exactly chosen them yet."

My eyebrows rose. None of them? They would have graduated at the same time I did, months ago, but they hadn't formed teams yet?

"Well," said Sativa, cutting me off before I could ask about it. "Give it a shot, newbie."

I sighed. "Don't expect too much. I've already tried a hundred times."

Closing my eyes against the stuffy, noisy room, I ran through the mental sequence to invoke my familiar. It was an ancient rite, different from casting spells or working circles. I felt the source of the magic inside me surge as I called forth my bonded familiar—but when I opened my eyes, I was still alone.

I swallowed around a tight throat, forcing my chin up. I wouldn't cry in front of these witches.

Oliver and Datura were frowning, Sativa was pensive, looking around me as if maybe the familiar was hiding in my hair.

"Did you do it?" Sativa asked.

"Did you do it *right*?" Datura added.

"Do it again," said Oliver.

I tried again, and again, while they watched.

"This is so messed-up," said Sativa.

Datura shrugged. "I told you she was a screwup like us."

"D, seriously. Try pulling some magic in when you do it," Oliver suggested. "Maybe you need extra oomph?"

I pulled in a little, not wanting to make myself sick since I had no way of pushing it back out. Except for whatever happened during the attack, and I wasn't about to pull in *that* much magic—I would seriously hurt myself.

The pressure of the magic hurt my head as I tried and failed a fourth time. Tears of frustration pricked my eyes.

"Layla." Costi rolled in like a storm in full uniform, a tall spell caster trailing behind him. He took in my face and then snapped his narrowed eyes to my companions as if they had done something to me.

"I'm fine," I murmured automatically, squinting against the sky-lights that were now irritatingly bright, creating a halo around everything. I had pulled more magic than I realized. *A little* had always been tricky for me.

"Hey, Calamus," Sativa said to the spell caster. "Is this your new guardian?"

My already queasy stomach lurched. I met Costi's gaze. It shouldn't be shocking—we *needed* functional teams, now more than ever.

But I was supposed to be his spell caster.

"Hello, Sativa. Hello, Mountain Thunder," my replacement, Calamus, said with a polite smile, turning a curious eye on me. He looked to be around my age and classically handsome, with an athletic build and bright blue eyes. His glossy black hair was neatly trimmed around his ears. He was wearing formal crimson spell caster robes, finely tailored and immaculate. My mother would love him.

"This is Constantine Blackthorn," Calamus introduced Costi to the coven, who suddenly seemed to be on their best behavior as they greeted him.

"I can see why Blackthorn wanted to come over so urgently," he continued with a smile directed at me. "You're Layla, right?"

"It's nice to meet you," I said without thought. My head began to throb.

"I've been hoping I'd run into you. You're the talk of the Circle," Calamus said as he took my hand in his and shook it. "The spell caster who defeated a whole squadron of angels."

"That was you?" Oliver hopped back and forth. "The super spell? But how—"

Ignoring my covenmate, Costi cut a dark look at Calamus as I extracted my hand and murmured an incoherent thanks for the compliment. "Why is she all pale?" he snapped at Sativa. Her familiar—Inky—hissed at him, showing its rows of sharp teeth.

"I didn't do anything to her," Sativa protested, widening her eyes and then looking to Inky in alarm.

"That's interesting," Calamus said, frowning at Inky. "I've never seen a familiar do that before."

"Really? They always do that," I said. "I'm fine. I just pulled in too much magic."

I had been talking to Costi, but Calamus answered. "You're having backlash? Why don't you invoke your familiar and cast something?"

"I'm having an issue with that. I can't seem to invoke," I explained, feeling irritated.

"Of course. You must have burned out your magic after that giant spell."

"No, I… I've never been able to invoke."

Calamus's brows lifted. "Not at all? How were you able to cast? I've never heard of that happening."

I shrugged, uncomfortable. "Something's wrong. I… haven't been able to figure it out yet."

"I'll look into it for you," he said. "I have connections with the Arcaenum and the library. I'll find someone who can help."

"Really? You don't have to go to any trouble—"

"It's no trouble, Layla." Calamus smiled warmly.

"Grey," Costi barked, causing me to jump. "We should get back to it."

"Of course," Calamus said, his expression frozen into politeness. He clasped his hands together.

I caught Costi's icy gray glare with a questioning gaze. He exhaled and ran a hand over the back of his neck. "You okay?"

My lips parted. I wasn't okay. I wanted him to walk me back to my apartment and hug me again like he did at the hotel. "I'll… go rest soon."

He nodded once, his mouth set tightly. He made no move to leave.

Calamus hesitated. "It was really a pleasure to meet you, Layla. I'll get in touch soon. I'd like to ask you more about the trouble you're having. Maybe we—"

He cut off as Costi's eyes snapped to him. My breath caught at the dark, angry look. Fate, Costi did *not* like this spell caster.

"I suppose we'll leave you to it," Calamus said with a strained smile.

With a final glance at me, Costi turned to follow him through the training arena.

Chapter 6

LAYLA

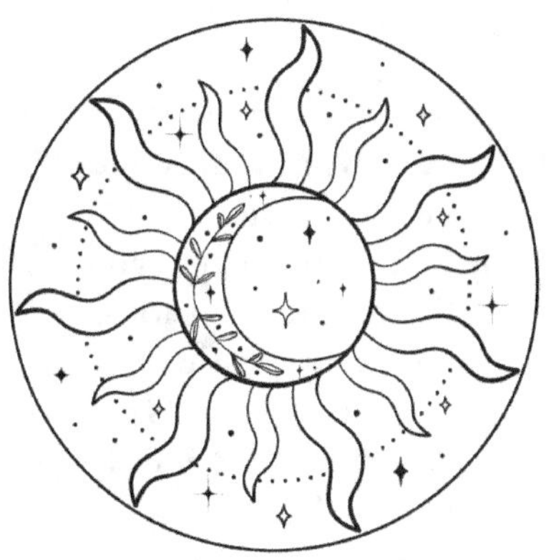

As soon as Costi and Calamus were gone, my new coven descended on me with three identical feral grins. I backed up, hitting the target on the wall.

"You've been holding out on us, Screwup." Datura bounced on her toes, her curls tumbling everywhere. "You cast a mysterious super spell."

Oliver rubbed his hands together. "*And* you have a hot older brother who's paired with the Mountain Circle's favorite golden-boy spell caster."

My mouth fell open as horror seized me. "I'm not related to *Costi*!" My face flamed at my outburst as confusion began to creep in.

"Oh. *Ohhhh. Costi*, is it?" Oliver chuckled.

Sativa laughed out loud. "That wasn't an angry sibling thing. That was pure possessive frustration. Our Layla has that poor guardian strung out."

I wished for fate to immediately turn me into compost and save me from whatever this was. "It's nothing like that," I said, waving my hands in denial. *It wasn't, right?* Of course it wasn't. "We've been friends since I was three years old. We just got attacked. We almost died. He's *worried*."

Sativa raised her eyebrows. "So, you don't mind if I go for him, then?"

Absolutely not happening. I choked, unable to form words while my covenmates laughed uproariously at my expression, drawing annoyed looks from the witches in the practice space next to us.

"We can't date guardians," I hissed, looking around to make sure no one else heard me.

Oliver snickered. "Who said anything about dating?"

Sativa rolled her eyes. "It's just some weird thing our parents made up anyway. Probably to make sure more spell casters get born. I'd give a guardian a try, at least once. I bet they're good in bed, very athletic."

"You would not," Oliver said, and turned to me. "She's been with the same three casters for over a year. They're practically married."

"Are we not going to mention that Grey had hearts popping out of his eyes and Blackthorn was about to murder him?" Datura gleefully piled fuel onto the raging trash fire.

"Oh no, we're *definitely* going to mention that," said Oliver excitedly.

"Rival fight!" Sativa and Datura howled in unison, pumping up their fists.

My face burned with embarrassment. My stomach lurched, and I swallowed down the urge to throw up as the magic I had pulled in wreaked havoc with my body. "I have to go."

"Layla?" Sativa cried after me as I hurried from the arena.

I fortunately remembered the way back to our coven apartment, where I just made it before miserably retching up the remains of my fruit bar into the toilet. I gave brushing my teeth an attempt, took a tincture of willow bark for the pain, then crawled into bed fully dressed.

My head throbbed with unreleased magic, but at least the nausea had subsided. I would have a headache for several more hours at least. I couldn't be sure how much I had pulled in—it was always more than

I realized. I should have known better.

I should have *been* better.

I wished I was someone naturally confident like Sativa, and well put together like Holly. Anyone other than me—this cold and uptight perfectionist who failed at the single task life had requested of her. Someone who couldn't even defend herself against mild teasing, who couldn't control her magic whatsoever, who needed Costi to help her with *everything* because she had no clue how anything worked.

A screwup.

* * *

I woke up hours later from a deep sleep, feeling cottony and thirsty, but it seemed most of the magic had worked itself out of my body. My skin always felt sensitive afterward. I imagined it was from the magic evaporating out of my pores, but I had no actual understanding of how it worked.

I stomped to the kitchen, washing out a glass because there weren't any clean ones and then filling it with water. My covenmates didn't seem to be home.

Now that I wasn't in pain, I was *angry*.

It wasn't *my* idea to join Mountain Thunder. What made them think they could just laugh at me like that? There wasn't anything going on with me and Costi anyway. Even if… even if I wanted there to be, he was an adult with an important role, and I was a hot mess barely out of school and four years younger than him. Not to mention the guardians would kick him out for even thinking about it.

His inked, muscular body, intense gray eyes, and the wicked grin hiding his golden heart came to my mind unbidden. He never talked about lovers, but if he wanted one, he could have his pick. The label of Troubled wouldn't stop anyone at all if they got a look at him.

He certainly wouldn't be fist-fighting his spell caster over *me*. There weren't a pair of witches in all the Circles that would start a rival fight over me. The notion was ridiculous. I was beginning to realize that my new coven was absolutely *obsessed* with drama, and if they didn't find some, they would make it.

I dug around on the messy counter and in random cabinets until I found a container marked Baked Rosemary Crackers with a date last week. I sniffed them to confirm that they were, in fact, recently baked rosemary crackers before nibbling on one absently.

I sighed, some of my anger dissipating. That was probably all it was. My covenmates liked stirring things up. This wasn't personal. They seemed nice enough. I might have even appreciated their snarky humor if I hadn't just fled for my life and had my world destroyed. If I made an effort to get along with them, I thought we could be friends. At least Sativa and Oliver seemed willing. Datura might come around if I didn't let her get to me.

I took my bounty back to my room with a fresh glass of water and noticed a note on my door I hadn't seen on my way out.

Sorry if we went overboard. Harvest party tonight, want to go? —S

Sativa left her number below, so I texted her with my response.

Hey, this is Layla. Sorry if I overreacted. I pulled too much magic and got sick. Yes to the party, let me know what time.

There. That was perfect. I'd go to a party with my coven and try to bond with them. Maybe I could find some fun gossip to share.

That sucks, Sativa texted back. ***Hope you feel better. We're leaving at 9, you can walk over with us.***

My mood lifted. Because of my summoning failure, I had missed all the graduation parties and had been drowning in stress since then. I could definitely use the chance to unwind.

It was only early afternoon, so I had time to kill. My mind automatically supplied me with a plan to go to the library and research familiars, which caused a flare of annoyance. Fate knew being dutiful had gotten me exactly nothing. No, I was going to go eat the worst junk food I could get my hands on, find a pretty dress, then waste my night away at the Harvest party and get drunk.

I threw on some street clothes and stepped out the door. The witch with the shaved hair I had seen my first night was kneeling in the garden, pulling weeds. I paused.

"Hey," I said, causing them to look up and smile. "Want some help?"

"Oh, sure." The witch gestured to the unfinished section, where a huge number of invasive seedlings had started growing in the mulch.

"I'm Juni," they said, waving with a dirty hand. "They/them, please." They had a round face with expressive brown eyes—rare for a witch. We tended toward blue and gray.

I knelt next to them and started creating my own pile of pulled weeds. "I'm Layla, she/her."

Juni grinned. "Don't be weirded out, but everyone knows who you are."

"That *is* a little weird, though," I said.

"Are you doing okay? Mountain Thunder seems a bit, uh… they just graduated, and I think they're going through a phase, you know?"

"Yeah, they're a lot." I looked around at the other apartment buildings that circled the central garden. "You're in a coven?"

"Yup!" Juni pointed at one of the other apartments to the left of ours. "We're the Dark Water Coven, six members, six years."

"Wow. The Northern Sea Circle only has—had—ten spell casters total." I dug out a particularly well-rooted weed with my thumb.

"Oh, we have at least thirty here, maybe even more. I think there are seven covens currently. Plus the new one with the rest of the Northern Sea casters. There are thousands of witches in the Circle."

So many witches in one place—it was actually kind of incredible. "So, do you go out with teams and stuff?"

Juni nodded. "It's not nearly as eventful as a big angel battle. I'm mostly involved in burning out infestations after the guardians find them."

A less eventful life sounded perfect.

We pulled weeds without talking for a while. Juni didn't seem like the type who needed to fill silence, and we settled into a peaceful rhythm. Warm sunlight filtered through the trees. My heart gradually resettled to the sound of bees buzzing around the late-summer garden flowers as we worked.

"Where can I find the unhealthiest food in the entire Circle?" I asked when we'd finished the bed.

With a conspiratorial smirk, Juni gave me directions to the main part of the community, which I had only briefly glimpsed this morning.

The Mountain Circle was beautiful. Houses crept up the sides of the hills, balanced by tall pillars, the entire community nestled between the rolling green mountains the Circle was named for. The walkways between the numerous buildings were bustling. Eateries, coffee houses, libraries, apothecaries, plant growers, ceramics studios, furniture builders, artists—everything a witch needed could be found here.

I checked to make sure my mother wasn't among the crowds as I made my way to the cafeteria Juni had recommended. And just like that, I had found a reason to stay at the Mountain Circle. The buffet was *incredible*! It was light-years ahead of the one we'd had back home, with trays and trays of traditional witch dishes, popular outside foods, and recipes that seemed like local specialties.

Grinning gleefully and not caring who saw me, I piled a plate with every fried thing I could find, fully intending to go back for desserts. Behind the cafeteria was a tree-lined courtyard crowded with pretty wood-inlaid tables where I found a seat to devour my hoard. A pleasant, warm breeze brought the scents of flowers, and the forest above the buildings made a beautiful backdrop.

I was about a third of the way to the bottom of my plate, concentrating on my epic task, when a shadow fell over my food.

"Layla," said Calamus's mildly surprised voice. "Are you eating alone?"

Costi's spell caster, still in his formal wear, paused in front of my table holding his own tray of food.

"You could join me. Um… if you want to." I swallowed nervously, thinking of Datura's declaration that he was interested in me.

He set down his tray, looking from his nicely balanced meal to my glorious mess of carbs. I refused to be shamed. I had earned my junk food by almost dying.

"I'm glad I caught you. I plan on going to the library this evening to look into your invoking problem," Calamus said.

"This evening? You're not going to the Harvest party?"

He gave an easy laugh that took his face from handsome to stunning. "Not me. Do you want to come to the library with me?"

"Oh! I was… going to go to the party."

His smile stayed in place, but something in his eyes shifted. Disappointment, maybe? "Next time, then."

"You really don't have to go to extra trouble. I can check the library myself. I was planning to."

"It's no trouble, really. I'm a circlewright as well as a spell caster, so I often study in the evenings. I have a great interest in magical history," he said as he cut salad leaves into smaller pieces.

"You do both? That's impressive." As an initiate spell caster, I had practiced a few circle spells, but most casters gave them up once they summoned their familiar. Circle spells were slow and time-consuming. Usually, only witches who couldn't pull enough magic to cast would put in the years of dedicated study needed to become a competent circlewright.

Calamus dropped his eyes to his food as he smiled again. "I feel it's important to have a well-rounded magical education. I hope to contribute something new to the body of witch knowledge with my cross-disciplinary studies."

"I'm sure you will," I said, my mind elsewhere. I had overestimated the amount of fried food I could cram into my body and was regretting taking so much. But I was unwilling to admit defeat.

"I'm very curious to hear about you. Tell me about yourself," he said, raising his eyes to my face and recapturing my attention.

I pushed some noodles around with my fork and tucked a tendril of loose hair behind my ear. "There's not much to tell. I'm just a typical witch. Nothing interesting ever happened to me before this."

"Something tells me you're not 'just typical,'" Calamus said with a warm look that made me wonder if Datura wasn't so far off about him after all. I didn't know how to respond, but he cleared his throat lightly and continued. "Can you tell me about what happened with your familiar? Did it just stop answering your invocation?"

"Well, it never appeared to begin with." My cheeks heated. "I worked the summoning circle… uh… several times, and it didn't seem to work. But during the attack, I saw a spell form and was able to cast. Apparently, it was pretty powerful."

"I've truly never heard of anything like this," he said, a small line appearing between his brows as he pondered. "I *definitely* want to look into it now."

"Thanks for your help." I offered a shaky smile, then sighed. "I took way too much food."

Calamus glanced at my ravaged plate without comment and cleared his throat again. "May I ask you about something else?"

I nodded, curious, and moved my plate to the side.

"You seem close with Blackthorn," he started.

My wariness rose. "We've always been friends, ever since we were little."

Calamus raised his eyebrows. "That's unusual. It doesn't bother you that he's Troubled?"

"Of course not!" I bristled. "He's always been the best friend anyone could ask for."

He let out a soft laugh at my reaction. "You're so passionate and warmhearted."

I blinked. I'd certainly never been accused of that before.

"Maybe you can give me some advice, then." He leaned forward, bracing an arm on the table. "I had a guardian previously, but the security coordinator suggested that I pair with Blackthorn instead because we're both high level."

"You don't agree?"

"Oh no, we're well matched. My casting is very strong. With a skilled guardian like him, I can take point in angel exterminations. But I don't think he likes me very much." Calamus looked lost.

Yeah, I could see that. The polished look, the smiling, the studying—Calamus was the golden ideal of witch society. Costi wasn't the envious type by nature, but Calamus was everything he would never be. I knew it would bother him.

"He's wanted to be a guardian his whole life," I said after a moment. "It wasn't just a last resort for him. He takes it seriously. He won't jeopardize that."

Calamus nodded slowly.

"He doesn't always talk a lot, or smile, but he's a good man. The best."

He regarded me evenly. "I see." He smiled. "He's lucky to have such a loyal friend."

I tried to return the smile. "I need to get going," I said, pushing back my chair.

Calamus stood up with me. "Of course. Thank you, it was so nice getting to talk with you."

"I'll see you around," I said, carrying my plate to the compost and dish collection.

I released a stuck breath as I stepped back out onto the walkway. Something about Calamus put me on edge. I wasn't sure I could measure up to his standards.

That wasn't fair, though—it was my own insecurity talking. He was kind, intelligent, and pleasing to look at. A spell caster.

You could do worse, my mind whispered.

Wasn't Calamus exactly what I'd always pictured in a lover? I didn't feel an immediate spark, but I'd just been through the worst few days of my life. Why wouldn't I fall for those baby blue eyes if I got to know him better?

I found a large clothing exchange a few doors down with an open front displaying racks of outfits that no one was using. Witches would return clothes in good condition when they outgrew them or no longer wanted them, leaving an ever-rotating supply of new outfits.

Signs directed me to the dress section, and I scooped up a few party dresses to try on at home. I had a pair of sandals that would match any of them.

On the opposite side of the walkway was a tailor with a pile of fabric grocery bags stacked in front of their small booth. I picked a bag, and the large witch hunched over a sewing machine behind the counter lifted a hand in thanks without raising their eyes from their work.

My final stop was the provisionary. It was a slender but deep building with a single row of shelves on one side and banks of refrigerators on the other. The shelves and coolers were full of containers of prepared foods, where I picked up a tin of the same fruit bars Sativa had given me this morning, a bag of seasoned snacks, and a box of assorted cookies. I stashed my goodies in my bag and folded the dresses on top.

At the front, there was a carafe of iced, sweetened coffee and a stack of mismatched glasses, so I poured a cup to go and wandered back to my apartment.

Juni had abandoned their gardening at some point. I finished my coffee and picked up weeding another of the beds until the sun began to dip low against the hills and my covenmates showed up to get ready for the party.

Chapter 7

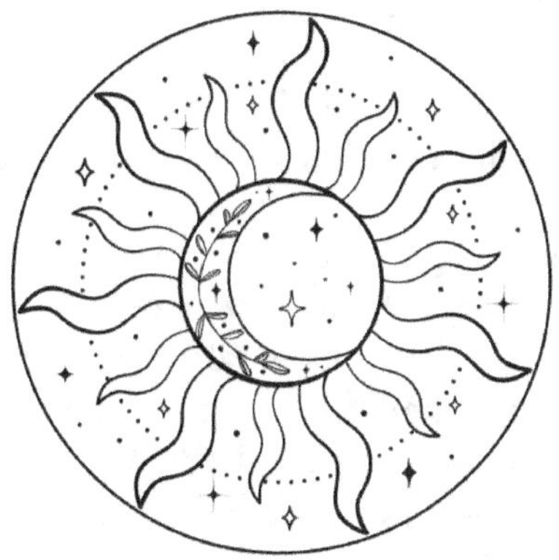

Ash was in a mood. Hell, *I* was in a mood. But Ash was usually the responsible one who would keep me from doing things like crashing the Harvest party so I could stalk a pretty spell caster. Tonight, Ash had been all too supportive of sneaking out of the barracks.

We weren't adjusting well to our new Circle.

I'd dragged one of the standing tables over into the shadows to hold our drinks. Hard liquor and leaning against the wall in the dark didn't seem to be helping much.

"I hate it here already," Ash said over the music. They'd put their hair up, but neither of us had bothered to change out of our uniforms. Black was great for sneaking around.

Ash had just arrived at the Mountain Circle after making it through the battle that three of our fellow guardians didn't. To top it off, their new assignment—one of the Mountain Circle casters—had already been giving them trouble.

I made a noise of agreement, but my mind was elsewhere. I should never have agreed to transport Layla here. I had been doing so well, staying the fuck away from her. A year of convincing myself *ruined* by the feeling of her in my arms.

I'd tried my best to avoid her, dreading when the time came to talk about the plan for me to be her guardian. That was a conversation that would never happen now, but the problem remained. I wanted her. Couldn't have her. Didn't trust anyone else to defend her.

I had to get it through my head—not becoming her guardian was a *good* thing.

I needed to focus on the problems at hand. *What exactly are the angels up to?*

And what was wrong with Layla's magic? That, I was allowed to think about. Having functional spell casters was more important than ever.

A third witch sauntered over to us. Holly. I was sick of her antics lately. She was dressed for the holiday in a harvest-gold number that showed off her long legs. She'd let her dark hair grow out longer in the past year, and whatever she'd done to style it tonight had fluffed it up like she was trying to look more like Layla. I hated it.

She smiled teasingly, propping her hand on a hip. "Are you two allowed to be here?"

I grunted. "Probably not. There's a bunch of guidelines."

Holly raised her eyebrows at me. "And you're supposed to *follow* the guidelines." She turned to Ash with a smirk. "And I can't believe you of all witches would condone this *scandalous* behavior."

Ash's eyes glinted. "What do you want, Holly?"

She stepped back. "Fate, the two of you are a real treat tonight. Sneaking out, drinking alone, being grumpy in the corner." Her calculating gaze slid back to me. "I was hoping we could talk."

Frustration boiled through me, and I clamped it down. I breathed in, then out. I didn't need to take my feelings out on her. "All right."

Holly turned a pleading look on Ash. "Give us a minute?"

Their nostrils flared, and they waved a hand in her direction. "Oh, by all means, just pretend I'm not here." Ash moved about five paces down, just barely out of hearing distance. They threw themself against the wall and crossed their arms with a glare.

Dark amusement trickled through me. Ash was *vicious* when they were pissed. We were both Troubled, after all.

"Does Ash hate me or something?" Holly asked, trying to pull me farther away.

Ash thought Holly was only in it for herself. That she used people. Thing was, they were right. I shook my head. "You'll have to ask them," I said, waiting for her to get to whatever point she had.

We'd been friends growing up, but it was Layla who kept us together. Without her in the middle to keep us nice, we battered our strong wills against each other. I was more than over it.

She was quiet a moment before her shoulders rose and fell with a deep sigh. "Costi, I know I messed up. But I want to try again. With us."

Surprise jolted me, chased by hot anger. Like Hell. *Like Hell.* "Yeah? After you said you didn't wanna be seen with me?"

"You're *still* mad about that? You *know* why. I wouldn't have been able to get where I am if everyone knew I was dating… someone like you. If you'd just *waited*—"

"What, I was just supposed to be grateful you'd slum it with me?"

Holly sighed. "Things are different now. I think I'll be able to get a position with the Arcaenum. I've been talking to some of the administration there. I can teach you how to make witches respect you. We can convince them you're no longer Troubled—"

"You want me to pretend. Be someone I'm not." She was living in a fantasy world anyway. There was no way to recover from being Troubled. Once you had a label like that, it stuck.

"Don't be naive. You're a bad day away from getting thrown out of the Circle. I'm trying to *help* you." She rested her hand on my chest. "You can get past this if you try."

"You're right about one thing. Things *are* different now."

Holly turned behind her to see where I was looking. *Who* I was looking at. Layla was a vision in black and crimson, swaying to the bright music, laughing with one of the Mountain Circle spell casters. Brilliant, kind, and passionate beneath her shy exterior. Guileless. Everything I'd ever wanted.

Holly whipped her head back to me. "You can't, Costi. She's a spell caster."

I had nothing to say. I knew I couldn't.

She made a disgusted noise. "*For fate's sake.* You've always been obsessed with her," she hissed. "It's *weird.* It's not *healthy* to be fixated like this. You have to stop. She'll never return your feelings, and if she did, she'd *doom* you. She's keeping you from being happy."

Nothing could have been further from the truth. Whether she returned my feelings or not, Layla was the one thing keeping me tethered to this world.

I scrubbed a hand through my hair. This was getting old fast. "Why are you bringing this up again, Holly? We didn't *work.*"

"That's not true." She slid her hand to my shoulder. "We could work."

I dislodged her with my good arm. "If the Circle decides I'm not Troubled, you mean."

Even in the dim light I could see her cheeks flush with anger. "Damn it, Costi, that's for *you.* Don't you *want* to get better?"

"There's nothing *wrong* with me."

"Besides lusting after a barely grown spell caster?"

Rage boiled through me so hard, the music washed out as my ears rang. How *dare* she go there. Layla was twenty years old. She wasn't a child. "So this *is* about her. That why you've been ignoring her? Breaking her heart? You think she's in your way?"

"You're such a hypocrite! You're so tied up about *me* not wanting to tell anyone. It would be ten thousand times worse with her."

I didn't respond. The way I saw it, there was a huge difference between *won't* and *can't.*

"Costi, just leave her alone already. Someone who cares about you is right in front of you." She reached out to caress my jaw.

I threw her hand off me *again.* "You *care* about me? You got a *fucking* messed-up way of showing it." I grabbed my whiskey from the bar table, downing it in one swallow and slamming the tumbler back down.

I looked again. I couldn't help myself. My body was a compass that always pointed to her. I stared through the crowd, and Layla's blue eyes latched on to mine.

***

LAYLA

The party was already humming when we arrived at a large community house with a wraparound porch, witches spilling out of the building into the warm twilight.

The house backed into the side of a hill, the front lifted up on stilts, accessed by a tall staircase that seemed like it would be a hazard after a few drinks. Glowing witch lights had been strung across the porch and inside, where partygoers talked and laughed above the thumping music.

The Mountain Circle, pieced together with the remnants of Northern Sea, had collectively decided we were not afraid tonight. We were celebrating Harvest.

Sativa, Oliver, and Datura were dressed to the nines in coordinating black outfits. Sativa's short dress showed off her golden legs, her long, straight hair gleaming. Oliver's crop top showed a strip of toned stomach above his fitted pants, his hair styled artfully to look messy. Datura wore a flare-legged bodysuit that clung to her curves and had pinned her wild curls up around her head, garlanded with a woven crown of her namesake flower.

In keeping with our unofficial coven theme, I had also picked a black dress from the selection I had borrowed earlier in the day. The sleeves were short, with a sweetheart neck. The skirt flared out into an A-line, and black ribbon laced over panels of crimson on either side. I had left my hair down in its natural waves and made up my eyes with liner and mascara. A pair of black sandals that tied up my calves completed the look.

I was so ready for dancing and fun.

"Florin!" Sativa shrieked as soon as we walked in the door.

"Sa-ti-va! Happy Harvest!" Florin, I presumed, twirled around and raised his glass at us, nearly spilling some of whatever was in it. One of his companions laughed and helped him hold it upright as they waved us inside.

"Hey, Mountain Thunder, looking *good!*" someone in the crowd boomed, causing whistles and cheers. "Layla Rosen, you're a badass angel cooker!"

A stunned laugh bubbled out of me. Fate, everyone *did* know who I was. That was so weird. At least I felt… a little more welcome.

A mix of young witches filled the house, caught in the glow of dozens of sparkling witch lights dangling from the ceiling. There would have been a more solemn ritual for the holiday going on, but we would let the older witches enjoy that without us tonight.

"Come dance with us, Newbie," Datura demanded.

Oliver twirled me around, and I grinned. "I've graduated from Screwup!"

"We have to celebrate by dancing!" Oliver declared.

"Wait, I have to find something first," I told them as Oliver pulled Datura to the dance floor.

Sativa was occupied by Florin, who was gesturing his way through a story that had everyone around him howling.

I scanned the room with intent and saw exactly what I was looking for. *At last!* An entire sideboard filled with desserts. I snatched up a cookie in each hand. If we were about to get fried by angels, I wanted to eat sugar first.

There was a bar stocked with liquor bottles—some locally made and some popular outside brands. Beer, soda, and mixers were stuffed into a huge tub of ice next to a drink cooler labeled Harvest Punch that looked promising.

Stuffing the last of my baked goods—the first round, anyway— into my mouth, I filled a tall glass of ice with bubbly punch. Sweet fruit and alcohol fizzed on my tongue. Perfection.

I noticed Juni sitting nearby with a group of friends in a huddle of chairs and couches.

"Hey!" I waved, heading over. "You look amazing." Juni was decked out in an adorable purple-sequined bodysuit that dipped under one arm and flared jeans.

"Hey, Layla! Love the dress. Thanks for finishing the weeding. This is my coven." They gestured at the tangle of witches sprawled over the furniture, drinking away.

"Dark!" one of them cheered. Juni and the rest responded with "Water!" lifting their drinks in the air.

I laughed. "How's it going?" I said, perching on the edge of an unused chair.

"It *was* going awesome, until Zac killed the vibe." Juni leveled a not-entirely-serious glare at their covenmate, a lanky witch in black cargo pants with a silver chain.

"I did not!" Zac protested. "I'm just saying if the angels have weapons, something's going on."

Juni pointed at him. "And *I'm* just saying we came to this party to not think about that."

"What if they do have weapons, though? Are they… are they organizing or something?" Another of the Dark Water casters spoke up.

Juni groaned. "Here we go again."

"They don't think. They're just creatures," said a witch with spiked hair that had been tipped with green.

"All the old stories have angels talking and waging war like people," Zac pointed out.

"Yeah, you just said it—*stories*. It's all mythology," Juni countered.

"I just think we should be ready. Something's different." Zac crossed his arms over his chest and leaned back.

My stomach twisted. It was the same fear I'd had.

"You were there," Zac said, and the entire coven suddenly focused their attention on me. "Did they have weapons? Did it seem… organized?"

"I… didn't see most of it. I cast too much and passed out." I fidgeted, not sure if I should share the rest. "But I heard they had staffs that could shoot burning light."

The Dark Water casters looked at each other uncertainly.

"That's it," Juni declared, poking a finger into Zac's chest. "It's not enough for you to murder the vibe in cold blood, you have to piss on its grave too? Layla, let's go. I have an urgent need to dance!"

I laughed, breaking the tension.

Juni led me to an open spot on the dance floor. The flashing lights, moving bodies, deep beat, and Juni's horrible dancing soon had me smiling and thinking of nothing as I swayed to the music.

Song after song unwound the deep tension I had been carrying.

"Can I cut in?" a large, grinning witch with a bushy beard yelled, clearly not dressed for the party in a dusty T-shirt with "LAKESIDE POTTERY: WE DO IT WITH CLAY" emblazoned on it.

Juni threw their arms around him with a scream, and the pair sealed their lips together, not even bothering to pretend to dance anymore.

I chuckled at Juni, who gave me a wave without coming up for air.

My throat tightened unexpectedly as I twirled off by myself. Longing and envy seared through me. I wanted that kind of freedom. Juni wouldn't be able to keep their lover, but that didn't seem to be stopping them.

Spell casters had to marry spell casters and have baby spell casters. I'd never once questioned that. My parents had broken that rule, and my mother made damn sure I knew it was the source of all her misery. It had never even crossed my mind to make out with a handsome potter on a dance floor.

Or a guardian. The thought bubbled up out of nowhere, lodged itself in my mind, and then wouldn't leave. A guardian who would kiss me like he did everything: aggressively and on his own terms, with his entire heart.

I wasn't sure what made me look up. Through the crowd, I locked eyes with Costi. *How long has he been watching?*

He was leaning with his boot propped up behind him against the far wall. Beside him was another Northern Sea guardian I had seen around—Costi's friend Ash, I thought.

Holly was with them, I realized with a jolt.

She whirled and glared at me as Costi stepped past her. I couldn't see her expression, but I suddenly felt small and awkward, standing in the middle of the dance floor alone. Ash clamped a hand over Holly's bicep, stopping her from following.

With almost frightening intensity, Costi stalked toward me like a storm rolling in off the ocean.

My body reacted instinctively, warring with itself. *Freeze. No, go to him. No, run.*

I made a panicked dash toward the nearest exit, which turned out to be one of the wooden porches. It was unlit. The breezy night air cooled my heated skin as I sucked in a shaky breath full of the taste of the forest.

Of course Costi followed me. He slid the door closed. The sound of the party muffled, leaving only the droning of night insects.

I swallowed heavily, backing up against the railing.

"I just wanted to talk to you." He prowled nearer. He was in all black as usual, his tight-fitting uniform that showed off his strong arms, the edges of his tattoos splashed near his collarbone. He had pushed his hands through his already messy hair. I liked it way too much.

"You look… so good," he said, running his eyes over my body.

I shivered despite being overheated. "You look pretty good too." I tried for nonchalance, but I couldn't catch my breath.

What am I doing? This wasn't good.

"You think so?" His lips tilted up on one side in a teasing smirk.

"Maybe a bit." I bit my lip against a loopy grin.

"Just a bit?"

I rolled my eyes. "You don't need me to tell you you're hot."

He chuckled darkly. "Yeah, I think I do." He moved closer to me, trapping me against the wooden railing with a hand on either side. "You gonna tell me?"

"Tell you what?"

"Tell me you think I'm hot. I wanna hear it."

My mind sped out of control, barreling past flashing red warning signs. "I think you're hot."

He gave me a wicked half grin that stopped my breath. A final step swallowed up the space between us until he was pushing me against the railing, pressing our bodies together. He smelled delicious, like salt water and alcohol. My body thrilled.

"What's that?" he murmured in my ear. My heart careened helplessly as this turned into *way* more than I bargained for.

"I said you're hot," I whispered.

"Hmm?" He ran his nose along my cheek.

"You're *hot*, Costi. You're *so*—"

I gasped out loud as his lips landed behind my ear—

He whipped his head around when the door slid open and a partygoer popped their head through as music spilled from inside. "Hey, is Florin out here? Oh… sorry."

We jumped away from each other, awkwardly pulling tangled arms and legs back into their own spaces. I glanced at Costi in the warm light from the open door—his face mirrored the exact kind of stunned that I was feeling.

What in the sacred name of fate were we just doing? This was bad, bad, bad. My heart pounded in my chest. No one could see who we were in the dark, right?

"I should take you home," he said, then coughed. "To… to your apartment. To bed. By yourself."

I clamped a hand over my mouth to stifle a hysterical laugh. I'd known Costi my whole life, and I couldn't *ever* remember him being flustered.

We slipped back through the party, not touching. Outside, a row of solar lights led from the community house to the main walkway. It was a bit of a walk, but Costi seemed to know the way. We were quiet. He seemed lost in thought.

When we got close, I showed him where my coven lived. We stopped at the door, standing in the porch light.

"We need to talk," he said. His face was carefully blank.

"Yes." I worried my lip between my teeth.

"Tomorrow?"

I nodded.

He exhaled a breath and leaned into me. He ran both hands up my bare arms, curling them around my biceps, holding me in place. I shivered. He dipped his head and I tilted mine up, lining up my parted lips with his but not quite touching.

A door banged shut somewhere nearby. We startled backward.

"I… Good night, Layla," he breathed, rubbing his hand behind his neck.

I stood with a hand over my burning face as he disappeared into the darkness.

* * *

Inside, the apartment was dark and still. I mechanically got ready for bed, my mind whirling.

Went home early, I texted Sativa. **Thanks for the invite. Happy Harvest!**

I was screwed. So, so screwed. Our childhood friendship had drifted into something else entirely, and I hadn't even noticed. But it was so obvious—the way I never got crushes on anyone. Even after he graduated and went off to training, I'd never even really considered dating. I always wanted to run all my thoughts by him. Fate, I'd followed him around for *years*—

I buried my face in my pillow and let loose a strangled sound of frustration.

How long? It might explain a lot. Why he'd been distant this last year.

Fate, fate, fate, this was so bad.

Or is it?

No, of *course* it was bad. Costi was the exact opposite of who I was supposed to like. Something was going on with the angels, and I just knew it was worse than anyone was letting on. Costi needed to concentrate on his job, and I needed to figure out where my familiar was, *quickly*. I couldn't tell *anyone* about this; they'd throw him out of the Circle for less than what he'd done tonight. And my mother... I didn't want to think about what she would do.

Late into the night, I heard Datura and Oliver come home, whispering and laughing in that way they had.

I forced myself to stop thinking and try to sleep. Eventually, it worked.

* * *

I dreamed of Costi pinning me with his hard body against the railing, eagerly trailing his lips down my neck in the dark.

I squirmed against him with delicious friction, chasing the sensation building in my core.

It felt like the buildup of magic. It *was* a buildup of magic. I pulled more while pain and pleasure battled to destroy me.

"Help me," I begged.

"I got what you need, Layla," he growled, his face tucked into my shoulder.

"*Please.*"

With the logic of dreams, he sang harshly into my ear in Greek, such a beautiful voice.

My whole body became liquid fire, boiling, burning—

***

COSTI

It was still dark out, but I needed to clear my goddamn head. I was starkly sober now, and I didn't appreciate it one bit.

The room in the barracks I shared with a dozen guardians was stifling and full of obnoxious snorers. It would serve them right if I woke them all up, but I tried to be quiet as I slipped on a shirt and my boots. I didn't want to talk.

Outside, a hint of dawn was just starting to brighten the sky, and a cool breeze ruffled my hair. There was a hiking trail on the north side of the Circle, and I made my way there. I missed the ocean. This place had too many damn trees.

What in the name of Hell was I thinking?

The guardians had a point. We were supposed to protect the spell casters in battle. Catching feelings made people do reckless things—like putting your whole team in danger to save your lover. Not to mention the shredded mess she'd make of my heart. They'd been working on her for years, convincing her to be a good girl and marry a caster.

It didn't matter how good she looked in a dress, how sweet she was to me, or how she parted her mouth—Layla Rosen was *not for me*, and I needed to stay the fuck away from her. *Not* chase her through a crowd and put my lips all over her.

Holly was right about that too. I *had* always been obsessed with Layla.

She seemed to attract bullies for no good reason, and someone had to look out for her. Holly and I both clung to her, a North Star in the night.

As I got older, I half-heartedly pursued romances that didn't go anywhere. Thought maybe I wasn't into that sort of thing. I was focused on becoming a guardian and proving I wasn't a waste of space.

Then Layla grew up.

A year ago, I saw her across the commons at the Northern Sea Circle, walking two paces behind her classmates as they laughed and talked without her. She was wearing this short skirt that swayed around her thighs, and just like that, I was a hundred percent gone. All the fond, protective feelings I had for her flipped to something potent and dangerous.

After that, I tried to stay away from her. I knew I couldn't have her. But she kept coming to me. And I kept fanning that flame. Holly had her head stuck up her own ass and was making Layla miserable. I *couldn't* leave her alone and friendless.

Even if I was the worst sort of friend.

The hiking path was barely visible, and I somehow veered off into the woods. I didn't care—I had a good sense of direction, and I'd just go back the way I came later. This part of the woods was open enough to walk through easily, tall trees shading out the underbrush.

I hadn't gone far when I hit the creek. It was obstructed by rocks, and water had backed up, forming some kind of natural pool. Ferns and vines drooped over the banks. Something about the place felt magical, almost sacred.

Layla would love it here.

I groaned out loud, dropping my head into my hands and scrubbing at my face. I *had* to stop thinking about her. When I'd told her we needed to talk after the party, I'd fully intended to make her *mine*, and damn the consequences. The worst, most reckless idea I'd ever had, and I'd had plenty.

She didn't need some Troubled fuckup blowing up her life. What she needed was a friend to help her figure out this stuff with her familiar. I'd already interrogated Grey about his demon but hadn't learned anything useful.

I scowled, thinking of the caster who'd taken Layla's place. He'd spent the evening at the *library*, looking up shit for her. I hated him, but that was the least of my problems.

I scanned the lightening sky above the trees for the hundredth time. There was no way the angels didn't know exactly where this Circle was. They'd been scouting. They probably knew where all the Circles were.

What are they waiting for?

* * *

LAYLA

I was already scrambling to the bathroom before I realized I was awake. I threw open the toilet lid and vomited up the meager contents of my stomach.

Oliver looked me over from the doorway, taking in my unchanged party clothes and what was probably a raccoonish smear of eye makeup.

He pointed at me. "Too much Harvest punch."

I slammed the door in his face and heard him laughing in the hall.

It wasn't the Harvest punch, I thought as I scrubbed my face and brushed my teeth in miserable slowness. I had pulled magic in my sleep while dreaming of… of…

I was in way over my head. My heart twisted painfully as I wished I could talk to Holly. She used to be the one to help me work through my problems. But my old friend was gone, replaced by someone grown-up who looked like her, someone who touched Costi casually in dark rooms and had no time for me.

Much later in the evening, I still hadn't emerged from my room except to crawl to the bathroom and back. I slept away my raging headache and choked down one of the fruit bars I'd picked up the day before. I had told Costi I'd talk to him today, but I *definitely* couldn't face him right now. Not after realizing I'd had a crush on him for half my life. Not after that *dream*. I needed to retreat into the forest immediately and become a patch of moss.

There was movement outside from my covenmates, but no one had bothered me. I supposed Oliver would run with the Harvest punch hypothesis, and I was fine with that explanation.

A text pinged.

Holly: *Can you come outside?*

My breath caught. Fate, I had conjured her by thinking about her. Talking to her was a *terrible* idea. After seeing her last night, I had a suspicion about what had come between us. I wasn't sure I wanted to confirm it.

With sinking dread, I pushed my feet into a pair of sandals and stepped out.

Holly, sitting on the bench in the garden, stood up when she saw me. She was wearing a yellow sundress that emphasized her curves, her dark hair done up in waves and pulled back into a ponytail, achieving a sophisticated look I could never hope to match. The garden lights cast a warm glow over my former friend, fireflies blinking among the plants.

My heart squeezed. I shouldn't have come out. This wasn't going to be an apology.

She smiled at me faintly. "Hey, Layla. It's been a while."

"Yeah," I said, wary.

"I see you joined a coven. That's great."

"Did… did you need something?"

She pressed her lips together before continuing. "We need to talk about Costi."

I knew it. "Yeah, no. I really don't think we do." I turned to go.

"Whatever this *thing* you're doing is, you need to stop," she called out, arresting me.

I whirled back around. "I'm not *doing* anything—"

"Layla, you're being defensive. Listen to me. He worked very hard to become a guardian, and he has to work hard to stay there. You can't get in the way of that."

"I would *never*—"

"You already have," Holly said with exaggerated patience. "You made him wait around for months after his training while you dithered about your summoning circle. You made him drive you here while he was *injured*. Every time you have any little problem, you make him drop whatever he's doing and come fix it for you."

Her words were like blades to my gut. Tears streaked from my eyes, and I scrubbed them away angrily.

"This is exactly what I'm talking about." She gestured to my face. "Your constant breakdowns are distracting him. I don't think you understand how serious this is. Joining the guardians is the last chance for witches like him. The Arcaenum won't hesitate to remove him from the Circle if he can't cut it. Layla, you're not *good* for him."

"Oh, and you are?" I said bitterly, finally catching on to what this was really about.

"Yes," she said frankly, widening her eyes. "He needs someone to stabilize him, not drag him under with them."

"It isn't like that," I insisted, wrapping my arms around myself.

Holly sighed. "I'm not trying to hurt your feelings. I love Costi, and I want him to be happy. He's in turmoil because of you. Can't you understand? You need to let him go."

I said nothing, looking away. Telling me to let Costi go was like telling me to remove the blood from my body.

"Guardians agree not to form attachments with spell casters when they join. It's better for everyone that way. Think about it. You'll eventually have to marry another caster. How will that affect him?"

"I don't… I don't want to…"

"He's not *allowed* to be with you, Layla," she said bluntly. "Tell him you don't want him so he can move on with his life."

"With you."

"You have to, Layla," Holly demanded. "This isn't good for either of you."

I stared into the shadowy garden trees. The lights of the Mountain Circle flickered in the dark hills above. My heart ached. Holly was right. Costi and I were forbidden to be more than colleagues. We were pushing it with our friendship. Now that I had realized what he meant to me, it wouldn't be enough. I would always want more.

"I… I'll talk to him."

Holly frowned. "Layla—"

"I said I'll talk to him!" I wrenched the door open and slammed it shut, leaving Holly outside.

Chapter 8

LAYLA

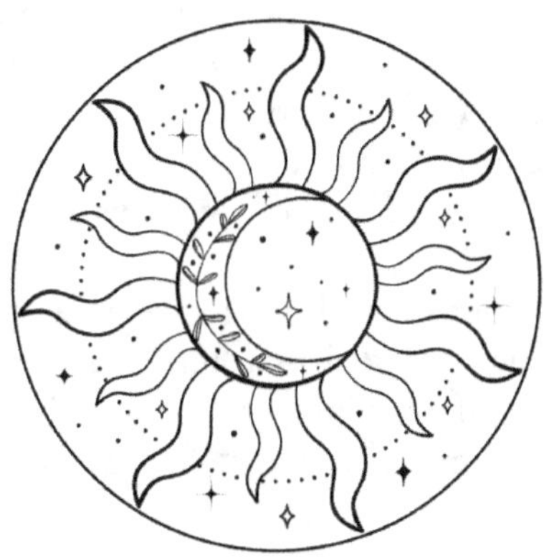

The next morning, I woke up determined. I needed to fix my problems myself and stop dragging everyone down.

I dressed to impress in a burgundy skirt and scoop-neck top and took the time to put on some makeup. After forcing a proper breakfast down my throat, I marched myself to the library.

The tall ceiling was dotted with skylights that let natural light into a cozy reading area in the middle, branching off to other rooms with rows of bookshelves.

"Good morning," I said to the witch behind the counter, who was bent over a ledger of some sort, writing by hand.

"Oh, good morning," she said. Around my age, she had the look of an outsider, with pale skin and long red hair. From time to time, outsiders were found who could sense magic. We tended to adopt them into the community.

"I'm looking for some books," I told her, immediately cringing. I was at the library—of course I was looking for books. "I'd like to read about the history of familiars. Anything about familiars, really."

She tilted her head, looking me over. "You're Layla."

"That's me." I grimaced through a smile. This reputation thing was getting really weird.

She glanced away. "I've been helping Calamus research some circle spells for you."

"Really? Thanks, that's amazing," I said genuinely. "You don't have to do everything, though. I can do some research."

She brightened. "I like looking through the historical records."

I chuckled. "You and Calamus must make a great pair, then."

Her face flushed a bright red. *Oops.* I wondered if Calamus knew. He seemed like the type not to notice.

Not that I had any room to talk.

"I can show you where the history books are," she said, changing the subject.

The history section turned out to be larger and less dusty than I had imagined. Bright witch lights lined the neat shelves. Like our library at the Northern Sea Circle, they hadn't installed electricity in this building to minimize the risk of fire. Some of our books were ancient, and witches kept limited copies in our small communities around the world.

I scanned the spines and picked some interesting titles at random. I would look through more systematically if I didn't have any luck.

Witch history seemed to blend with mythology at some point. I had studied our past in school, including the story of the millennia-old alliance with Hell, the supposed realm of our demon familiars.

Of course, we witches could objectively prove that angels and demons were flesh-and-blood creatures, but the modern understanding was that we were all a normal part of evolution, albeit one the outsiders didn't understand. Our ancient stories were nothing more than attempts to explain what our ancestors had not understood. The non-magical had folded a lot of the same stories into their religious systems, which just proved my point.

I ran my fingers over an ancient illuminated manuscript showing a scene of two beings locked in magical combat—an angel and a demon straight out of the outsiders' myths, looking nothing like the vile winged creatures we battled or our tiny, pale familiars.

The story went like this: The angels believed they were superior to all other beings. They ranked every type of being from their most favorite to their least, and then each individual according to the angelic notion of power. They insisted that everyone adopt this hierarchy and vow to serve those above them.

The ranking system was called Inperium, and the angels fought bitterly with anyone who opposed it.

The demons were their strongest opposition. As punishment, they were locked in a prison—Hell. The angels then set their sights on humanity, commanding their worship. The story claimed that many of us fell willingly into Inperium.

Our ancient witch ancestors were not swayed, though, and laid down their lives to oppose the angels. Blades, fire, bullets—those things could only wound an angel. No matter how maimed, they would recover. Only magic could *kill* an angel, but the circle spells of the witches were too slow and unwieldy to be used as a weapon.

The alliance with Hell changed that. The demons had a way of *casting*—flinging magic with their hands, without a circle. Keeping their one advantage, they only taught witches half of the process so that every caster needed a demon ally to supply the spell.

The story neatly explained every facet of our existence—why we needed to fight the angels, why we hated hierarchies, and why we required a demon familiar to cast spells. It was too clean to be anything *but* a myth.

I didn't think ancient stories would help in my case, but I hoped I would find accounts of demon behavior from the past hundred years or so and see if anyone had ever encountered a problem like this before.

I brought a small stack of books to the front, and the red-haired witch scanned them out on a battery-powered tablet.

"I'll set aside anything I think of that seems useful," she promised.

I felt a little more myself after stopping for lunch on the way back to my apartment. I had a plan. Calamus and the library witch were going to help too. Between the three of us, we were bound to uncover something.

I drew up short. My mother was standing on the garden path in front of my building. She lifted her furious face, and I knew there was no chance of escape. She advanced on me, and I stepped backward, nearly tripping on the walkway.

"Where have you been?" she hissed. She clamped her hand around my upper arm. My books spilled onto the ground.

"Let… let go. I'm *sorry*." I tried to twist away, but she squeezed to the point of pain. I stumbled as she dragged me farther into the garden, where no one would see her. "I… I was only trying to—"

"Trying to what? Sneak around with that Blackthorn man? Go out partying and drinking? Ignore my calls?"

"I wasn't sneaking around. He was assigned—"

"Neither of you were *assigned* to be on the seawall in the middle of the night. Don't think I didn't put that together."

My heart beat wildly as I inched away into the garden bed, backing myself against a tree. She was blocking the path. "I wasn't doing anything wrong." I raised a shaking hand to my arm, which was throbbing from where she'd grabbed me.

"Layla, I've warned you about him. About *this*. Look what happened to me. I married a spell caster, and fate is *punishing* me."

"I'm not doing anything like that. I—"

"Stop *lying* to me!" she seethed. "You think I don't know what you're doing behind my back? How do you think it looks when I don't even know where my daughter is? When I had to ask around to find you?" Her face was contorted with anger, and her normally smooth hair stuck to the sweat at her temples.

I clutched myself miserably, tears dribbling down my cheeks. "I'm… I'm sorry…"

She stared at me a moment, then sniffed. "I heard about your spell casting during the attack."

I said nothing.

Mother gave a wan smile. "So, you did your summoning after all. Why didn't you tell me?" After a moment, she continued in the velvety voice she used on people when she wanted something. "I recently met the Mountain Circle's security coordinator. She's a delight."

My eyes flicked to her nervously.

"She has such a heavy responsibility, vetting and assigning all the new Northern Sea guardians. Not all of them are up to Mountain Circle standards, sadly."

My breath stalled and my body turned to ice as her threat hit its mark. Witches like Costi didn't get a second chance. If they decided he couldn't make it as a guardian, they would ask him to leave the Circle.

She said, "Please answer my calls and texts."

"I… will," I rasped, looking down at the wavering mulch.

"And stay away from the guardian."

My head snapped up and I opened my mouth, but no words came out.

My mother's lips pinched with rage. Her voice was like a knife at my throat. "You'll do as I tell you, Layla."

Blood rushed to my head so fast, I felt faint. *Do as she tells me?* Witches didn't try to control each other like this. With *threats*. It wasn't done. It went against everything we held sacred.

If she was aware of my reaction, she didn't comment. She sighed. "This new Circle… it's different from Northern Sea. It'll be good for us. I can feel it. I have a plan to make things better. You just need to *help* me instead of fighting me."

"Wh-What plan?"

"You needn't worry about the details. Just focus on yourself and your spell casting," she said. "We're in a new era now, and I'm prepared to make the most of it. For both of us."

She stood over me a moment longer before nodding to herself and leaving me alone beneath the oak tree.

I slid down the rough bark onto the ground as raw emotion clawed up my throat. She'd never been this bad. She'd never hurt me before. What was I supposed to do now? I couldn't tell Costi. My mother would—

A shadow fell over me.

"No," I whimpered. But it was too late. I raised my head.

Costi took in my huddled form and my tear-streaked face, and I swore the color of his eyes darkened like storm clouds. "What in Hell's name is going on?" He dropped to a crouch in the mulch in front of me.

His gaze snagged on the nasty red mark blooming on my arm, and he froze. "Who was it, Layla?" His voice held a cold fury I'd never experienced from him.

I shook my head, eyes wide.

"There's a *handprint* on your *skin*," he pushed out through gritted teeth, breathing harshly with the promise of immediate and terrible violence. "If it was that *fucking* spell caster, I'll—"

Which spell caster? "No," I mumbled, fresh tears spilling.

Spitting out curses, he slid his arms around my torso and pulled me off the ground and into his arms. His voice was gravel as he ran a careful hand down the back of my head. "Fate, baby, don't," he said into my hair. "Hell, you're shaking. I've got you. I'd never hurt you. *Please* tell me what happened."

I should have pushed him away and told him to go. But I had no one else. I didn't *want* anyone else.

"You can't do anything," I breathed, clinging to him.

"The Hell I can't," he said, tightening his hold.

I raised my face and braced my hands against his chest. "My mother—"

Costi stiffened. "She's done this before?"

"No. Not like this." I took a shuddering breath. "I've never… She was so angry. She threatened you. She… she told me to *obey* her."

The last part came out as a whisper as the shameful admission spilled out. It was worse than scandalous. Commanding another witch to obey you was Inperium. It was *treasonous*.

Costi said nothing as he held me.

"Sh-She needs help," I admitted. "A mediator or… the councilors?"

"Not the Arcaenum," Costi said gravely.

"What?"

He pulled back slightly to look down at me, sliding his arm down to my waist. "Something's not right here."

I swallowed, nodding slowly. Something *did* feel off with the Mountain Circle, and Costi had a knack for seeing the bigger picture.

I looked at him then, taking in his black uniform and the sheen of sweat that clung to the side of his face and neck. "You were training?"

Costi nodded. "Running. But I wanted to see you. It's a damn good thing I came when I did." He brushed the pad of his thumb over my cheekbone, wiping away the moisture.

"You sh-shouldn't have come. I don't want you to lose your position because of me."

His eyes narrowed. "You been talking to Holly?"

Fate, this man. It was impossible to keep anything from him. "She's right, though. I don't want to be the reason you get thrown out of the guardians, not after you worked so hard to get in."

"She doesn't know what she's talking about. She's meddling. I already told her to knock it off."

"My mother said she'd get you disqualified," I said.

"Let her try," he growled.

"I think—"

Costi shook his head. "No."

"Maybe we should—"

He pressed two fingers over my open mouth. "Layla," he said, his breath hitching. "Don't."

He leaned in, pushing a hand through my hair and holding my eyes with his. "I'm not about to leave you alone. You get what I'm saying?"

He was so close, I could feel his breath on my lips, still stopped by his touch. I nodded, unable to do much else as he stroked his other hand along my scalp.

I suddenly remembered the party. The *dream*. My body flushed hot.

I shivered as he traced his fingers over my mouth. He pulled himself away with a shudder.

"Come on," he mumbled, guiding me gently back to my apartment. Inside, it was dark and quiet. I trailed behind him into the kitchenette. He rummaged around in the freezer, pulling out an ice pack that he wrapped in a towel.

Looking me over, he frowned at the bruise forming on my bare upper arm. He pressed the ice pack onto it, and I raised my other hand to hold it in place, our fingers brushing. Costi's phone vibrated from his pocket. He ignored it.

"Don't you need to get back?"

His eyes confirmed that he did, but his mouth was set obstinately.

"Don't get in trouble because of me," I said.

He scoffed.

"I'll be fine," I promised.

"Call me right away, okay? If your mom shows up again. Try to stay away from her. This isn't right. I'll tell the security coordinator."

"You can't tell her. My mother said they're friends."

He cursed. "Of course they are. Keep your eyes open. I've been talking to some people, and I'm gonna find out what this is all about. We'll figure it out."

My heart warmed. "Be careful," I told him.

He nodded once. "You too."

I thought I would break down when he left, but instead I just felt numb. My mother hadn't always been this way. I thought she had even been happy when I was young. She was the success story of a regular witch who married a spell caster for love and had a powerful child, proving society wrong. *What happened to her?*

After retrieving my bag of library books, I went into my bedroom. I flipped the lock on my door and fished out one of the history texts, sitting on my bed. The faded fabric cover and yellowed pages smelled of old paper.

There wasn't a section helpfully labeled "Problems with Your Familiar," and I had no idea what information would be helpful, so I started from the beginning.

The book was a full, anthropology-style investigation of demon familiars, written fifty years ago.

A lot of it backed up common knowledge: familiars had never been found in the wild, they seemed intelligent but didn't speak or communicate, they didn't interact with each other, and they always answered the call of their spell caster, but they would recall themselves after a short time if no spells were being cast.

There were also some strange tidbits I'd never considered: the tallest familiar the author had measured was four feet, their eyes seemed to be sensitive to light, and they had never been able to do an autopsy on one because their bodies would disappear back to wherever they came from if rendered unconscious or dead.

A dead-on-arrival demon was a line of inquiry I hadn't considered, but reading further, I found that if a spell caster lost their familiar in battle, they could and did summon a new one.

The bond between spell caster and familiar was for life. Demons seemed to age roughly the same as humans, and older spell casters would sometimes find their familiar unresponsive when being invoked—presumably claimed by old age.

There was also a chapter on natural summoners, like Sativa. It happened to some young witches who could pull large amounts of magic—according to the author's detailed notes, it was a one-in-a-thousand phenomenon. It typically occurred in the witch's early teens, but the how and the why of it wasn't clear.

What was *unknown* about demons was a much longer list: where they went when they weren't with their witch—the mythological Hell or elsewhere; if they were Earth-like mammals that ate and reproduced; what the nature of the spells they passed to us was; and if they possessed humanlike reasoning or if they worked by instinct. Were they allies? Pets? Did they feel *enslaved*? Uncomfortably, we had no way of knowing.

I found nothing about invisible or missing familiars, and nothing to suggest this kind of thing had happened before.

I started skimming faster through a long section with charts and eventually groaned, setting the open book aside on my bed. Maybe I was going about this the wrong way.

"Come on out, shy little demon. I'm not mad," I invited the empty air, patting the bed. "You did such a good job with those angels! I'd love to work together."

An overtired, loopy giggle escaped me.

"No? All right then." I decided it was probably best to get some sleep.

* * *

"Fate, what happened to your arm?" Sativa asked as she set down her handbag on the table I'd just cleared. "Did you walk into a door?"

"Something like that." I had been on a cleaning spree since the morning. My mission was to destroy this mess before the mold gained sentience. I clasped the fragile sense of purpose like a lifeline.

Sativa sighed. "You don't have to do all this. No one cares."

I looked away. "It's not like I'm doing anything else."

"No luck, then?" She propped herself against the counter, watching me load a bag of rinsed-out containers to return to various eateries for sanitizing and reuse.

I shook my head.

Despite her assertion that no one cared, she began to help sort through a pile of papers. "Maybe you don't *need* a familiar. What if you're, like, the next evolution of witches?"

I snorted a laugh. "I doubt that." I paused, trying to remember. "It felt... like there was something. A force outside of me creating the spell."

"That is how it feels," Sativa agreed, nodding.

Perching on a stool, I sat next to her. "Are you doing okay?" I asked seriously.

She widened her eyes. "Me?"

I nodded, feeling a little awkward. "You and the others. I've only been here a few days, but... I can see you're not practicing casting. You haven't picked guardians. Is something... wrong?"

Something in my recent conversation with Costi had stuck with me.

Sativa looked away in a rare gesture of self-consciousness.

"I'm sorry. I didn't mean to—"

Before I could finish apologizing, Oliver and Datura tumbled through the door, apparently trying to go through together instead of one at a time.

"Hey, it's us," Oliver said.

"Funny enough, I could tell," Sativa deadpanned, abandoning my question.

"Here, Screwup. I brought you lunch." Datura shoved a container and a fork at me.

I blinked in surprise. "Thanks, that's... actually really nice of you," I said.

Oliver gasped loudly. "No! Don't you dare spread those kinds of rumors. My Datura is a wicked, poisonous flower." He flung his arm around her neck and tried to pull her into a headlock.

I laughed despite myself. "*Did* you poison it?"

She scoffed, shoving Oliver away. "Guess you'll find out."

My phone started chiming, causing my heart to flip in dread. I'd been keeping it on since yesterday, when Mother had suggested that if I didn't answer her, she would go after Costi. He'd said he wasn't afraid, but I wasn't about to test her.

"Excuse me," I murmured, taking my phone and my probably-not-deadly lunch to my room. "Hello, Mother," I said without emotion.

"Hello, sweetheart," she said approvingly. "I have a nice surprise for you."

I consciously controlled my shuddering breath. I couldn't imagine this being good. "Oh…"

"Fate blessed me with running into one of our new councilors— our recent assembly speaker, Cedar Grey."

I was sure fate had nothing to do with it. Mother had a way of getting in front of people.

"His son Calamus was with him. What a charming young spell caster!"

"Yes." I hadn't known the witch who'd spoken at the recent meeting was Calamus's father, but now that I thought about it, I could see a resemblance.

"Layla, I was very surprised to hear about the problem you're having with your familiar. You didn't share that with me." Her tone fell.

My body went cold. "I-I'm sorry…"

"I heard that Calamus kindly offered his help. He said he's already come up with a solution."

"He did?" I blurted. "What is it?"

"I didn't have time to listen to all the details, darling, but he had to get special permission from the Arcaenum to try it. His father and I agreed that he should talk through it with you over dinner this evening. Doesn't that sound lovely?"

Anger flared through me. She wasn't even subtle. Bitterly, I wondered how Calamus would like the bruise on my arm. Did Mother know Costi was his guardian?

"Yes, Mother," I said. What else could I say? She had me, and she knew it.

I'd always thought the people in the old stories were hapless and silly, letting the angels demand things of them. Why didn't they simply refuse? I hadn't realized how… *easy* it was. Everything someone could use against you as a weapon.

"I'll send you the details. Wear something nice, sweetheart," she reminded me.

"Thank you, Mother," I said cooly.

After punching off the phone, I angrily dug into the lunch Datura had brought. It was a curry with rice and a side of fried potato dumplings, which I appreciated. I'd seen the side-eye Calamus gave my dastardly carbohydrates. I wondered what he thought of this dinner plan our parents had cooked up.

The food did my mood some good. Bringing my dishes back out to the kitchen, I found Datura and Oliver on the couch with their heads bent together over a tablet as they scrolled.

I slammed the container down with a bang. They looked up with matching startled faces.

"It was *delicious*, and I feel *fine*. I can't count on you for *anything*," I scolded Datura in mock fury.

I hid my smile by pretending to storm away in a huff as she threw back her head with a loud cackle.

Chapter 9

LAYLA

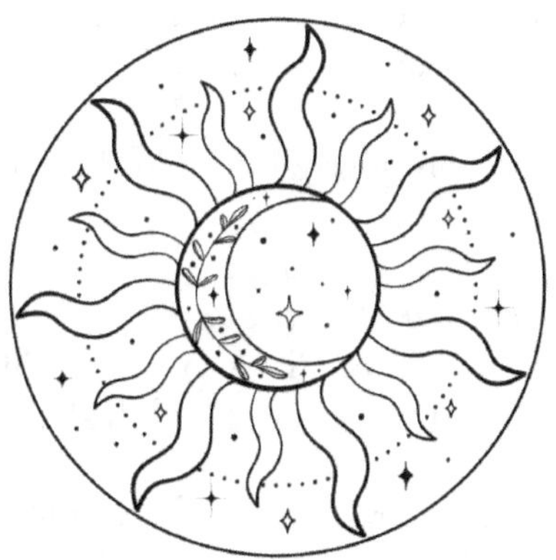

Hours later, it was apparent that Datura had indeed not poisoned me, so I couldn't get out of going. I wanted to know what Calamus had discovered, but I was mortified. Was this supposed to be a real date? I cringed with the idea that he would think I was in on it, artlessly trying to get his attention by having my mother set us up.

Then there was Costi. I badly wanted a friend to talk to about this. And I needed to talk to Costi about… other things as well. But I had only stared at my phone all afternoon.

Maybe, once we met up, Calamus and I could ditch the dinner idea and go to the library to talk.

I pulled out one of the skirts I normally wore, then thought better of it. If Mother checked up on me, I had to look like I was taking this seriously.

"Gross," I said as I pulled on the simple wine-colored dress that I had rejected for the Harvest party because it was too plain. "Gross, gross, gross."

My lace-up sandals finished a look that could be interpreted anywhere between summer-casual and dressy, which felt like compliance without complying. Perfect.

Mother had texted me the time and place. My heart sank as I took in the romantic venue—an outdoor eatery with a tiled patio shaded by an excessive growth of leafy vines dangling from the overhead trellises. The small tables dotted with flickering candles looked full. Maybe it was too crowded for us?

My hopes were dashed on the rocks and my soul washed out to sea as Calamus stood up and moved to meet me, carrying an armload of flowers.

"You look incredibly lovely," he said, presenting me with the cloying bouquet.

I gave a nervous, unconvincing laugh. *Fate stuff me in a hole and leave me to rot. He* does *think this is a date.*

"Thanks, um… you always look great," I said without real feeling. My mind flashed on the way Costi had looked at me at the Harvest party.

Calamus led me to the table. I'd never seen him wearing anything but formal crimson spell caster robes—a fitted tunic with a long, flared outer jacket. Tonight was no exception. He was attentive, smart, and kind, but he didn't do it for me.

There's really only one person who does it for me, I thought with a slow shiver of awareness. Costi wouldn't be caught dead in a fancy eatery. I remembered stolen evenings, laughing and running, pulling out mismatched snacks to share on a seaside rock or a rooftop under the sunset.

Calamus had already poured me a glass of water from the pitcher. Seeing that I had joined him, one of the attendants brought us the first dish of the evening's menu, a cold summer vegetable soup and a basket of warm bread slices. There wasn't any room on the table for the flowers, so I sat with them awkwardly in my lap.

"I'm glad you agreed to meet me," Calamus said, smiling gently. "I'd really love to get to know you better."

"That's great," I said, trying to think of a way not to drag this out.

Concern clouded his handsome face. "What happened to your arm?"

"It's nothing." I stirred my soup around unenthusiastically. "I heard you might have an idea about my familiar."

"I suppose I should tell you about that first."

"If you don't mind," I said. "I've been worried about it."

"I spent some time researching various texts about familiars without much success," he began.

I nodded politely, nibbling on the bread. I'd done the same.

"I think I mentioned my interest in circle spells. I've been helping compile a database of sorts, cataloging ancient forms that are no longer used. You're probably surprised that nothing like that exists already, but there are *thousands* of circle spells that have been lost to us."

"I never considered that before," I said, trying to sound interested. Circle magic was slow and boring, and after working the summoning circle so many times without success, I was ready to leave it behind forever.

Calamus nodded, impassioned. "Circlewrights have largely been reduced to making witch lights and other things of that nature, but in the past, they were much more involved in our fight against the angels."

I made a noncommittal sound, shifting the overly perfumed bouquet of flowers in my lap and giving up on eating entirely.

"So, I searched through the database, and I came across something that I think can help you."

I perked up. "You found a circle spell to find lost familiars?" Maybe he *was* onto something.

"Something almost as good." He smiled. "I found one to contact Hell."

I blinked rapidly in surprise and schooled my expression. "That's… interesting," I said diplomatically, all hope I'd had of a real solution draining.

"Apparently, we maintained regular communication even up until four or five hundred years ago," Calamus continued. "The spell itself is a thing of genius. There's a sort of object of power on the opposite side—in Hell, I assume—then we work the circle on our side—"

"And the councilors agreed to let you try this?" This was pure fantasy, a complete waste of everyone's time.

"Well, yes," he said, surprising me. "The Arcaenum understands the potential benefits of renewing our alliance."

"Oh…"

"But of course, we'll start with asking them about your familiar. Hazel, the library assistant I mentioned, has been studying everything about the demonic language that she can find for years. She'll be able to translate."

I released a slow breath. A demon language? Calamus had a familiar—he *knew* they didn't have a language. And he'd somehow convinced the Arcaenum to try this? Were they just humoring him because his dad was one of their councilors?

I was saved from replying right away by the arrival of the next course, which I frowned over. It was a salad with a variety of beans, covered with chunks of red. *Roasted beets?* Disgusting.

"Calamus, to be honest, this all sounds… pretty implausible."

He nodded. "I can see why you might think so. In the modern era, we've come to think of certain aspects of our history as a sort of metaphor, but there's quite a lot written about all of it. I think, and there are many who agree with me, that it has more of a basis in reality than we commonly believe."

I didn't point out the long tradition of the non-magical writing up *very* detailed and elaborate religious systems. The presence of a lot of writing didn't convince me at all.

I pushed my food around while Calamus speared a beet and ate it, as if it wasn't an abomination. "The Arcaenum… they really think the old stories are real?"

"They do. They've put a lot of trust in me. It's exciting to work with them on this," he said with genuine warmth. "I'm planning to campaign for election in a few years, so I appreciate the opportunity to see how the process works."

Somehow, that didn't surprise me at all.

Calamus regarded me with a gentle look. "What are your future plans, Layla?"

And just like that, this conversation was veering into *nope* territory.

"I haven't really thought very far ahead…" But that wasn't exactly true. This thing with Calamus? It was exactly what was expected of me. What I had imagined for years. Right until Costi backed me against the railing, put his lips on my neck, and slammed a destructive spell into my life path.

"You just graduated a few months ago. And you've been through a lot recently. I suppose you have time to figure everything out."

"Yes. Well, this has been really nice…"

Calamus looked startled. "Are you finished eating already?" His eyes wandered to my mostly untouched vegetables, but he wisely kept quiet.

"Sorry, I'm getting pretty tired. There's a lot to think about," I hedged.

"Oh. Of course." He stood. "Let me walk you home."

I pushed back from the table, petals spilling everywhere. "I'm… sure you're busy. There's no need to go to all that trouble."

"It's no trouble, Layla," he said with a smile as he hurried to catch up with me.

I kept my eyes trained on the bricks as we walked together down the main pathway of the Circle past who knew how many witches. Calamus, standing out in his crimson spell caster robes, was greeted excitedly by at least a dozen voices as I sank farther behind my flowers.

"Do you like music?" he asked, pointing to an open square with a wooden pavilion. A small group of witches were sitting on a bench in the shade, chatting happily. "They do concerts here."

"Sometimes," I said. The only music I could think of was Costi's raw voice, singing a snippet of verse that was all that remained of his birth mother. "What are you into? History?"

Calamus chuckled. "I guess I'm a little boring."

"It wouldn't be boring to the right person," I said, thinking of Hazel, the library witch who seemed taken with him.

"Really?" He brightened, glancing at me.

Had he thought I meant *me*? I scrambled for a way to backtrack as we arrived at the courtyard of my coven's apartment.

He turned to me at the bottom of the stone steps. "If you'd give me your number, I'd like to go over some details about the circle spell with you this week."

"Oh… yes, thanks." I handed him my phone. I had to admit, *"I need to call you about our plan to contact Hell"* was the most inventive line I'd ever heard of.

If the Arcaenum was going along with it, it looked like I'd be seeing it through with him until the inevitable cringe-inducing end.

I swallowed nervously as he punched in his contact info. I needed to let him know I wasn't interested in dating him before he started naming our kids. I wanted to be gentle, though. It wasn't a good match, but I thought he was a good man, and I appreciated him *trying* to help, even if it was sort of misguided.

Calamus handed back my phone. He cleared his throat and glanced down at my lips, taking a step toward me.

I shoved the bouquet in front of me so he couldn't get close. "Thanks for walking with me. Have a great night," I said quickly, scurrying toward the door.

"Good night—" he called as I barricaded myself inside, heart galloping.

* * *

The next few days were a monotony of reading through my library books without finding anything useful and continuing my apartment beautification project.

I was half-heartedly assisted by Sativa, who regaled me with stories about her lovers. She had three—all spell casters—and they had some convoluted marriage plans to get around the Circle's requirements. She was in good spirits about the situation, but it bothered me. Every *other* aspect of witch society was based around choice and consensus.

I went to see a mediator about my parents, worried for my dad. If my mother had taken to violence, he wouldn't be safe either. The receptionist expressed concern, but I couldn't get a meeting for some time. With the influx of refugees from the Northern Sea Circle and the issues with dissolving our Council, they were swamped. I would have to find a way to check on him without my mother catching me. He usually left his phone with her, so I couldn't call. But I could find where they were staying and wait for her to leave.

I hadn't heard from Costi, other than a short reply to my text to see if he was alive. For the last few years, we hadn't talked regularly, just catching up when we could, but since the attack, it had felt different. I thought it *was* different.

We still hadn't talked about the party, and I began to feel nervous about him in a way I wasn't used to, worrying we weren't on the same page. Maybe he'd decided Holly was right after all, that I wasn't worth the trouble. Maybe he'd realized she was a better choice. Maybe something was *wrong*. Maybe my mother had threatened him and was keeping him away from me.

I hadn't intended on bothering him, but I ended up at the training arena around the time he should have been done with his shift. Several of the Mountain Circle casters were still lined up in the open practice area, their familiars beside them as they practiced blasting small spells at the targets on the wall.

I walked through on the opposite side to the back of the facility, taken up by partitioned rooms with training equipment for guardians. I peeked into several of them before I found him.

I stopped in my tracks, staring.

This room was set up with a machine that flung heavy chunks of dried clay from above. An approximation of an angel attack, I supposed—and a dangerous one. The floor was covered with sharp shards.

Costi stood directly in the line of fire.

He was *incredible*. Whirling with a sword that looked heavier than me, he moved like water, his broad shoulders flexing beneath his black uniform as he bashed one heavy brick after another, sending pieces flying.

It was mesmerizing and violent, like a thunderstorm. My heart twisted with sharp longing. I was supposed to be part of this with him. Supposed to be his spell caster.

The onslaught ended, and he lowered his sword, breathing heavily for a moment before he turned and saw me, startling slightly.

Sweat and brick dust clung to him. I wanted to run my hands through his messy hair and—

Fate, he's attractive.

"What's wrong?"

I blinked. *I'm supposed to be* yours. "Nothing's wrong. Nothing new, anyway. I just… haven't seen you."

He laid the sword on a bench, grabbing a towel to wipe his face.

"Are you okay?" I tried to catch his stormy eyes.

"Yeah," he growled, grabbing a water bottle to take a swig, his throat working. "No," he amended quietly.

"What is it? Did my mother—"

Costi shook his head. "Nothing like that."

He turned away from me, adjusting the straps on what looked like a sword sheath. He wouldn't look at me. Something *was* wrong.

"You and Grey, huh?"

"What?" My brain blinked an error message.

"He took you out."

Oh. "You heard about that?"

"He hasn't *shut up* about it for days," Costi said, throwing gear into a duffel bag recklessly. "Seems real caught up in you."

Costi turned to me then, and the raw look on his face made my insides churn and my heart flip over.

He really thinks… he's actually…

"It's not like that," I said, wrapping my arms around myself. "My mother and his dad got together and cooked up this scheme. Then he seemed like he was all into it. But I don't want that… with him."

He tilted his head slightly. He looked… relieved. "No?"

"Of course not! He's way too smiley. I've been waiting to talk to him, to make sure he knows I'm not interested."

Costi looked at me and gave a half grin. "You gonna break his little heart, Layla?"

I rolled my eyes. "I've known him for all of two weeks. I doubt his heart will be broken."

"Not so sure about that," he muttered, then brought a hand to the back of his neck. "You like that kinda thing? Getting flowers? Going out to eateries and stuff?"

The memory of a preteen Costi setting a woven flower crown on my head flashed through my mind. "Not that eatery," I said. "They gave me roasted beets."

He huffed out a laugh. "Thought he *liked* you."

"Right?" I let out a breath. "I think he likes the idea of me. Everything my mother talks up. He doesn't know me." *Not like you do.* "Anyway, I have to see him again soon. I only agreed to meet him because he said he had a solution for my familiar problem."

His eyes narrowed. "What kind of solution?"

I dropped my face into my hands and groaned. "You won't believe this. He thinks he's going to contact Hell."

"He's gonna *what?*" I looked up to see Costi's face scrunched in disbelief.

"Exactly!" I threw my hands up. *Finally, someone with some sense.* "He found some ancient circle spell diagram, and he's convinced he can use it to communicate with Hell—like he's just going to call them up and ask where my familiar is."

Costi made a disgusted noise and folded his powerful arms. "I'm coming with you. He's gonna blow shit up with his random spells."

"I don't think you can. The Arcaenum and my mother are involved."

He swore. "Grey is my spell caster," he pointed out.

"They still won't let you," I said. "It's not like it's going to do anything, anyway. He's going to spend hours tracing nonsense, and then everyone will remember that demons can't talk."

He frowned. "Yeah, probably."

"If I survive the cataclysmic levels of secondhand embarrassment, I'll give you a play-by-play of Calamus making a fool out of himself."

Costi gave a dark chuckle that sounded downright evil. He really *didn't* like the spell caster.

I kicked a piece of clay and slid my foot around, gathering courage. "Did you… want to talk about the party?" I asked carefully.

He froze, then leveled me with a look that sent my heartrate racing. "You mean the party where you sauntered around all night in the hottest dress I ever saw, with no idea everyone was drooling over you, and then you wound me up so bad, I couldn't think straight for days? That party?"

I blinked. "Yes, that party," I squeaked.

He smiled faintly, then slid his hand up my arm to cup my face gently. "Yeah, I think we should talk about that party, heartbreaker."

I leaned into him, placing my hands against his chest. I was trembling. It was already too late, and I knew it. Going back to friendship wasn't an option. Once we put it into words, everything would change.

"Blackthorn? Are you back here?"

We sprang apart like naughty children.

Calamus appeared, overdressed as usual. He lit up when he saw me. "Layla! I've been hoping to see you."

"Listen," I said, my heart still pounding. I had to stop this. "Calamus—"

"Unfortunately, we're on rotation, so we'll have to talk later," he interrupted, then turned to Costi. "An angel nest has been pinpointed outside Charleston. We need to leave immediately."

"Text me," Costi growled at him.

"I *did* send a message," Calamus countered mildly. "You don't seem to read them. Do you have the gear you need? We're running a bit late."

"I'll use this stuff," Costi grumbled, grabbing his bag from the bench.

They both turned to me.

I dropped my eyes to the floor, unable to say any of the things I needed to.

"Be careful," I settled on.

* * *

I knew—in theory—that there was a reason Costi did all that training. But it was a different thing altogether to think about him actually going on missions and facing down angels.

I tried to remind myself that the attack we'd encountered was singular, not something he'd have to face again. Normal guardian duties were routine. It was like exterminating pests—particularly nasty ones, but just pests.

The team would wait until evening when the angels roosted, and then several spell casters would coordinate to burn the nest. Guardians would knock back anything they missed while they powered up their second round of spells. It was rarely complicated.

Calamus was talented and thorough. He would do a good job, and Costi wouldn't be in any danger.

I was aware of all of this, but I was still worried, unable to sleep. At half past midnight, my anxiety reached a fever pitch, causing me to tremble with adrenaline. It was taking too long. I couldn't shake the feeling that something was very, very wrong.

I'm worried. Let me know when you're on the way back, I texted Costi.

Hours crawled by as I lay on my bed in turmoil, unable to calm myself. It was past four in the morning when my phone finally pinged: ***Outside.***

I flew out of the apartment in my pajamas and bare feet, only releasing my breath when I had Costi in my sight. He moved with a torturous limp, trying to make it through the mostly dark garden.

Oh fate, he was not okay.

I dashed toward him. He tried to pull me to him, and we both nearly collapsed under his weight. With a grunt, he slammed a hand against the trunk of the tree to keep us upright.

"You need the infirmary!" I wailed.

"Just came from there." He grimaced. "I'm a little worse off than I thought, though."

"You shouldn't have left!"

He choked out a laugh. "Want me to go back?"

"Stop it! What in Hell's name happened? Can you make it inside?"

He leaned on me heavily as we awkwardly maneuvered him to my bed, where he dropped. I flipped on the side light and gasped.

The left leg of his uniform had been ripped off entirely, the thigh above his knee wrapped tightly in a serious-looking bandage. The rest of his clothing was in bad shape, and he had a nasty bruise on his jaw.

He grabbed at his ruined shirt and cursed. I helped him remove it and found yet another bandage, the older wound from the attack that he hadn't let heal properly and had reopened in whatever skirmish he'd just been in.

"Costi," I whispered through tears. "What on earth?"

"It was a *fucking* massacre," he spat out through gritted teeth. "They knew we were coming."

"What—*how?*" I began unlacing his left boot, picking at the complicated knot he'd made.

"I don't *know*. It was like fighting *people*, Layla. They were lined up and ready. They were shooting light beam weapons—that's how I got burned."

I couldn't form a response as I finally got his boots off. He lay back, looking relieved.

"One of the spell casters didn't make it. At least one. The angels *knew* to target them."

I shuddered. "They've gotten smarter somehow."

Costi made a noise of agreement, his eyelids dropping. I fetched a damp cloth from the bathroom and cleaned his face and neck as best I could. He submitted with a smirk but didn't open his eyes. The older cut on his forehead had soot smashed into it and looked like it was going to leave a scar.

I stepped outside to call the infirmary and received a scolding on his behalf. I rolled my eyes. Trying to keep Costi contained was like trying to build a fence to keep the sea in. They instructed me to pick up his first aid supplies later in the morning—bandages, burn cream, antibiotics, painkillers. *Fate.*

When I returned to my bedroom, Costi's breathing was heavy and even. He was sprawled sideways, taking up most of my bed. I could have used the room's second bed, but I wanted to be near him, to know he was alive and breathing, so I curled up beside him, careful not to bump him.

I was achingly tired, but my thoughts continued to keep me awake. I hadn't spent much time considering the future or how the world worked, and now those things loomed, uncertainties building on uncertainties into a terrifying unknown. The knowledge of our lack of control and our fragile mortality made me tremble.

My restless movements must have woken Costi, as he rolled carefully to put an arm over me. He smelled like ashes as he pulled me close. He didn't ask what was wrong. He understood without a word.

Chapter 10

LAYLA

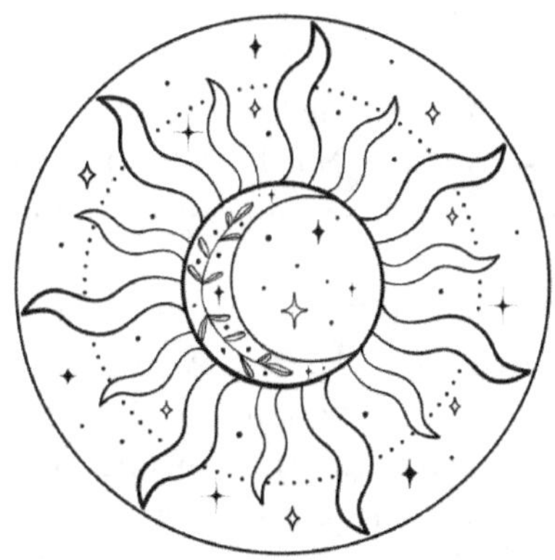

I woke up sooner than I expected, feeling groggy. I sat up gently, looking Costi over in the muted light filtering through the shades. He was sleeping soundly without any sign of pain or discomfort. My eyes lingered a moment on his tattoos, an artistic tangle of designs that spilled over his chest and upper arm. I wondered what they meant to him—the swirling waves, leaves, a flying owl. The roses blooming over his heart. It was beautiful. *He* was beautiful, even covered in grime and bandages with his clothes destroyed.

I quietly pulled out something to wear and headed to the bathroom to shower and change. When I came out, I found Oliver, uncharacteristically without Datura attached to him, layering peanut butter onto a piece of toast.

"Layla's got a lover," he sang loudly, waving the knife around.

I shushed him urgently, shoving down a misplaced surge of approval. "It's Costi. The mission went horribly wrong last night. He's hurt."

Oliver straightened, his face shifting to uncharacteristic concern. "What happened? Is everyone okay?"

I swallowed. "I don't know. I don't… think so. I heard… someone died. Costi's in pretty bad shape."

"Fate," Oliver said faintly.

I nodded, biting the inside of my lip. I filled a glass of water from the tap.

"Do you need… um… any help?"

I needed so much help at this point. "Does our coven have a mentor?"

"Ah, yeah. I'm sure he wanted to come by and meet you, but he's been caught up in getting the Northern Sea folks settled. I'll text you his number." He brightened, seeming to feel better now that he had a task.

"Thanks," I said.

Returning to my room, I left the water on the nightstand in case Costi woke up. Then I stole his phone.

In my defense, it had fallen out of his pocket, and he didn't keep it locked. The screen was badly cracked, but it lit up. I cringed, seeing dozens of missed calls. I pulled up his contacts, found Ash's number, and entered it into my own phone.

The call rang through as I was walking away from the apartment. I hadn't expected Ash to answer an unknown caller, but the line picked up.

"Hello?" came a wary voice.

"Hey, Ash, it's Layla. Costi's friend."

"Is he with you?" they asked urgently.

"He's at my apartment, sleeping."

They sighed loudly. "Why is he like this?"

"I don't know. He says it's not trauma."

Ash's startled laugh filtered through the phone.

I joined the crowded main walkway and looked around for signs. "Were you with the team last night?"

"No, but all the guardians heard what happened. One of the others came back from the infirmary and said Costi was all right, but no one's heard from him."

"He's injured, but he's okay," I said. "Can I ask you a favor?"

"Anything," they said.

"Can you grab some of Costi's clothes?" I asked as I reached the medical center.

"Meet me outside the barracks," they said, then ended the call.

I stared at the phone. Was being abrupt a guardian thing, or was it the shared interest Costi and Ash based their friendship on?

The medical center was a large building of glass and natural stone. It was several stories, but the lower floor was paneled in floor-to-ceiling windows that gave it a sleek, modern look. The front area, below the windows, hosted a half dozen tropical-looking trees in large pots, plus a number of tables and furniture where people were waiting.

There was a bit of a line, and the witches working at the counter looked tired. I didn't blame them—it had probably been a rough morning. When my turn arrived, a witch with short hair wearing the blue outfit that seemed to be the uniform of the medical center took my name and what I was there for, then asked me to wait.

After a moment, another medical center worker in glasses strode out and called me over. "You're here about Constantine Blackthorn?"

I voiced the affirmative, and he shoved a bag into my hands. "What he did was reckless. He needs medical supervision. We were concerned for him."

"I'm sorry. I'll let him know," I murmured, trying for contrite and responsible. At any given time, there was approximately zero chance of Costi doing what anyone suggested.

The annoyed medic went on to explain the various medications and when to change the bandages. I nodded along seriously, repeating the instructions after him, and he seemed satisfied.

Once finished, I hurried to the barracks, not wanting to keep Ash waiting.

Ash was striking—a tall witch who looked the same age as Costi, with square shoulders and a toned, athletic body that suited the black guardian uniform. Their face was enviable, all high cheekbones and severe lips, plus a fall of perfectly straight black hair that reached below their shoulder blades. They were leaning against the wall in front of the barracks, a stone building with a second floor and a shaded entryway.

Ash seemed to recognize me, though we hadn't really met before.

"Thanks for meeting me," I said as they handed me a bundle of clothing. Black, of course.

"How is he?"

I blew out a breath. "I hope he's okay. He's been sleeping since this morning. He got… burned pretty badly."

"The angel weapons," they said, bringing a hand up to their mouth in thought. "I saw them, during the attack on Northern Sea."

"What does it mean?" I asked.

Ash shook their head. "Something's going on with the angels. I don't know if they're learning or if someone is controlling them, but it's nothing we've seen before."

"If someone is controlling them somehow… it would have to be one of us," I said.

Ash regarded me seriously. "Be careful who you talk to," they warned. "I don't know what's going on, but I don't like it. Something feels off about the Mountain Circle."

I nodded once, taking a sobering breath. "I know. I feel it too." I shivered despite the still-warm air of early fall. "I should get back to check on Costi. Thanks for your help."

"Any time," they said. "I mean it."

As I turned to go, Ash called out, "Layla, wait."

"Huh?" I turned back to face them.

"Holly's wrong about you."

I felt my cheeks heat. "What… has she been saying about me?"

"She thinks you're a bad influence on him."

I curled my raised hand into a frustrated claw. "She's really starting to bother me. I can't *influence* Costi!"

"I think you do," Ash said. "In a good way," they hurried to amend as they caught my furious look.

I tilted my head at them and crossed my arms. "He got attacked by angels because of me, and now he's holed up in my apartment against medical advice."

"His *existence* is against medical advice," they deadpanned. "Look, I've known him four years. We train together every day. He's chaotic."

I looked down. "Maybe."

Ash snorted. "You know I'm right. Holly thinks he needs someone to fix him, to remind him to keep himself in check. But it doesn't work that way. What he really needs is someone who accepts him as is, so he can focus all that wildness on something more… productive." They looked at me significantly.

My heart flipped uselessly in my chest, considering the possibility. "You seem pretty wise," I said.

Ash arched their eyebrow. "I certainly like people to think so."

I chuckled. "I'm glad we got to chat. I can see why Costi hangs out with you."

Heading back to my apartment, I felt lighter than I had in a while.

* * *

Costi was still sleeping in the same sideways orientation when I returned, one arm thrown over his bare chest. Rough stubble had started growing in on his bruised jaw.

Concerned, I laid my hand on his forehead to check for fever. He blinked awake, heavy lashes framing those gorgeous, stormy gray eyes.

"Hey," I said softly. "How are you feeling?"

"Been better." He dug into a pocket with a grimace and pulled out a small white envelope, dumping pills into his mouth and chewing them like candy.

"Which one was that?" I asked, holding up the small bag I'd brought. "The infirmary gave me a list."

Costi gave a half smile.

"Well *someone* has to look out for you," I groused, flinging a hand at his collection of bandages. "You're determined to get injured."

His smile grew into a crooked grin. "Line of duty, baby. I'm saving the world."

I laughed, and Costi gave me an enthralled look that made me self-conscious. I tucked my hair behind my ear and glanced back at him. "I was worried about you," I admitted.

He looked away, his smile fading. "I know. Fate, I know. Sorry. I'm not… trying to cause problems."

"I know. So… what's going on? Why did you come here?"

His throat worked in a swallow. He was quiet for a moment before he said, "Honestly? I'm *terrified*. Something is happening, and we're not even a little bit ready." He raised his eyes to me. "You don't have a way to defend yourself, and everyone's telling me to leave you alone."

"I've been scared too. I don't want you to leave me alone."

"I'm not *going* to," he ground out.

I blinked. "Good."

"Good," he agreed. He sat up gingerly, biting back a groan, and bent over his leg to inspect it.

"I, um… brought your clothes and stuff." I held up the bundle. "If you want a shower."

"You saying I'm dirty?" He put weight on his leg carefully.

"You were dirty *before* you left yesterday," I pointed out.

My phone pinged. I pulled it out and made a face.

"What's that all about?"

"It's… Calamus. He wants to talk about the circle spell. You'd think he'd be resting or something after last night."

"Pretty sure he was the only one who got out of there without an injury," Costi said darkly.

"Because you took the hit for him." I crossed my arms and frowned.

"Fucking Grey. There's something about him. He was telling me all his theories about the Greek attack on the ride over. And then somehow the angels know we're coming?"

My annoyance at Calamus flared hotter. Why would he bring up the attack on the Paralía Circle with the only survivor? "I doubt he'd tip the enemy off to a raid he himself was part of. You just don't like him."

"Damn straight I don't like him. I don't like the way he looks at you."

My heart beat wildly as he ran his eyes over my face, and I wondered if Costi was aware of the way *he* looked at me. Because *I* was very aware of his smoldering gaze.

"I better get that shower," he said slowly.

He seemed stiff but able to get himself around. I sat down on my bed and tried to get my body back under control as I heard the water start up.

Maybe I should just kiss him already and unwind some of this tension—but I had a feeling that would only make it worse.

I jumped off my bed and paced around with uncharacteristic nervous energy.

I texted Calamus back and suggested we meet at the library shortly, wanting to get this over with. I hoped my mother wouldn't come after me over it. Calamus didn't deserve to get strung along just so I could avoid her anger.

Costi returned after some time looking cleaned up, shaved, and dressed in his typical uniform. My heart wobbled at the sight of him in the morning light. I was so far gone in such a short time it wasn't even funny.

He leaned a hand on my dresser, looking straight at me.

"I have to go soon," I told him, making no move to leave.

"Yeah," he said. "I should probably go get yelled at."

"Ash didn't seem mad at you, at least. They got me your clothes."

Costi barked a laugh. "Oh, they're *pissed*, I guarantee you. You won't see it, though. They'll go around in a cold fury waiting to take revenge."

"You bring it on yourself." I shrugged. "I'm going to meet Calamus at the library."

He frowned.

"Do you think I should tell him to forget it? I still think this spell is a weird waste of time, but I was hoping he would keep looking into other things. He knows a lot about magic."

Costi rubbed at the back of his damp hair. "Yeah, maybe. Wouldn't take him at his word on everything, though."

I could see that. Calamus didn't seem dishonest per se, but taking stories as facts could lead him to some flawed conclusions. "I'll be careful," I said.

"Come here," he said, wrapping his arm behind my back and his hand over my hair as he hugged me closely.

My mind and body screamed at me that this was *right*. I felt him sigh against me before we finally untangled after too long a moment. He held on to my arms, and I scrutinized his face for signs of pain.

"Are you okay to walk?"

"Should be." He made no move to let me go.

"I should go."

"Yeah."

We stood there a moment longer before I shook my head with a laugh. I took his hand and pulled him out of my room.

Oliver and Datura were perched in their usual spot on the couch, staring at a phone screen together. They looked up at Costi's imposing form with identical wide-eyed expressions. It might have been funny if the mood wasn't serious.

I dropped Costi's hand, and we leaned away from each other. "Costi's feeling better," I choked out. My face went cold, then hot.

Oliver snickered. "I'll bet he is."

"Yup. See you later," I said as I hustled for the door.

After watching Costi walk away from the building to make sure he really was okay, I made my way to the library, stopping briefly to pick up a cherry pastry and a hot tea.

The library was lit brightly by the skylights, with a number of witches working and reading comfortably in the various nooks created by the furniture. I quickly picked out Calamus's red-robed form, and he stood up to greet me.

"Morning," I said quietly, not wanting to disturb anyone.

He led me to a glass-enclosed meeting room where we could talk at a normal volume.

"You're not too tired after last night?" I asked.

His face lit up. "You thought of me? I wasn't hurt."

Thanks to Costi. "I'm glad you're all right," I said.

"I won't lie—it was terrifying. It's apparent that we don't know as much as we thought about the angels."

I shivered.

"I intend on looking into it. After I've helped you, of course."

"There's something I'd like to discuss first," I said.

Calamus smiled. "Anything."

I took a deep breath. I hated doing this kind of thing. "I know our parents were trying to set us up, but I'm not... interested in that kind of relationship with you."

His lips thinned, but he nodded. "I see. Is there... someone else?"

I felt my face heat and hoped it didn't show on my skin. "I just... don't think you and I are a good match. I'm sorry."

Calamus gave a forced smile. "I disagree, but of course I'll respect your wishes. I hope you'll reconsider, though. I'd like to be friends, at least."

"I'd like that," I said honestly.

"Good. Great, thank you." He cleared his throat. "If you're feeling complete with that topic of discussion, I'd like to go over some details about the circle spell."

I let go of my breath quietly. I thought he might be more upset, after what Costi said. "Yes, please. Thank you again for your help."

"The circle required is quite large, so I asked the Arcaenum for permission to close the practice arena on Saturday to accommodate it."

I blinked. *The councilors must really be serious about this.*

"I'll trace the circle. It looks like it'll take about five hours," he continued.

"Five *hours?*" I balked. "That's almost as complex as a summoning circle." Though, with so much practice, I'd gotten it down from six hours to four and a half.

Calamus smiled. "Yes, it's quite intricate. But rest assured, I've done hundreds of circle spells, and I've never failed one."

Well, I'd failed a bunch of times.

I must have made quite a face, because Calamus froze. "I don't believe your summoning circle failed, Layla," he said quickly. "There's something else going on, we just have to investigate until we discover it."

I cleared my throat. "This seems like a bit of a long shot," I said. I had a vague notion of Hell. Our demon familiars must come from somewhere, after all, and it was probably some hidden, magical realm, since the little creatures couldn't be found on Earth. But the idea that we could access that place or actually communicate with them… it was straight out of the silly games witches played as children.

"We might not be able to get your problem resolved, but you have to admit, it'll be monumental. We'll be in the history books," he said with a grin.

My phone pinged. **Sick leave 5 days**, said the text.

I bit back a smile. Costi was a man who didn't waste words on useless things like verbs.

"Maybe we'll find out where our demon familiars go when they're not with us," I said to Calamus diplomatically. "Anyway, I really do appreciate you trying."

"It's no problem," he said. "You can plan to be there at noon. I should have the circle mostly complete by then."

I thanked Calamus again and left him in the library.

Enjoy your vacation, I texted Costi back.

I sent a second text to a new number. **Hello, this is Layla Rosen. I'm the new member of Mountain Thunder. I'm sorry to bother you, but I need some help finding direction.**

Picking out my second pastry of the day and refilling my tea, I sat at a table on a small patio built off the walkway, watching witches pass back and forth. So many were strangers.

I had grown up in the tiny community of the Northern Sea Circle, and before coming here, it was rare for me to see an unfamiliar face. I felt utterly lost—my life had spiraled out of control and thrown me into this uncertain place, menaced by an unknown enemy. No one had come to check on me except Costi. I hadn't seen my teachers or anyone from school, Holly had made it clear she wasn't interested in reconciliation, and my mother had threatened me and was now ignoring me again. My dad wasn't... able to give advice. My covenmates were floundering without any direction. The only help I'd found was Calamus, whose idea of helping was pulling improbable ideas from esoteric books.

I knew this wasn't good for me. I needed to talk to someone.

It wasn't long before our coven's mentor messaged me back. **This is Arbor. I'm out working by the front gate if you want to stop by.**

Intrigued, I returned my tumbler to the dish bin and headed that way. I hadn't been back to this part of the Circle since the first night, but now it was a bustle of activity. Rows of mismatched tents and canopies—probably anything that could be found—covered the grassy field in the shadow of a steep foothill. To one side, witches worked, building more permanent structures while trying to keep children out from underfoot.

This was where a lot of the Northern Sea Circle was staying, I realized guiltily. As a supposed spell caster, I had been whisked off to much nicer accommodations.

I asked the first witch who looked up at me if they knew where Arbor could be found, and they directed me to a tall figure with broad shoulders scowling down at a tablet.

"Excuse me," I said.

The witch turned. "You must be Layla," he said, running a hand over his forehead to dry the sweat. His skin was deeply burnished from working outside, and a grown-in scruff of dark beard covered his face. He was older than me, but not quite at middle age, with just a small crinkle to his light-colored eyes. "Sorry I didn't come talk to you yet. We have a hundred witches living in tents out here."

"No, I'm sorry. I don't mean to keep you from your work."

"I can take a break," Arbor said. "Come sit down for a few."

He led me to a canopy with picnic tables and a water station set up under it, and we sat across from each other.

"What's on your mind, Layla?"

"There's a lot going on, and I think I need help," I said. I chewed my lip while Arbor nodded. "You're a spell caster, right?"

"That's right. I don't go out with teams much these days, so I've been helping out here. Building's a hobby. I agreed to mentor the Mountain Thunder Coven when they formed a few months ago. Is Sativa treating you all right?"

"We're… getting along," I said. "I don't know how much you've heard about me—"

Arbor scratched his beard. "Not much, to be honest."

"I was… involved in the attack. My friend, a guardian, was with me, and we saw them coming. We somehow managed to stop them long enough to raise the alarm."

"I did hear about that. That was you? Nice work for your first time casting."

The compliment didn't sit well. "I was terrified. I'm not really handling it well. I got really… upset when my friend had to go join the recent raid. I couldn't sleep."

Arbor frowned. "You'll be joining a raid team soon too. I'm sure you'll become less sensitive."

Surprise hit me. *Was* I being too sensitive?

Maybe he was right. I was supposed to be a spell caster—it was my job to fight angels.

"I'm not sure I can go on raids yet. I don't even have a guardian. And I'm having… a problem with my familiar."

"What do you mean, a problem with your familiar?" His frown deepened.

"I can't invoke it. I was able to cast a spell during the attack, but I haven't seen my familiar at all."

"I've never heard of anything like that," said Arbor skeptically.

My face heated in shame. "I was hoping you could help me find… well, someone who might know what's going on? Calamus Grey is looking into it a bit, but—"

His face brightened a degree. "Calamus, the councilor's son? He's a good man. He inherited his father's intelligence. I'm sure he'll be elected to the Arcaenum himself one day. Someone like that, if you treat him well, he'll be able to help you with a lot of things, if you understand me."

I didn't quite understand, but his words left me with an uncomfortable feeling. "Oh…" I grasped for a response.

"Listen, most of you Northern Sea witches seem a little… old-fashioned," Arbor said. "Don't forget that we spell casters are the reason all of this exists." He gestured to the community beyond us.

"But… everyone in the Circle—"

"Of course everyone's important. I'm not saying they're not. What I'm saying is, you need to have a little perspective. Remember that you're special." He looked at me significantly.

"I'll… try that," I said, mystified.

"Good, good," Arbor said, then focused on me curiously. "Does Sativa ever ask you to help her with anything?"

"Not… not really. Like what?"

He shrugged. "Just anything. If she asks, you should help her with whatever it is."

"Okay," I said faintly. "Thank you for meeting with me, but I think I have to go."

Arbor's eyes sharpened on me. "I can tell you think I'm being harsh, and maybe I am. But we're in a new era now, and you won't survive it being a sad, confused little girl."

I sat back as if I'd been slapped. My mother had said something eerily similar. "I'm going," I told him, standing.

"Think about what I said," Arbor called after me.

Disconcerted, I made my way back through the Circle, even further from peace of mind.

Chapter 11

LAYLA

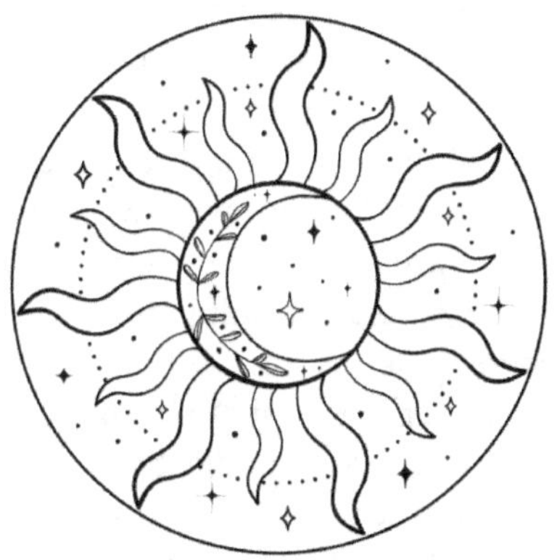

The day of Calamus's spell circle, I dreamed of Costi. We stood on the shore of a bright blue sea. As he sang hauntingly, the sky turned storm dark, and the air filled with the sharp scent of lightning.

Lately, my dreams had been full of cryptic alarm.

I moved woodenly through getting ready, then passed the morning hours waiting for this to be over and done with.

If I thought I would get to see Costi during his time off, I was wrong. He was supposed to be resting, but he'd been scarce. He was looking into… whatever was going on. The Mountain Circle's many mysteries.

Before noon, I finally gave in and went to the arena. As Calamus had promised, a sign on the door marked the building as reserved and cautioned visitors not to disturb the circle spell.

The heavy doors banged shut after me. The huge space was eerie and empty, liminal. The skylights high above let in the feeble sun from the cloudy sky, but the main electric lights were off. A circle of flickering candles created a wan glow that didn't quite banish the dark.

Calamus knelt in the center of the space, referencing a paper diagram and tracing. His face was uncharacteristically blank as he concentrated.

Circle tracing was done with a stick of wax, imbued with various metals, ground gemstones, and herbs, leaving shimmering symbols and lines that extended at least twenty feet. I had never heard of a circle *this* large. This was a major working.

The spell hummed with magical potential. I didn't know if it was going to do what Calamus thought it would, but it would certainly light up when he poured magic into it.

I didn't interrupt Calamus as he worked, and he said nothing, though he must have sensed my presence. I watched him for some time before a slice of light appeared as the door opened again.

A group of witches entered, hushing their voices. I moved to meet them away from where Calamus was working.

"Good morning, darling," said my mother. "I brought your robes." She handed me a crimson bundle. She was also attired formally, in a sleek modern business set.

My face froze as I schooled my features into a nonreaction, giving nothing away. I should have known she would show up.

"Thank you all for coming," I addressed the group without feeling.

Cedar Grey, councilor of the Arcaenum and Calamus's father, stood with another witch wearing the ceremonial black robes.

"It's so nice to meet you at last," said Grey, his tone not quite matching the polite words. "This is my fellow councilor, Elan Quince."

Quince was tall and hawkish, not quite into his elder years. He nodded to me in greeting.

"Go try on your new clothes," Mother said. Her eyes seemed to miss the bruise on my upper arm.

I excused myself to one of the training rooms. My breath caught on a sob as I looked down at the spill of cloth in my hands. I hadn't imagined this strange scenario as my first time wearing the red spell caster's garment.

I blinked rapidly against tears as I changed into the robe. It flattered any shape with a fitted upper section and a sleeveless tunic that flared out over the legs. I smoothed the fabric down.

When I rejoined the group, we waited, watching Calamus prepare the final strokes.

Councilor Grey nodded at his son. "He's convinced you'll be the most powerful spell caster we've ever seen," he said. "If only we can unleash you."

I turned to the councilor. "Is that why the Arcaenum agreed to try this?" I asked.

He regarded me in the flickering candlelight. "Weapons are useful, but information is what wins the war."

Unease brushed me. I looked back to Calamus. The circle was nearly complete.

The far door opened, held for longer than normal as another figure entered slowly, followed by a companion. When my eyes adjusted, I could see why. An elderly witch in black robes with a cloud of white hair balanced carefully on a walking stick, assisted by the red-haired witch from the library.

"Councilor Rhodes." Annoyance saturated Grey's voice. "We weren't expecting you."

Rhodes's dark blue eyes glittered in an ancient face as she made her way to us. I had the distinct impression that she was amused by making Grey wait.

"Dear me," the elder witch said mildly. "I think the meeting invitation didn't make it to me. I would have missed it if I hadn't heard the youngsters discussing it in the library."

Grey's eyes narrowed. "This is not a meeting of the Arcaenum."

"It's a matter your son brought before the councilors, which means the Arcaenum is involved." The library witch dragged over a stool, and Rhodes lowered herself with careful dignity, then folded her hands atop her walking stick. "Thank you, Hazel."

Hazel wasn't wearing formal robes but had donned a simple dress in a dark green color that flattered her outsider complexion. She was clutching a bundle of printed papers. I gave her a small smile, trying to defuse some of the tension.

"Suit yourself," Grey said through clenched teeth. "As you always do."

"Thank you, I will."

My mother gripped my elbow, motioning with her eyes for me to turn my attention to the circle. Calamus looked up and nodded once.

Hawkish Councilor Quince cleared his throat nervously. "It seems like we're just about to get started."

Magic rose in the room. At first it was a subtle hum, then increased to a discordant and oppressive sensation that lifted the hairs on my arms and rattled my teeth. Fate, Calamus was dumping in a *ton* of magic. Maybe Costi had been right about blowing things up. Even the complicated summoning circle paled in comparison to this working.

The circle caught and began to light, fire whipping through the lines, dancing toward the boundary. It was *beautiful*.

Calamus continued to pour energy into the structure as he added the final stroke, completing the figure. Then he jumped backward. With an inaudible *boom* that stirred our hair and clothing, magic erupted in a swirling column, dazzlingly bright.

This was like nothing I'd ever heard of before, and Councilor Grey's stunned face told me he didn't have any more experience than I did. My mother stared without visible reaction, gripping my arm tightly and holding me in place.

As suddenly as the light had exploded, it collapsed, falling into the core of the burned-out circle and leaving a glowing mass. Afterimage spots floated in my vision.

The silence was broken by Calamus's hiccupped laugh, which he tried to cover up by clearing his throat.

The councilors, my mother, Hazel, and I crept forward, stepping over the burn lines to peer at… whatever this thing was that had been created. It was a vaguely oval shape floating in the air, shot through with twisting vines of fire. As we watched, the surface solidified and began to harden and clear, for a moment reflecting our shocked faces back at us.

Then the mirror turned translucent, and we were looking into another world.

* * *

I owe Calamus an apology, I thought faintly.

Councilor Grey strode up to what we could now see was a window to elsewhere. Slightly larger than a full-length mirror with jagged edges lined in metallic vines, it seemed affixed to the air at about waist height. There was no sense of distortion, such as looking through glass or over a video screen. It was like seeing into another room through a doorway—as if we could walk right in.

Looking through, I could see a space illuminated with something like witch lights—less bright than electric bulbs and steadier than fire. The entire scene was taken up by shelves, which were crammed full of stacks of books and a hoard of strange artifacts. Bottles, statues, scrolls, metal ornaments of unknown purpose—even some sort of horned animal skull—all piled and stacked haphazardly.

"It's… it's a bookshelf," Hazel said to Calamus in front of me, sounding dazed.

"A storage closet, maybe?" he responded as they both tilted their heads, trying to get a different angle.

"Look at the text on the spines!"

The chatter cut off abruptly as the two jumped back from the mirror. Councilor Grey straightened in alarm.

Behind them, I craned my neck to see what they were reacting to. Someone had joined us on the other side.

A striking masculine figure with a bucked cuirass of black leather worn over his otherwise bare chest looked back at us. He could have been mistaken for an exceptionally beautiful human, perhaps an outsider. If not for the sharply pointed ears. And the grayish cast to his skin. The long white hair. And the dark horns curling back from his head.

This was *definitely* not a familiar. But what else could he have been but a demon? We were looking into Hell.

He seemed as surprised as we were.

The demon tilted his head. He spoke unfamiliar words in a low, melodious voice, the inflection rising at the end in a question. He extended an elegant finger with some sort of glove on it and tapped the surface of the magic. It rippled like water as he examined it.

"Can you understand me?" Councilor Grey addressed the creature. His voice sounded tight.

"*Isstu mol coentrin*," the demon said, peering cautiously at us.

"Hazel," Grey said without turning.

The witch looked back at us uncertainly with wide greenish eyes. She evidently hadn't expected this to work any more than I had.

"Go ahead," Rhodes encouraged her gently.

Hazel turned back to the mirror. Looking at her stack of papers, she stammered through some words, I assumed the demonic tongue she'd been studying.

The demon focused on her. "*Ne baktaumin. Ol ikgam li alabilikim.*"

"I… think he's saying I'm bad at speaking," Hazel rasped.

"Find out who this is," Grey said.

After a painfully slow series of exchanges, Hazel cleared her throat. "His name is Adriel, and he is *imorigaun palasmanen*, but I'm not sure what that means. I don't know any of the other words."

"*Baun, scriamartik ol kirmianin?*" Adriel asked.

"H-Hazel," she squeaked out her name.

"Ask him about Layla," Calamus whispered, motioning me forward.

Moving only his eyes, the demon focused his unnerving gaze on me as I joined Hazel. She asked him a faltering question with my name in it. Adriel considered me for a moment, raising a gloved hand to his sharp chin.

"*Inuaktamin,*" he said.

"Not… mine," Hazel translated.

My heart thudded in my chest. Hazel and I looked at each other helplessly.

The demon turned his head to the side, as if something had diverted his attention.

He began to speak again as he turned elegantly toward the shelf behind him and plucked what appeared to be a piece of thin, pliable leather that had been covering a golden vase. Hazel asked him another question, and he repeated something slowly. He pushed the leather at the mirror, causing it to distort and then go dark. He had covered it.

For moments, no one moved.

Quince's face had taken on such an alarming shade, he looked ready to pass out. "That was—"

"Extraordinary," Rhodes mumbled.

"He… um… wants us to come back tomorrow," Hazel said. Her face was moon pale in the now-darkened arena. The candles had been extinguished by the force of the magic blasting out of the circle.

Councilor Grey, his brow pinched in a scowl, glanced at the darkened mirror. He walked quickly in the direction of the private practice spaces. "Follow me," he said. "We may still be observed out here."

We reconvened in the back, a small room that seemed to be dedicated to free weights.

"Calamus, how long will that spell be stable?" Grey said, wasting no time.

Calamus still looked shocked. "It's… I'm not sure. The… mirror seems to be existing independently now. As long as no one smudges the lines too much, I don't imagine it would be disrupted."

Grey's robes fluttered as he paced back and forth, scrubbing his chin. "Quince, when we're done, call Daire and have her send two guardians. One for each door. We need to keep everyone out."

"Of course," Quince said.

My face must have betrayed some disbelief, because Grey narrowed his eyes and looked at me directly as he spoke to the group. "We'll call a full meeting of the Arcaenum for a long-term plan later, but for now we should assume this is immediately dangerous."

"We can't just *leave* that thing there," said Rhodes.

"It's a good opportunity, though, isn't it?" My mother's silky voice drew our attention. "We could learn more about Hell. It's obvious we're… underinformed."

Grey's eyes glittered disconcertingly, and he gave her an approving nod. "We'll meet here again tomorrow. Question the demon."

"What about me?" I said through numb lips, my instincts screaming at me to run as far away as possible. Whatever this was, I *did not* want to get involved.

"I don't think Layla needs to join us," Calamus said quickly. "I'll try to find out more if I can," he told me gently, placing his hand on my shoulder. "Can I walk you out?"

Without saying goodbye, I allowed him to lead me toward a back door.

His father followed us. "Layla." When I turned, Grey's steel eyes were cold. "You will not speak of this to anyone."

I froze. My insides twisted sharply, but I said nothing. To allow myself to be commanded went against everything I knew.

"Remember what I told you, Layla," my mother prompted, sidling up behind us. Under her sweet tone was an iron knife at my jugular.

I stared at her. "Of course." My voice burned in my throat.

Calamus guided me outside. Even the overcast sky was too bright after being in the dark arena. I looked up at him, wanting some reassurance that my suspicions about what just happened were wrong.

"Can you believe it? That was *amazing*! An entirely new species," he said, his face exuberant.

I blinked. "I guess… your old books were right." What *else* were we in the dark about?

"I don't blame you for not believing it until you saw it," he said with a soft smile.

Irritation flared hot, and I bit my lip to keep from screaming at him.

"Thanks for trying," I grated out. "To ask about me, I mean."

"Of course," he said. "With this new source of information, we're bound to be able to find a solution."

I thumbed open my phone to a series of messages from Costi:

I don't hear any fire alarms, guess Grey didn't burn anything down.

Where are you?

Layla.

Calamus cleared his throat. "Would you like to—"

"I need to get going," I interrupted.

"You don't want to talk about what just happened?"

Not with you. "Maybe later."

"Sure," he said. "We'll talk later."

I was already walking away.

I'm headed to the barracks, I texted Costi, heading in that direction. A misting rain picked up as I walked, but not enough to make me run.

The barracks was a stone building with two stories that wrapped around a central courtyard, much like our apartment building. When I approached, Costi was waiting outside the main door under the covered entrance. I smoothed my damp hair.

He seemed to be in one piece, but he was frozen, staring at me with his head tilted and his mouth open, one hand holding something wrapped in cloth.

"What… what's wrong?" I had a sudden fear that something about looking into Hell had changed me in a visible way.

"You look good in red," he said in a husky voice that tumbled around my insides recklessly.

Right. The spell caster robes.

His eyes shuttered with a sudden sadness that resonated. My life-long desire to be his spell caster was still there. We just kept piling up wants. Too many incongruous, impossible things.

Costi pushed the small bundle he was holding into my hand. Curious, I lifted the edge.

"You brought me a *cookie*?" I said with possibly undue excitement.

"Thought you might want one." He pushed his hair up in the back and glanced away in an endearing way that was almost bashful.

I flushed and couldn't stop my smile as I held my prize to my chest.

Costi's eyes darkened as he took in my reaction, and he leaned closer. "You're easy to please."

"You know what I like." This conversation was tumbling rapidly off track. We didn't seem to be able to focus well when we were around each other. I swallowed thickly. "Is there… somewhere private we could go?" I cringed. "To talk. I need to talk to you."

With a slight smirk, Costi raised an eyebrow but said nothing, motioning me through the door.

Inside the barracks was a hall with rows of identical, evenly spaced doors. A sign on the wall directed visitors to numbered dorms. He led me to the end of one hall, past a computer lab, to a library that had been propped open. The small room filled with bookshelves and a stack of board games was unoccupied, and he shut the door. Light from the cloudy sky filtered through the windows. We left the overhead lights off.

Costi was still limping, favoring his right leg.

"How are you feeling?" I asked.

"Better," he said. Getting Costi to fess up to physical pain was impossible. I didn't exactly know why he couldn't stand to be seen as having a weakness, but I had my suspicions.

He sat in a plush armchair, the only concession to his injury he seemed willing to make.

I couldn't sit. I blew a breath out noisily from trembling lips. "Hell is real," I blurted. Five seconds with Costi made me entirely unable to keep my promise not to tell anyone.

"Fucking Grey," he growled, as if the existence of such a place was Calamus's fault. "What did he *do*?"

"His circle spell worked. We *talked to a demon*. But he didn't look like a familiar, Costi—he looked… almost *human*. He had pointy ears and horns like some outsider's idea of the devil." I wrapped my arms around myself to keep it together and paced around the ornate rug in front of his chair. "What does it mean? Is *every* old story real? Are the angels gathering to impose Inperium?" Now that I admitted everything out loud, panic was starting to seep in.

"Layla," Costi said, grounding me.

I paused and turned to him. "I don't know what's going on," I said, trying to be calm. "My mother, my coven mentor, the councilors, they all seem… wrong."

He made a rumbling sound of disgust. "They're using the attack to make changes without agreement."

"Calamus's father warned me not to tell anyone about what happened today."

Costi didn't reply. His mouth was set seriously, his eyes narrowed in calculation as he looked into the distance, contemplating.

"We didn't find out anything," I murmured, drawing his attention back to me. "About me."

He held out his hand. I put the cookie into it, and he gave me a faint half smile, setting my snack on an end table before reaching for me again.

I tentatively placed my hand into his, and he wrapped his fingers around it, pulling me to him until he could hook an arm around my waist and tumble me into his lap. I made a surprised squeak. He pushed his fingers up into my hair and held me against him.

"Tell me," he said.

My throat tightened at his tender tone. He'd always been able to draw every hidden worry out of me.

I sank into his warm embrace, careful not to press his injured leg. We shouldn't be doing this—not in public, and definitely not while he was in uniform and my crimson clothes marked me as *off-limits*. But I couldn't move. I needed this badly.

"The… *demon*… said I wasn't his."

Costi considered my words quietly. "What does that mean? Is someone else… like him involved?"

"I don't know," I whispered, leaning my head on his shoulder.

"Your magic was different," he said after a quiet minute.

A vague memory of him mentioning that after the attack brushed through my mind. "What was different?"

Costi ran his fingers along my scalp and through my hair as he thought for a moment. "Caster magic is kind of like fire."

"Yeah," I said, starting to feel sleepy.

"It's always like that, as far as I can tell. Different sizes, different intensity, but always fire. That's the only thing I've ever seen. Everyone I asked said the same thing."

My heart flipped. "You've been asking around?"

"I wanna get this figured out for you," he said. "The fight was intense. Thought maybe I was seeing things, but…"

"What did you see?"

"Your magic was like water, like you pulled it up from the sea. And huge, bigger than any spell I've ever seen. It was *boiling*—it burned all six of them dead immediately."

I kept my head tucked against him as I stared sightlessly at the bookshelf across the room. I felt… a connection with his words, my stomach churning. I'd been raised to kill angels, but it was something else entirely to be confronted with scalding them to death by the half dozen. But I knew, without a doubt, that spell had come through me.

"What does it mean?" I asked quietly, but neither of us had an answer.

The rain picked up outside, spattering against the windows, throwing the library into shadow. With no one to judge us, I clung to him, the only constant in my life that I could count on.

We stayed like that, quietly, until the night fell and the rain ended.

Chapter 12

LAYLA

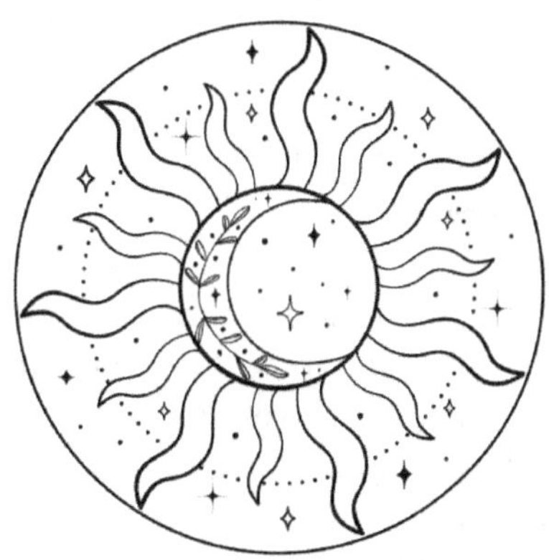

The weather had broken overnight, leaving a cool morning breeze. Wearing a light cardigan over my black outfit, I sat outside the cafeteria with a muffin and tea. It would be Mabon in a few weeks, the autumn equinox. It was one of my favorite holidays, filled with fall decor. I wondered how the Mountain Circle celebrated as I picked up the dishes from my breakfast and looked around for the dish bin.

"Layla, good morning," a voice startled me.

I turned to see Artemesia Rhodes, one of the Mountain Circle councilors I had met yesterday, leaning on her carved wooden walking stick. She was a tiny, elegant witch with hair gone entirely white, set in tight curls that haloed around her head. Her lined face was grave, with serious deep blue eyes. She wore the formal robes of the Arcaenum. This was official business.

"Hello, Councilor," I said uncertainly.

"Walk with me a moment, won't you?"

The councilor led me to a nearby trail that looped a wooded area. A jogger passed us with a wave, but otherwise it was secluded.

"I don't much care for Cedar Grey," she said without preamble, hauling herself forward using her stick as leverage. "I can tell you feel the same."

I choked. "I'm sure he's… It's just that…"

Rhodes, breathing heavily, sank down onto a pretty carved bench lining the path and gestured to the space next to her.

I sat beside the councilor and cleared my throat. "I don't agree with keeping secrets."

Rhodes gave a nod of approval. "Layla, I'm a very old woman. I'll be ninety-three in the spring."

My eyebrows rose.

She waved a hand dismissively. "Now don't you start. My point is, I've seen a lot of life, heard every idea."

"You weren't shocked. About the demon, I mean."

"Not shocked, no," she said. "In my day, it was common knowledge that we used to communicate with our allies in Hell. *And* that the Angeloi once had a more direct involvement in this world."

I shivered, looking away. *Angeloi.* The unfamiliar word made me uneasy. "What does it all mean?"

"It means we need to be ready. *You* need to be ready."

"I don't know what to do," I admitted. "I'm not sure I can be of any help."

"I believe you can," Rhodes said. "There is something special about you, Layla."

I blinked at her. That was wishful thinking at best.

"I'd like to formally invite you to join the Arcaenum as a delegate."

"*What?*"

Rhodes's grim demeanor cracked for a moment as she cackled gleefully at my reaction. "That's right, young witch. I'm here to rope you into politics."

In our councils, delegates represented a variety of special interests. "What would I even—"

"Don't worry about all that," she said. "Just attend and see what comes of it."

I chewed the edge of my lip as I gazed into the woods. It didn't sound like a terrible idea. I wanted to know what was going on. "If you're sure—"

"I am," Rhodes insisted.

I rubbed my fingers over the wooden texture of the bench absently. "Something's happening, isn't it?"

She regarded me soberly, her back straight. "Yes," she agreed. "It's been coming for a long time. We underestimated the Angeloi *severely...* what they've been doing, what their plans are."

My heart pounded. "What... what are they planning?"

"They are always planning Inperium."

"You're saying we have no idea what they're up to," I whispered. "We've been sitting here, just dealing with small infestations, while they—"

"You have the gist of it, yes. We became complacent. We forgot that a hierarchy means someone is above them. Controlling them."

I was racked with shudders, trembling uncontrollably. "You knew about this?"

Rhodes shook her head. "I've done what I could. My hands are tied, in certain ways. And there were other, more immediate problems."

Councilor Grey and the witches who supported him.

"I'm too old to fight, Layla," she said. "I've tried to gather allies, but there are few. So very few."

I took a deep breath. "I'll go to the next meeting," I said, not wanting to overpromise. Despite her apparent faith in me, I doubted I would have anything to contribute, or that the Arcaenum would suddenly spill their secrets.

A cardinal called loudly from the trees. The familiar sound brought me a measure of calm.

Rhodes gestured toward the Circle. I lent her my arm to help her stand and then walked with her slowly toward the main walkway.

"You were a guardian?" I asked as we walked, thinking of the way she carried herself.

Her eyes sparkled. "You can tell, can you? I'm the only Troubled witch ever to be elected to the Arcaenum. It's why they don't like me much."

I gave her a polite smile. Silence stretched between us as I thought of a hundred questions and stopped myself from asking them. Rhodes was kind, but she had an agenda. I was learning not to trust someone right away just because they seemed like they were on my side. I would wait, see how this played out.

"Fate keep you, Layla," the councilor said solemnly as we reached the main path. She turned and walked slowly away, her stick thumping on the stones with the rhythm of her steps.

* * *

The next week passed quietly, at odds with my inner turmoil. Every noise made me jump. I wanted to shake every person who smiled at me and tell them Hell was real and the Angeloi were coming for us. I needed to be doing research—*something* to figure out my magic—but I was on edge and couldn't concentrate.

Costi had been busy doing physical therapy on top of his normal intense training. I'd told him briefly about the Arcaenum meeting, but I'd been trying not to bother him. We both needed to get our heads in this game.

It was true, I had caught a bit of a crush, but it couldn't go anywhere. It *couldn't.* The sooner I got that through my head, the better. The space was good for us.

Calamus had offered to escort me to the Arcaenum meeting, which he apparently attended regularly as a guest. We both wore our formal red spell caster robes. His eyes had lit up when I walked outside to meet him.

Calamus is kind, intelligent, and good-looking as a bonus, I told myself, trying to listen to what he was saying as we walked. *He likes me. He would be a good match. He would—*

My feet, my breath, and my thoughts all came to a screeching halt when Costi's storm-cloud gaze slammed into mine from where he was waiting in front of the meeting hall. My body rebooted itself with a fluttering of my heart. With one look, all the distance I'd been forging, all the sensible things I'd repeated to myself—*all of it*—collapsed.

Costi's eyes raked over me before flicking to Calamus, and I wondered if he was over being angry.

"Looking nice and healthy, Grey," Costi called out, glaring at the spell caster.

Yikes. He was very much *not* over it.

Calamus gave him a thin smile as we approached. "To what do we owe the pleasure?"

"It's a Council meeting. I'm here to meet the Council."

"It's a closed session," Calamus said.

Costi smirked humorlessly. "Door looks open to me."

Calamus held up an arm, blocking the entrance. "I'm sorry, Blackthorn, but you aren't invited. The guardians already have a delegate."

Costi tilted his head. "You gonna remove me, Grey? Physically?"

Calamus snatched back his arm. "You're *threatening* me now?"

"Maybe we should tone it down just a bit," I said.

Both men ignored me.

"You can take it however you want," Costi said to Calamus. "I'm coming with Layla."

Calamus clenched his fists. "Your behavior is out of control. It's clear the interventions aren't working with you. I'm having you removed as my guardian."

"Suits me just fine," Costi growled. "Try not to piss off an angel with a laser stick next time. The other guardians aren't as fast as me."

"This is outrageous!" Calamus fumed. He turned to me. "Layla, you can't seriously—"

"Finish that sentence, Grey. I dare you." Costi's teeth flashed in a terrifying half grin.

"Cut it out!" I pushed myself between them before they came to blows. Not that Calamus would survive the first punch.

I whirled around and marched inside. They could stand out here *comparing sizes* all day if they wanted to.

The Arcaenum chamber was an auditorium set up with folding chairs in concentric semicircles around a central speaking platform. A few councilors and other witches who were probably delegates or guests milled around a refreshment table, chatting. I threw myself into a chair in the back row next to the wall.

Costi and Calamus were close behind, apparently having decided not to throw down for now. Calamus folded himself elegantly into the seat next to me, and Costi kicked back against the wall on my other side.

Just great.

"You've been avoiding me." Costi leaned down to murmur into my ear, making me shiver. "You hanging out with *him* now?"

"You were busy," I whispered. "I was trying to—" I glanced to my other side and noticed Calamus looking overly interested. "Can we talk later?"

Costi made a deep noise that could have been agreement.

"Good morning, everyone," Councilor Grey said over the crowd, causing the assembled witches to start taking their seats. Between the thirteen councilors and dozens of delegates representing all sorts of interests, the hall was full. I saw Councilor Rhodes's poof of white hair.

I recognized Councilor Quince, the hawk-nosed witch who had been with us for the summoning circle. He stood and convened the meeting. "Point of discussion number one," Quince announced. "A spell caster died, and several guardians were injured in a failed extermination."

I looked back and caught Costi's eye. They were *just now* discussing this? It had happened almost a *week* ago.

The delegate for the spell casters, a middle-aged witch with gelled black hair, spoke up. "That raid was a disaster. Spell casters are exceedingly rare—we cannot be expected to go into dangerous situations."

"The spell casters accepted our apology," the delegate for the guardians said. She was tall and slender in her black uniform, about my mother's age, with her hair pulled into a tight bun.

"That's Daire, the security coordinator," Costi told me quietly.

Calamus glared at him. Costi glared back and recklessly leaned closer to me.

Fate, they're determined to keep this up.

"We did, but words aren't enough in this case," the spell caster delegate said. "I would like to put in a proposal that two guardians be assigned to each caster, in case of an emergency."

Daire snapped to attention. "Absolutely not. We don't have those kinds of numbers."

The spell caster delegate put his nose up. "*Something* needs to be done. If the guardians would have done their job and assessed the building before the team went in—"

"They *did* assess the building," Daire cut in.

"We need to carry shields," Costi called out, interrupting.

The room went silent, and all eyes swung to our little group in the back. It hit me that Costi hadn't only come here for me; he was here for this.

Quince gave us an annoyed look. "Is this your guardian, Layla?"

"No," said Calamus at the same time Costi said, "Yeah."

"You haven't been assigned, and she's not a spell caster." Calamus crossed his arms.

"It just so happens that I'm available as of this morning, and she's wearing spell caster robes," Costi said with a shrug.

"Sit down, Blackthorn. You aren't a delegate," Daire said. "How did you even get in here?"

"Are these your guests, Calamus?" Councilor Grey said, scowling.

Calamus shook his head with wide eyes. "No, Father, I—"

Councilor Rhodes stood from her seat near the front. "I invited them," she said, sounding pleased. I decided I liked her. "It is, of course, still our prerogative to appoint delegates for areas of special concern."

Grey's eyes flashed. "You have *one* allotment remaining, and there are two witches here. You have an agenda, and you're trying to install mindless partisans."

"Very well, then. Rosen is my appointed delegate."

"And what *area of special concern* is she supposed to be a delegate for?"

"You know what," Rhodes said ominously. "Point of discussion number two."

Grey said nothing to that. He turned to Costi. "Blackthorn, you're not a delegate. Please remove yourself from the chamber."

"I'm her guardian," Costi insisted. He crossed his arms and leaned back against the wall.

"That is *not* your assignment," Daire said, pointing angrily at him.

"This is a procedural matter. Can we *please* get back to the matter at hand?" Quince looked ruffled.

"Love to," said Costi loudly, holding out a hand in invitation. "The *matter at hand* is that I brought you one of those angel glow sticks. Figure out what blocks it and get me a shield before more of your spell casters die."

The meeting erupted as his words registered and everyone started yelling over one another. Apparently, that hadn't been common knowledge.

I rolled my eyes. He hadn't bothered to mention it to me either. Knowing him, he had clobbered the angel that burned him and stolen its weapon in retaliation.

Costi chuckled behind me.

"You enjoy stirring people up way too much," I said without turning.

Quince clapped his hands. "Quiet, please!" Most of the chatter died down, so he continued. "Young man, the Arcaenum has a process. We may not yell out in the middle of the meetings—there are many witches with points of discussion, and it isn't fair to them to interrupt. You must confer with your group's delegate, who may bring your concern to the councilors."

"Lemme confer with my delegate real quick," Costi said, then leaned over to murmur into my ear. "Layla, baby, talk some sense into these assholes before I start flinging daggers."

Fate. Tell me he did not *actually bring weapons into the Arcaenum chamber.* My cheeks heated, and I cleared my throat nervously. "I invoke my privilege to speak as a delegate."

Quince sighed and pinched the bridge of his nose. "Go ahead, Delegate."

"My… uh… constituent is concerned about the weapons the angels seem to be using. He has procured a working model for testing purposes and would like to propose adding a shield to the guardians' standard equipment." There, that sounded very diplomatic.

The audience of witches boiled over into speculative chatter once again.

Rhodes spoke over the din. "Security Coordinator Daire, could you please explain what this is about?"

Daire's face darkened in anger. "A *dangerous* idea that we *already* discussed."

"Not as dangerous as going out there defenseless," Costi shot back.

Quince interrupted, "Guardian Blackthorn, *please.*"

Rhodes returned to the discussion. "Coordinator Daire, are you saying you have an angel weapon in your possession but didn't share that information with the Council?"

Daire bristled. "It's a guardian matter."

"You didn't bring it to a vote or anything," Costi said.

"It doesn't *need* a vote, Blackthorn. We're not messing around with unknown weaponry," Daire seethed.

"We need to know what these weapons do, how we can stop them," Costi argued.

As the councilors muttered uncertainly, my annoyance flared. They weren't *convinced*?

"I invoke my privilege." Another of the delegates stood, a lanky witch with a thinning hairline. "Angels can't make things like weapons. I think this was probably a fluke, something they stole from the non-magicals. Now that you got it away from them, they won't have it anymore."

Murmurs of agreement filled the meeting space as my anger simmered. They hadn't heard about the same weapons being used against Northern Sea? And even *I* knew the outsiders didn't have any laser staffs! This wasn't a fluke, and these witches were too comfortable to notice the danger—just as Councilor Rhodes had suggested.

Costi groaned behind me, only loud enough for me to hear.

"This is so useless," I said. "Calamus, you saw the weapons. An angel was trying to kill you. You talk to them."

Calamus looked disappointed in me. "I'm not sure I agree with setting off random weapons to test them."

Costi barked a laugh. "You were fine with opening up a *Hell portal*, though."

"You're not supposed to know about that," Calamus said to Costi, then looked at *me* accusingly.

Quince fixed our group with a glare, and I ducked my head like a child caught chattering in class.

"If I may?" Cedar Grey had been watching silently until now. His voice wasn't loud, but it stopped the side conversations instantly. The members all turned their attention to him. Uneasiness trickled through me. How did he do that? "I sympathize with your position, Blackthorn. Young guardians often want to lash out with more violence than is strictly necessary. We all know it's difficult to be Troubled."

"I'm asking for *shields*," Costi growled.

Grey held up a hand. "You can leave the strategy to the security coordinator. I'm sure she knows what equipment you need."

"They *shot* at us. A caster *died*. Your *son* was standing behind me." Costi's voice was grim.

Grey nodded. "And you did your job, for which we are all grateful, I'm sure."

My vision whited out. What in Hell's name were they telling him? To get injured, to *die*, because they didn't want to think about a small change to the guardians' uniform?

I felt myself stand up, my chair scraping the floor. "You can't do this," my voice said, sounding far away.

Grey raised his brows over wide eyes. "And what am I being accused of now?"

"None of you are listening. You're not getting it. The angels knew our team was coming. They've figured out how to use weapons—that night and during the attack. They're *doing* something—"

Grey gave me a patient smile. "I understand the attack on Northern Sea was traumatic for you, Layla," he said. "You were worried for my son, and I appreciate that. I know he cares for you as well."

I felt my face flush deeply with anger and shame. "You can't… You're using guardians as human shields—"

"There's no need to worry," Grey said soothingly. "The guardians' job is to protect their spell casters. They're well trained."

"Is this matter somewhat settled?" Quince asked. "It seems like a personal argument at this point, so it might be more appropriate to discuss it elsewhere."

The entire room looked at me—a traumatized, lovesick little girl who had no idea what guardians were for. Grey had set me up expertly. I flung myself back into my chair and crossed my arms over my chest, smoldering.

Quince sighed. "Now, with that out of the way, point of discussion number two. It looks like this meeting is going to run over today—"

"Point of discussion number two," Councilor Grey interrupted with a mild smile, "is that the training arena is, unfortunately, closed indefinitely for emergency repairs."

Quince cleared his throat. "Yes, well. Thank you, Councilor. Moving on. Point of discussion number three: housing for the Northern Sea refugees is progressing more slowly than anticipated…"

My mouth popped open in shock as Quince continued speaking, and Grey looked straight at me with eyes that made me go cold. He then moved his eyes slowly, deliberately, to Costi and then back to me. He raised an eyebrow, daring me to call him out.

I'd never been so livid in my *life*. I stormed out of the meeting hall in a flurry of red robes and let the door slam shut without looking behind me. Outside, I sucked cool air into my lungs, unable to see anything through my frustrated tears.

"I'm so done!" I yelled into the air, not caring who was around.

"Layla," Calamus said, hurrying after me. "That was uncalled for."

I whirled on him. "You *agree* with them keeping secrets from the rest of the Arcaenum."

Costi prowled up behind Calamus with a scowl.

"*Think*, Layla. There are reasons we might not want everyone to be involved. You can't just storm around like this." Calamus crossed his arms over his chest, frowning. "Blackthorn is a bad influence on you."

"You should go, Calamus. Go back inside," I said through gritted teeth. Costi moved close to me so our arms were touching.

Calamus narrowed his eyes at Costi. "There's something else we need to address. Layla has an overly kind heart, and I cannot continue to stand by while you take advantage of her. Guardians are forbidden to form attachments to spell casters for a reason."

"*Calamus Grey*," I yelled, stepping forward to jab a finger into his crimson chest. "Don't you dare."

"He's been *looming* over you all day—"

"Go on back to your meeting, Grey," Costi said menacingly.

Calamus sneered at him, disgust marring his normally serene face. "Don't bother coming to training tomorrow. I'll ask Daire to reassign you immediately." He turned and trod angrily back toward the entrance.

"Can't say it's been a pleasure working with you," Costi called out as Calamus yanked the door open, then turned back to me. "He thinks I'm gonna take advantage of you, but he's just going to leave you alone with me?" he muttered as he gently pulled me to a secluded spot behind the building. The woods pressed in, but a space had been cleared for some electrical equipment.

With his hand still clamped around my bicep, he bent his head over me while I waged an internal war between screaming in frustration and crying. Honestly, he *was* kind of looming.

"Useless *asshole*!" I shrieked, not even sure which of the Greys I was talking about at this point. "They're trying to cover everything up—the weapons, the demon," I hissed. "Why?"

Costi shook his head, releasing me.

"But you have suspicions?"

He was quiet for a moment. "You first."

I paced away from him and back. "They don't want to change. They're afraid of acknowledging the situation because it'll force them to do things differently."

Costi nodded. "Some of them, yeah."

I looked up at him. "What else?"

He ran a hand through his hair. "Say you wanna make someone do something. Something they don't want to do. What would you do?"

"Find out what's important to them and threaten them with it," I said, thinking of how my mother and Grey had both gone after Costi to get me to comply.

"What if you don't want them to realize what you're up to?"

I stopped pacing. "You think they're hiding things to… to manipulate people somehow?"

He nodded. "If they have all the information, they can twist it into anything they want, make it support anything they want us to think."

I considered it. "And then what?"

Costi looked out into the trees, a line of concern forming between his eyebrows. "Nothing good."

Chapter 13

LAYLA

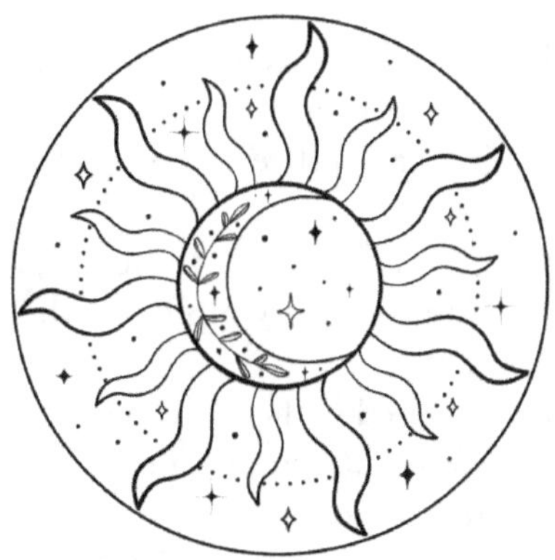

Something woke me. My room was still dark, but outside, there was some sort of commotion. Moving back the curtain, I could see porch lights flickering on and the flashing of a witch light being carried in the distance. Suddenly wide awake with adrenaline, I left my room to see what was happening.

As I reached for the handle to peek outside, a loud banging caused me to jump back. It sounded like someone beating on the door with both fists.

"Sativa!" a voice called.

I yanked the door open, and a long-haired witch in a nightgown rushed in. I heard my covenmates emerging from their rooms with various protests and questions.

"Sativa!" the witch cried, tears streaming down her face as she ran. Outside, I could see other witches running, doors opening. Fear seized me. I quickly shut the door and locked it.

"Fern, babe, what's happening?" Sativa drew the crying witch into her arms.

"People are going wild outside," Datura said, standing next to Oliver. "Are we being attacked?"

"Not us, other Circles!" Fern sobbed. "Cypress and Saltmarsh are sending distress calls and fleeing for their lives, and no one can get a hold of *anyone* from Hillsong. We're next... oh fate, we're next!"

Sativa ran her hand down Fern's hair. "Shh, you're safe," she said, but she looked up at me uncertainly.

Panic slammed into me as an emergency signal blared from everyone's phones.

Oliver looked down at his screen. "Shit. *Shit*. We're... we're being called up," he yelled over the tone.

"Us?" Datura grabbed Oliver's arm. "We don't even have guardians assigned!"

"It says all covens," I said through numb lips, reading through the stark, all-caps notification on my own phone. The alert sound ended, leaving us in stunned silence.

Sativa's familiar appeared by her side as she released Fern. "We... we'd better get ready. We should go get our robes."

"No! I can't!" Fern crashed into Sativa again.

"I'll grab the robes," Datura said as she jogged to their rooms.

"I can't do this," Fern wailed. "I never wanted this."

Datura tossed Sativa her spell caster robe, and my covenmates struggled into their formal wear. It was the only equipment we had—a bright red beacon to mark our locations in a skirmish so guardians could pick us out easily.

If the angels did have some intelligence after all, it would be a deadly liability.

Datura and Oliver both called up their familiars. The small demons glanced around warily, as if searching for the source of danger—did they understand that they'd been called at an odd hour? I tried to see if they looked like they'd been sleeping, but they gave no indication either way.

"Shit," said Oliver. "Shit, shit, shit."

"Stay here with Layla," Sativa told Fern. It was a given that I wasn't going. "Take care of her," she begged me.

I gave her a grim nod.

"Stay safe." My voice sounded small.

I locked the door after my three covenmates left. Fern huddled miserably on the couch while I paced.

"I… I think we should—" I felt lightheaded, hugging my trembling arms to my chest. I took a series of deep, calming breaths. A shard of self-loathing pierced me. I'd prepared my whole life to be a spell caster, and here I was, terrified. Costi would *never* cower in fear. If I wanted to be *anything* to him, it was time to *grow up*.

I forced myself up straight and assessed the apartment. If I couldn't help with the defense, at least I could make sure Fern and I were safe. I had no idea what we'd be facing, but it was probably best if the building looked unoccupied. I turned off the main lights and made sure the shades were closed in the main room and the bedrooms. In the dim glow of the single night-light, I moved items into the bathroom: a comforter, prepared food, bottles of water. From the kitchen, I took the fire extinguisher. It was heavy enough to bash at least one intruder.

"If we hear anything," I said to Fern, trying to project confidence though my voice was shaking, "get in the bathroom. It's the only room without windows." I sat next to her on the couch.

"Okay," she said weakly. "You're not going with them either?"

I shook my head, though it was probably too dark to see. "I can't. I don't have a familiar."

"Oh fate, I wish you could take mine. You seem really brave, like Sativa. I… I'm not cut out for this at all."

"I'm not brave," I murmured, thinking of how I'd panicked during the attack on Northern Sea. "Which coven are you from?"

"Brightstar. I'm one year ahead of you. My covenmates hate me because I haven't gone on any missions with them." Fern sighed. "I think after this, I'll have to drop out or something."

"You don't want to be a spell caster?"

"Fate, no. Do you?"

"Yes," I said, but then I thought about it for a moment. "I never really had a choice. It was just assumed."

"Exactly. If your parents are casters, they just throw you in, too, whether you like it or not."

I frowned. "Well, we're so rare, I suppose they have to."

Fern thumbed her phone on. In the dim light, I could see her with her knees drawn up, resting her head on them. "They don't *have* to," she said bitterly. "Other witches could learn to pull magic."

"*What?*"

"You didn't know?"

Initiate casters pulled magic instinctively, but could *anyone* learn to do it?

"But… they probably wouldn't have enough capacity for casting," I reasoned. "It's hereditary."

Fern made a small sound. "All I know is, I don't want any part of it anymore. I just want to be with Sativa. Our other lovers can give her children, and I'll help raise them." She checked her phone again, and I checked mine, even though I hadn't gotten any notifications.

"You're worried about her?"

"She's everything to me," Fern said lowly. "I can't stand the thought of her out there…"

"It seems quiet so far," I said, glancing at the window. I didn't see any flashing behind the shades. If there was an attack, would we hear it from here?

"Do you have someone out there too? Your parents?"

My throat closed. I'd been trying not to think about him. "Not my parents," I said thickly.

My phone pinged, causing us both to jump.

Where are you? Costi's message glowed on the screen.

"Is it someone outside? What are they saying?" Fern gasped.

"Hang on," I told her.

I texted back, ***At home, hiding in the dark. Where are you?***

Good girl. Costi's immediate reply simmered through me. A second text came through. ***Front line. No sign of angels.***

I let out a breath. "He says there's no angels so far."

Fern mirrored my exhale.

My phone dinged again. ***Stay where you are, Layla.***

Pay attention to your job, bossy, I sent back.

I'll show you bossy, he replied.

My stomach swooped, and I bit the inside of my lip to stop my reaction from showing.

"What kind of face is that? Fate, are you *flirting* right now? Who is it?" Fern leaned over, trying to see. "Costi—is that one of the Northern Sea casters?" She grinned.

I pushed my phone under the pillows with a groan. "Is *everyone* in the Mountain Circle addicted to drama and gossip?"

Fern giggled. "Pretty much, yeah." When I didn't reply, she continued, "Take my mind off everything and tell me about Bossy Costi."

My face burned as I choked on my own spit. How did she *read* that quickly?

Fern laughed again as I tried to recover from my coughing fit. At least I was entertaining her.

This could be bad. Costi was probably already in trouble for squabbling with Calamus. The last thing he needed was rumors about me.

"Listen, I've known him forever. We're old friends. He's just having fun. It's nothing like what you're thinking. I'm seeing Calamus Grey," I lied through my teeth.

Fern nodded. "Ah, gotcha. Calamus, huh? He's popular." She didn't sound convinced. After a moment of quiet, she yawned.

"Hey," I said. "I'm way too wired for sleep, but you should get some rest if you can. I'll wake you up if anything happens."

"Maybe you're right," she said. I pointed her to Sativa's room, hoping my covenmate wouldn't mind. She seemed to keep her lovers out of her space, but I got the feeling that it was more for the rest of us than herself.

"Calamus Grey didn't text you the first chance he got. Just saying." Fern closed the bedroom door before I could reply.

I know. Fate, did I know.

As the night wore on, I sat alone in the dark living room with only my tumbling thoughts, listening for danger.

I wasn't like Fern. I *wanted* to be a spell caster. Even though I hadn't had a choice, even though I was terrified, I wanted to stand with Costi and make the angels regret trying to kill us. I wanted the raw power I felt surge through me when I boiled them out of the Northern Sea sky. I wanted the Arcaenum to listen to *me* instead of manipulators like Cedar Grey and my mother.

I wanted to protect my people.

I had been going about this wrong, trying to find someone to help me. This was *my* life. I was going to figure out my magic *myself*. And if I couldn't, well, I'd find a different way. Maybe I could learn to throw down, become a guardian.

I decided then and there, I was *not* going to sit out another fight hiding in the dark. Come what may, I was joining this war.

Hours later, the sky brightened beyond the window shades.

The attack never came.

* * *

It was still early, and Fern hadn't reappeared yet. Costi had texted me once to tell me the status was the same. I could no longer sit still.

Throwing on some clean clothes, I cautiously peeked my head out the door. The movements of the Circle were hushed—just whispers and scurries.

I glanced to the sky nervously, then crept out and hurried to the large indoor cafeteria in the main part of the Circle. It seemed like everyone else had the same thought—the place was packed.

One of the councilors I didn't know, an elder witch with a bald head and a scraggly white beard, was addressing the crowd from a small platform. "…have been unable to make contact with the Hillsong Circle in Kentucky. We expect refugees from the Saltmarsh, Cypress, and Tidewater Circles to begin arriving today." The councilor paused, placing a weathered hand over his eyes. "We believe we are the only remaining eastern Circle."

My heart kicked up a wicked beat as gasps and cries followed the announcement. How could three—maybe four—Circles be attacked in the same night? This was coordination on a massive and devastating scale. An *army* of angels.

We had to be next. Even if the angels didn't know where this Circle was, there was no way they'd miss so many witches coming to one place. Those refugees were running straight to their doom.

Our doom.

"We are in touch with the Great Lakes Circles, the Canadian Circles, and farther beyond. They're on alert now and will send aid as they can. The eastern Circles had no advanced warning. They suffered heavy losses."

My body turned cold despite the sticky warmness of the crowded cafeteria. No one had really believed the angels would attack again. They'd thought the Northern Sea was a fluke, like the attack in Greece seventeen years ago. It had been long enough that they felt safe. They hadn't even been watching. Fate, even the Northern Sea's survival was down to Costi and me sneaking out to meet up at night.

"It is likely we will be attacked," the councilor said, then held up his hand to stop the panicked chatter. "We need to be prepared. Gather what weapons you can—angels cannot be killed except by spell fire, but decapitating or badly maiming them will incapacitate them."

Would Costi give me one of his daggers if I ask nicely?

The councilor continued, "Remain alert at all times. Our teams are on rotation now, with spotters watching the skies from the fire towers in the hills. But if you see *anything*, call the emergency line."

The councilor stepped down and was immediately surrounded by people clamoring with questions. Feeling grateful to the witches working in the kitchen during this chaos, I joined the line for coffee, filling an extra mug for Fern before hurrying home.

* * *

Our living room was full of witches, and they all turned to look at me when I entered. My three covenmates looked miserable and exhausted, with frizzy hair and drooping robes from being outside all night. Fern had emerged and was sitting on the couch, looking somber. But taking up most of the space were Costi and three other guardians. They wore full tactical gear—intimidating black armor, with riot helmets and massive swords strapped to their backs.

I felt young and small in front of them.

"Hey," I said, flushing and feeling awkward. I handed Fern her mug silently and placed mine on the side table.

Sativa gave me an annoyed look, widening her eyes. "As I was saying, Oliver can move over with Datura, and you two can take their room, leaving Salix with me."

I blinked. Was everyone moving in?

"Fucking fate," said one of the guardians. "Ewan snores."

The guardian next to him, presumably Ewan, grinned and punched him in the shoulder.

"I—" Fern started, then cleared her throat. "Can I stay here too? I can sleep on the couch."

Sativa looked at Oliver and Datura. Datura shrugged.

The third guardian, Salix, a tall Northern Sea witch I had seen around, spoke up. "I can take the couch. It's no big deal," she said, running a hand over her buzzed head.

Costi grabbed me by the upper arm and tugged me toward my room while the group started working out a schedule for the shower. He kicked the door shut behind him with a bang—he'd never cared what anyone thought in his life, so why start now?

Still holding my arm, he pulled me closer. "Thought I told you to stay put," he said into my ear.

I shivered. He smelled like lightning and fresh air.

"You did. Then I called you bossy and ignored you," I said.

"Hm." He looked down at me with an unreadable expression. His face was way too close to mine.

"What exactly is going on?" I said a little breathlessly.

Costi released me. "Turns out the practice arena, the only large indoor space in the Circle, is *closed for emergency repairs*," he growled. "We can't leave witches outside in tents anymore, so they emptied the barracks and told us to go bunk with our spell casters or family."

"And you came *here*?"

He smirked. "Not a very nice welcome for your new roommate." He threw his helmet on top of my dresser and started unbuckling his gear.

I balked. "They're not going to let you stay with me."

He shrugged. "Who's not going to? We've got bigger problems."

"Fate!" I squeaked and whirled to face the door as he pulled his shirt over his head.

He just chuckled.

This was already a disaster. We could barely keep our hands to ourselves in public, let alone a closed room where he was throwing his clothes off.

"Safe to look now, innocent little Layla," he teased.

I bristled, turning back around with my arms crossed. He had replaced his shirt. "I suppose you've had dozens of lovers and don't care about that kind of thing anymore," I said. My voice sounded more bitter than I liked. I didn't know where it had come from, but now the idea was like acid in my throat.

He raised his eyebrows with a half grin. "The number would shock you."

"I—"

Someone pounded on the door and called out, "Hey, Blackthorn, what are you doing in there with your *childhood friend?*"

"I'm gonna break your face, Ewan," Costi yelled back, but he was still grinning.

The door opened, and the two male guardians from earlier laughed at my expression.

"What a pretty *best friend*, Blackthorn," Ewan said with a grin of his own. He was a stocky witch with his hair shaved at the sides.

"Meet two assholes," Costi said to me, gesturing broadly at the guardians. "Hollis Ewan and Aeron Bay."

"Hey," said Bay with a warm, dimpled smile. His nose was crooked, as if it had been broken.

"This is Layla," Costi said, clamping a hand over my shoulder. "*My* pretty best friend."

Ewan held up his hands. "Relax, bro. We're not trying to catch it from Daire by messing with spell casters." He looked at me. "No offense, Layla. You *are* pretty."

"Um, none taken," I murmured. My face was about to melt off from blushing, and I wished I could dissolve into molecules. "You're Oliver's and Datura's guardians?"

"That's right," said Bay. "Your coven was the only new one without a team, so you got an emergency assignment. They said you're not casting yet, so no one's with you. Salix is with your other covenmate."

"And Blackthorn here's just looking for a comfy bed," Ewan said, reaching out to ruffle Costi's hair.

Costi grabbed the other guardian's hand, and they scuffled as they tried to best each other.

"Cut it out! You'll knock stuff over!" I cried.

The three guardians chuckled at me, but Costi released Ewan from the neck hold he'd been attempting.

Bay rolled his eyes. "Anyway, we came to give Blackthorn the rotation since he wasn't paying attention." He handed Costi a piece of torn-off notebook paper. "Looks like you and Grey are on the six-thirty shift."

"Better get some sleep, besties!" Ewan crowed.

"I know where *you* sleep," Costi threatened.

Ewan and Bay ducked out of my room, laughing and tumbling around loudly like rocks in a can.

In the hall, Datura was moving a basket to Oliver's room. "Thanks for the coffee," she said with a smirk, then toasted me with my own mug.

Fate, it's too crowded in here already. The stressed-out lack of sleep suddenly pulled on every nerve in my body. I closed the door and flopped down on my bed, throwing an arm over my eyes.

"You're going to get in trouble," I told Costi.

"I'm always in trouble," he said, but there was no heat to it. The second bed rustled as he sat. I supposed it was his now.

He wasn't wrong. "You're still partnered with Calamus?"

"Yeah. He didn't get around to talking to Daire." He was silent for a long moment. I nearly drifted to sleep before he continued, "I'm not gonna... let him get hurt or anything."

I sat up quickly. "*What?* I'd *never* think you would do something like that."

Costi's lips parted, his face caught in an unguarded moment, eyes luminous and vulnerable. It occurred to me that most witches would be quick to judge him. Did he really think I felt the same?

"Costi, I *know* you. You're a *good* man."

He swallowed and looked away. "No." His voice sounded like it had been raked across hot coals.

I shifted off my bed to sit next to him. He stiffened as I slid my arms around his middle. I blinked back tears. He'd been strong for me, but he'd had *no one* to comfort him. "Where's this coming from?"

"You're like... like a light," he grated out. He wrapped himself around me and pressed his forehead into my neck. "The only thing I could ever do for you is be your guardian, and I can't even do that."

My heart cracked. *I* was the defective one who couldn't summon a familiar. I cradled his face with both hands and tipped his head up so he would look at me. "You don't need to be anything for me. You're Costi."

"Layla," he whispered, gazing at me as if I was his whole world. His hands tightened where he held my waist. "I can't have you." He pressed his forehead to mine.

The truth of it hit me then. This was our permanent reality. We could have a friendship of sorts, but we couldn't have more than that. Ever. They'd punish him for touching me. They'd never let us build a life together. They wouldn't let us have what was simmering in Costi's eyes that I was sure he could also see in mine.

"I'm not really a spell caster," I whispered back.

He looked at me sadly. "I don't think they're gonna let me off on a technicality."

The only way would be to leave the Circle. Even though neither of us was particularly beloved by our people, could we live with ourselves if we left them to their fates?

"You should get some rest," I said. "You were out all night."

Costi made no move to let me go. "Now who's bossy?"

I quirked my eyebrow at him and used my weight to push him down onto his bed. He gave a surprised grunt, but I sat up and started picking at his shoelaces.

He said nothing, only watched me through his lashes as I tugged off his heavy combat boots. The moment they tumbled to the floor, he hooked one arm around my waist and hauled me down beside him. He pulled me close, draping me over his arm and shoulder, holding me against his chest.

I tucked my hot face under his chin, not daring to look at him. This was very different from when I slept next to him when he was injured. My body lit with breathless energy, but I was held motionless, intoxicated. I was treasured. *Safe.*

I can't have you, he had said.

But I don't think I can live without you.

Chapter 14

LAYLA

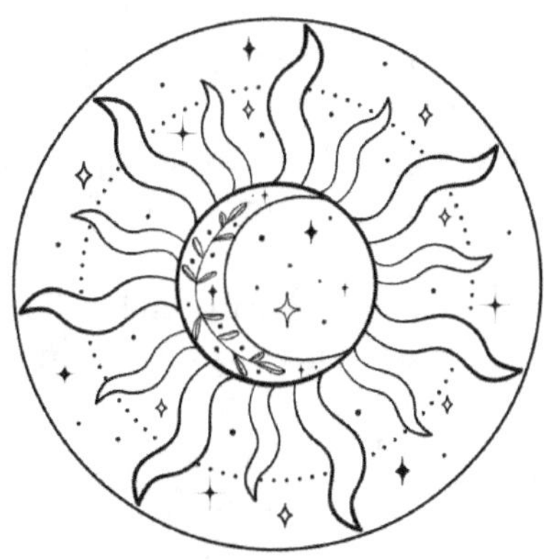

I woke in the early afternoon, thoughts tossing around my head like waves hitting the rocks. Even though I was still exhausted, I didn't think further sleep was possible.

Costi slept soundly as I gently pulled myself out of his embrace.

After setting him an alarm on his phone, I crept out to the bathroom and washed my face, trying not to notice the dark circles under my eyes. Sativa's new guardian, Salix, was asleep on the couch as I slipped out the front door.

I figured it was safe enough with our teams on constant patrol, and I needed to find Hazel urgently. I hurried through the Circle, watching my surroundings carefully. I saw others doing the same. Despite the breezy, sunny day, no one lingered outside.

I scurried into the library and was met with a crowd of unfamiliar witches. They took up most of the space in the center of the building, sleeping fitfully, huddled on sleeping bags and chairs. A child was crying piteously as someone tried to soothe them. Bags and piles of belongings were pushed up everywhere, and a table with water coolers had been set up on the back wall.

A teen was slumped in an armchair near the door, toying with a necklace.

"Is anyone from the library here?" I asked quietly. My stomach churned with unease.

The teen shrugged, looking at me with blank eyes.

Not knowing what to say to the young witch, I made my way to the library counter. It had been commandeered to hold brightly colored boxes of packaged food—a rarity from outside. Behind the counter, a hallway ran into a different part of the building. A light was on, so I went to investigate.

I found Hazel piling old books and papers into a box in a small conference room with a round table. "There you are," I said, startling her.

"Oh, Layla," she said. I couldn't decipher her tone, but it didn't sound overjoyed. She looked paler than usual, her greenish eyes wide and somber.

"What's going on out there? Are those—"

"The Saltmarsh Circle," she said, nodding. "What's left of them…"

"Fate," I exhaled, feeling sick. There was a crowd, but nowhere near the number of people that even a tiny Circle like Northern Sea had.

"You were looking for me?"

"I…" My problems suddenly seemed inconsequential, and I wanted to apologize and leave. But I had to try, or I'd be of no help at all. I breathed in. "Your database of circle spells. I'd like to look at it… if you'll let me."

Hazel frowned and glanced around to the stacks of papers and folders she was packing. "Right now?"

"I know it's not a great time, but I need to figure out the issue with my familiar."

She nodded slowly. "We need all the spell casters we can get."

"Exactly. I don't have any other skills," I said with a wry smile.

Hazel nodded again without expression. I cringed.

The redheaded witch pulled a tablet out of a bag hanging from one of the chairs. "You can borrow this. There's a copy of my work so far."

"Thank you. I'll bring it back," I said, then nibbled the corner of my lip awkwardly. "How are you doing?"

She blinked at me. "Huh?"

"I mean, we saw some pretty, um… unusual—"

"Oh," she interrupted, turning her face away as she busied herself with boxing again. "Oh, that. Yes, that was unusual."

I had clearly worn out my tenuous welcome. "Yes," I said with a weak smile. "Well, I'll get out of your hair. Thanks again."

"Good luck," Hazel said distractedly as I scurried out of the room.

Down the hall, I was relieved to see a back exit illuminated with a sign. I didn't want to see the Saltmarsh Circle witches again.

I paused outside to rub the fingers of one hand over my eyes. We would fare better—we were prepared. We were watching the skies. I had to believe that.

I stopped by the provisionary, where several witches were working to stack new food onto the shelves. My head spun. How many people lived with me now—seven? Eight if you counted Fern, who didn't seem intent on going home. Fate, and four of them were guardians who would probably burn through a hundred times the calories as the rest of us.

I wrapped Hazel's tablet in a cloth napkin so it would be protected, then grabbed a cardboard box from a stack in the corner and started piling in containers. I couldn't bring everyone a drink, so I added a tin of lemonade mix and some tea bags as well. There was a large open bin with bamboo forks, probably since there were so many refugees arriving. I took a few of those, too, not knowing if we had enough silverware for everyone.

"Thank you," I told the working crew.

An older witch, their curly hair streaked with gray, gave me a tremulous smile. "Thank *you*, spell caster."

I ducked my head and left quickly with a murmured reply.

When I arrived back at the apartment, juggling my heavy box against my hip while I wrestled the door open, Salix was sitting up sleepily on the couch. She was tall and built sturdily, probably a great advantage in her line of work.

"Hey, spell caster," she said around a yawn, running a hand over her shaved head. "I've seen you around Northern Sea. Didn't catch your name."

"Layla," I said, setting down the heavy box.

"Oh, the one who isn't casting yet. Is that all food? Fate bend me over a log, you're a lifesaver."

Salix helped lay out the containers as I turned on the toaster oven to warm up an assortment of hand pies. I pulled dishes out to stack them up and found a pitcher to mix the lemonade. We had a dish set for six, but one of the glasses was missing.

"I'll try to find us some more cups later," I said absently.

I ate my lunch quickly, and the full stomach and lack of sleep finally ground me to a halt. I was too exhausted to worry or think anymore.

Thank fate.

I crawled into my bed and fell asleep to Costi's even breathing.

* * *

The next day arrived, and the next, and still there was no sign of the angels. My covenmates and the guardians came and went at all hours, on a rotating schedule. I took on the unofficial duty of going out to procure food for everyone, with Fern helping by washing the dishes and rinsing out the containers to return. Afraid to leave the apartment, she busied herself with household chores, giving the rest of us a break.

I was able to pick up some news along with our meals. Refugees from the three Circles—Saltmarsh, Tidewater, and Cypress—were still trickling in. Some had fled west to Circles there, but most were coming here, believing in strength in numbers and hoping the mountains would form some natural protection.

The news was bad. Their Circles had been *devastated.* We had gained a huge number of witches to protect, but hardly any were spell casters or guardians. Most of them had been killed in battle.

There were rumors—angels viciously pursuing any witch they spotted, using glowing weapons to cut down the unprotected, setting buildings ablaze to flush out new prey. It was a wonder anyone had survived at all. The Hillsong Circle, in Kentucky, was believed to be a total loss.

Knowing an attack must be imminent, the new piecemeal Mountain Circle worked around the clock to prepare, bringing in food and supplies from the outside for all the new residents and trying to complete building projects. Witches were crammed into every indoor space available. We were burgeoning close to four thousand in a space built for less than half that.

Costi was on an evening shift, not due back until two in the morning, so I began to scroll through Hazel's database in between mealtimes. It was *extensive*, with dates going back five hundred years. Each spell had a numbered designation based on the book it was found in and a description of the effect, with Hazel and Calamus's cross-referenced notes about history, variations, and speculations on whether the spells would work or not. I decided to look through line by line instead of searching for keywords so I wouldn't miss anything.

There were circle spells for everything from growing hair to turning stones into metal—far more than circlewrights ever used these days. I supposed our slow circle magic had been mostly replaced with the technology of industrialization. It was a shame. We used to be a wonder of the world, but now our powers were outmatched by modern civilization in almost every area except defense against angels. And we weren't doing so great with that lately.

Lying on my bed, I flicked quickly through the endless list of spells. In the hall, Datura was helping Salix move one of the beds from Sativa's room into the bedroom with the other guardians so she wouldn't have to sleep on the couch. Briefly, I imagined giving up one of the beds in my own room, forcing me to share with my surly, attractive roommate. It would be a noble cause, to help other refugees.

I flopped over onto my back with a groan. I was getting nowhere with this. I hadn't come across anything useful, like a spell to shield witches from angel death rays. What in Hell's name had we been *doing* for the last half millennium? I'd seen at least ten spells for curing toenail fungus, and one to calm a crying baby that took an hour to draw. Maybe spend less time drawing out a circle spell and more time rocking the poor little thing.

Halfway through the database, a new section began, denoting a different book of spells, and I slowed my scrolling, paying attention. This one seemed a lot more serious—the first entry was a spell to create a quicksand trap. Not that great against flying angels, but moving in the right direction.

In this more interesting section, one line denoted a place where an unknown number of pages were missing from the tome. Farther down, Hazel had highlighted a spell in yellow that was labeled "creates a door." Maybe she meant to look into that one more, since there were no further details about what it meant. I imagined a circlewright hoping for a nice wooden door with a knob and knocking a big hole in the wall instead.

Scrolling farther, I finally read a line that made me pause: *traps a familiar.* Excitement shivered through me. Now *this* was promising—

A sound in the hall made me look up. My bedroom door banged open, and Costi rolled in like a hurricane, all anger and black combat gear.

I shot up and grabbed Hazel's tablet before it fell. "What the—"

He slammed the door shut and stalked toward me, throwing himself on my bed sideways with a frustrated groan. "Fucking useless," he growled, splaying a muscular arm over his eyes.

A light flicked on in the hallway—Costi had probably woken everyone up. My heart was still beating a million miles an hour. "What's useless?"

"Daire. The Arcaenum. They're gonna get people killed."

"What's going on?"

"The whole thing is fucked. They have five witches watching the sky from fire towers in the mountains, and their brilliant plan is to relay any sightings to the teams on the ground—in the *woods.*"

I balked. "That's a horrible setup! Spell casters can't hit anything in the sky if there's a bunch of trees in the way. They'll cause a forest fire while the angels just cruise in and murder everyone!"

Costi made a low sound. "Wish they'd make *you* security coordinator."

"They're acting like they still think of the angels as mindless creatures when it's obvious they're planning things. There has to be a way to make them understand. I'm still a delegate. Maybe I can get through to them."

"They'll kick you out."

"Probably," I sighed. "But I have to try."

"I'm going with you," he said.

"I don't need to tell you what a bad idea that is. They're not happy with you."

"Got a lot of bad ideas when it comes to you." He gave me a faint smile.

"You could have a little self-preservation," I said, poking him in the side.

"Where's the fun in that?"

* * *

The day was clear, but the cool of the oncoming autumn lingered in the air, and the sun hadn't quite made it above the mountains bracing the Circle. I huddled into my cardigan as I waited outside the cafeteria.

"Hey," I said to Calamus warily as he approached. "Thanks for meeting with me."

He sighed. He was dressed immaculately in his crimson spell caster robes as usual, his short dark hair neatly brushed. "You shouldn't be outside, Layla."

I bit back a retort, reminding myself that I didn't come to fight. "Let's go in, then."

I followed him into the crowded cafeteria. A few spots were still available for sitting, and we found a place at the end of a bench table.

Calamus brought over two mugs of hot tea and set one in front of me, ever polite and attentive. "I wanted to apologize for my behavior at the chamber. I shouldn't have taken my frustrations out on you."

I blinked. "I wasn't expecting an apology, but thank you. I'm… sorry I yelled at you."

He smiled. "Despite everything, I want us to be friends."

Despite everything? What does that *mean?* I breathed in, centering myself. "I want that too," I told him, hoping it was true.

He looked into my eyes. "How have you been? You're not frightened?"

"I'm not scared. I *am* wondering how we haven't been attacked yet."

He shrugged. "It does seem strange, but who can know these things?"

My annoyance surged. *Oh, I don't know, maybe spell casters who have teams trained for scouting? Maybe the security coordinator who's supposed to think about security? Maybe the council of people elected to make sure we know about these things?* Wasn't Calamus concerned about the angels at all?

I made a noncommittal sound. "How's the patrolling going? I heard they have you out in the woods." I wasn't about to mention Costi, or exactly where we were having conversations.

Calamus nodded decisively. "You're well protected. If any angels breach the perimeter, we'll destroy them before they get to the Circle."

I had to stop my eyes from rolling. The only thing he'd be destroying was the local wildlife and possibly the infrastructure.

I needed to ask my questions and get out of here. It was clear to me that Calamus and I would never be on the same page. "I was wondering if you could help me with something."

"Of course," he said with a smile.

"I borrowed something from Hazel, and I need to get it back to her. Do you know where she's staying?"

"That's easy enough. I don't know where she is, but I'll text her."

I gave a genuine smile. "That would be great."

Calamus nodded, typing into his phone. "There, done."

"Thanks. There's one more thing…"

"What is it? You can ask me anything," he said.

I felt my face heat. "I… I need to get in touch with my dad. But I don't know where my parents are staying. Is there a directory, or—"

Calamus's normal mask of mild indifference shattered into a look of horror that shocked me.

"What is it? What's wrong?"

He cleared his throat uncomfortably. "I'm sorry, Layla. I thought…"

Alarm surged through me. "Just tell me."

"Your mother is staying with us—my father and I—since the recent attack. She led me to believe your father wasn't… in the picture."

"*What?*" I said too loudly, drawing attention from those around us. I lowered my voice, but panic began to take over. "She can't just leave him. He's sick. Where is he? What if he's not taking his meds?" *I shouldn't have left him. I should have made sure he got here okay. I should have been more diligent about finding a mediator to help me.* "I have to go find him," I said through forming tears.

Calamus grabbed my arm before I could get up. "Stay, Layla. You can't go running around outside. I'll help you. If he's here, we'll find him."

My breathing felt too fast. *If* he's here. I tried to remember if my mother had mentioned him. Did she bring him with her? She wouldn't have left him in the Northern Sea Circle alone, would she?

"They said they got everyone out, but what if—"

Calamus took my hands in his. "They didn't leave anyone in Northern Sea. I promise I'll find him, Layla. Let me talk to the other covens and the housing coordinator."

"Okay," I said, blinking back moisture. This was so embarrassing, airing out my dirty laundry with *Calamus* of all people. "Thank… thank you."

"Oh," a voice interrupted. Hazel's eyes flitted to where Calamus's hands covered mine. I yanked them away, but it was too late. I cringed.

"You wanted to see me?" she asked uncertainly when we didn't say anything.

Fate, she looked like she was on the verge of tears.

I tried to compose myself and gave her a wobbly smile. "Hey, Hazel. Sorry, I asked Calamus to get in touch so I could give you back your tablet. I didn't know he'd asked you to drop by."

She regarded me suspiciously, and I wished a sinkhole would open below me. If I were her, I would think this was contrived to show off my conquest.

It's not me, it's Calamus being oblivious! I desperately tried to convey with my eyes.

I took the tablet out from my cloth satchel and held it out to her. "Thanks for letting me look through it."

"No problem," she said, taking it from me with a little more force than strictly necessary. She clutched it against her chest like a shield, looking like she would bolt at any moment.

Oh fate, this is such a mess. "I, um… found one that looked like it might work. I was wondering if… if you might help me with it. If you want to try it. I'm not great with circles," I told her, trying to broker some sort of peace.

Hazel flushed a bright red. "I'm not a circlewright," she said thickly, glancing at Calamus.

I withered. Fate, I had thought *Calamus* was oblivious, but here I was pulling up every single insecurity this poor woman had and throwing it in her face. I couldn't have done worse if I was trying.

"You found a circle spell?" Calamus asked me with interest.

Oh fate, he really is *oblivious.*

"He has a copy of the database. He can help," Hazel said, stepping backward. "I'd better… get going." She hustled away before I could tell her to be careful outside.

My insides curdled. I had to fix this somehow. "That was kind of her. She seems really sweet. Smart and beautiful," I said.

He frowned with mild distaste. "Who, Hazel? I suppose."

Yikes. Poor woman.

Calamus pulled out his phone. "Which spell were you looking at? I can help you with it if it looks viable."

I sighed. "JB47," I said, giving Hazel's designation. I had been trained in circle magic in school, but doing new circles was always difficult. A trained circlewright like Calamus would save me a lot of time and headaches.

He tapped a few buttons and raised his eyebrows. "*Traps a familiar?* Great find, Layla." He beamed a smile at me and opened the attached image of the diagram to examine it. "It's complete, and it looks straightforward. It'll only take an hour to trace. I'll find us a place to try it out."

I sighed. "Thanks, Calamus. You're doing a lot for me, and I appreciate it." He really was trying to be helpful. It felt shamefully one-sided, and I wished I could do something for him in return, but I couldn't give him what he wanted from me.

"It's my pleasure," he said, picking up my empty mug for me as he stood. He rested his free hand on my shoulder, looking down. "I have to go, but I'll get in touch as soon as I find out anything about your father."

"Hey, Calamus," Datura said to him as he passed. She and Oliver were heading for me with their trays of food.

My lips tipped down. They had a mischievous look, and I wasn't in the mood.

"Good morning," Calamus replied politely, nodding to them as he navigated away.

"No one brought us breakfast today!" Oliver cried as he slid into the seat Calamus had vacated.

"We're so hungry," Datura complained, squashing me over on the bench so she could sit too. I was trapped unless I wanted to bother the people on our other side.

Oliver clutched his belly dramatically. "We nearly *died*, but someone's too busy flirting to feed us."

"If you're starving, then *eat*," I said, stealing a strawberry from Datura's plate.

"So," said Datura, completely ignoring my suggestion, "when is it?"

"When is what?" I asked automatically, realizing too late that I'd just played into whatever she was setting up.

"The rival fight," she said with a sharp grin.

I groaned, sinking my head into my hands. I was glad they weren't at the last Arcaenum meeting or they'd never let this go. What counted as a rival fight? Did it have to come to blows?

Oliver pushed two orange slices into a pile of baked oatmeal. "In this corner, we have the brooding guardian Constantine, who inexplicably moved in with us and glares violently at anyone who looks at Layla—"

"Cut it out," I hissed.

"And in this corner, we have handsome Calamus, sought after by single witches everywhere and the Mountain Circle's most powerful spell caster, last seen with his hands all over our lovely prize."

"It was *one* hand, on my shoulder—"

Oliver mashed the two oranges together and tumbled them around, providing growling sound effects. He shoved one into the oatmeal with a dying gurgle.

I tilted my head at the mess. "Well? Who won?"

"Blackthorn," Oliver and Datura said in unison, then laughed riotously.

I rolled my eyes pointedly at them, but I couldn't fight the small smile that tugged at my mouth. Their antics had pulled me out of my own bleak thoughts.

The pair quieted for a few moments as they ate, and I sank back into my somber mood.

"Are you two okay?" I asked seriously. They'd never even seen an angel, hadn't trained with their guardians, and now they were responsible for defending against an imminent attack. To top it off, from what Costi had said, they were set up for failure.

I added that to my long list of worries—sometime in the weeks I'd been here, these two had wormed their way into my heart.

They glanced at each other, communicating without a word. Datura looked away with a sigh, and Oliver stirred his food around with a spoon.

"I suck at being a spell caster," Datura said. "I hate patrolling."

Oliver said, "I'm terrified constantly."

"I wish I could help," I told them.

Oliver brightened. "Any luck with your magic yet?"

"I have a circle spell to try. That's why I was meeting up with Calamus. But nothing yet."

"I just want you to get your magic. We'll hide behind you, you can fry the entire sky if any angels get close, and Blackthorn can slice up the stragglers," Datura said.

"That's mean," said Oliver as he lobbed a cherry at Datura, who dodged it. "If they pair up, then they *definitely* can't date."

"Fate help us, here we go again," I muttered, picking up the cherry from where it had fallen onto the bench.

"It'll be all forbidden and hot," Datura argued.

I set the cherry on the edge of her plate. "You two certainly have a lot of opinions on dating for people who don't seem to date."

Oliver grinned. "We're spectators, not participants."

"Commentators, not players," Datura agreed with a straight face.

"Why don't you ever pick on Sativa? She's got to have some drama going on with all those lovers."

"Oh, she does, but that's old news," Oliver said. "Yours is way more fun."

My phone pinged, and I looked down. There was a text from Calamus.

Good news, I found your father right away. He's staying with the Oak Grove Coven in G block. They said he's doing great.

Chapter 15

LAYLA

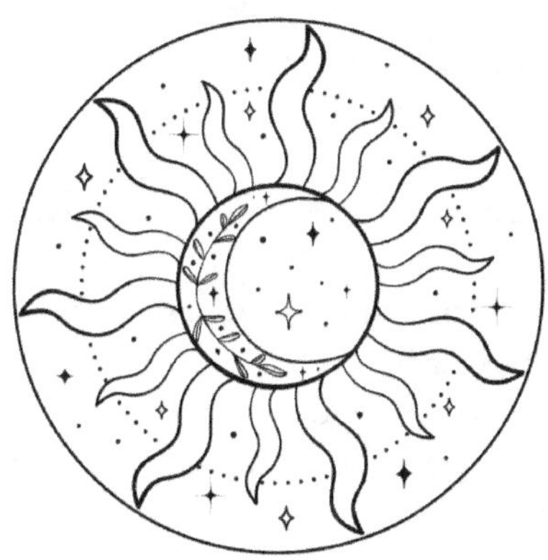

The one benefit of having a hoard of new people in the Circle was that they put signs up everywhere, so I found G block easily even though I hadn't been to that part of the community before. The apartments circling a courtyard looked similar to ours, but this block had a fountain burbling in the middle of the garden. A few early fallen leaves swirled in the water.

The bench across from the fountain was occupied, and my breath caught.

"Dad!" I skirted around the stone water feature to embrace him. His body felt thin, and his beard was shaggy, but he was alive. "You're okay, thank fate. I… I thought you were with Mother." I pulled back to look at him. His eyes tracked me—a good sign.

"She got tired of me, I think. Sorry, Layla…" He shook his head, as if clearing it.

"Don't worry," I told him, sitting next to him on the bench. "Are you feeling okay? Taking your meds?"

"I got new ones. I think they're… better. I've been sitting outside a lot."

"That's good," I said, hoping it was safe.

I sat with him, watching leaves fall. His condition had developed during my childhood, with him slowly growing more withdrawn and locked in his mind. I couldn't remember him before, but my mother often pointed out how different he was from when they got married. How disappointed she was. She blamed him for it, and I blamed her for that—driving a wedge between us that only got wider with time. This kind of mental illness wasn't anything someone could control. He was still my dad. Still the man my mother loved. But she had become obsessed with imperfections and couldn't see what she had right in front of her.

"You're okay?" he asked, breaking the silence.

"I'm… I'm okay, I guess." I held on to his arm and leaned my head against his shoulder. I should have come and found him ages ago. "I can't invoke my familiar."

"I lost mine that day. Maybe you're better off. We won't win."

My body chilled. "What day? What do you mean, we won't win? You said that before."

His mouth opened and closed, his gaze becoming unfocused. "The… host. The throne. Layla. The *eyes*. Don't… I need to…"

I shivered. He didn't always have the best grasp on reality, but this didn't seem like part of that.

"It's okay, Dad," I said. It sounded hollow to my ears. "You're okay."

"I'll… I'll go lie down…"

"Good idea," I said. "Do you want some help?"

"No," he said, getting up shakily. "No."

"All right. I'll come back and see you soon."

He turned back to me and swallowed. "You can't fight… *them*," he told me. "Promise me you won't."

I couldn't make that promise. I wasn't about to stand back and let the angels go unpunished if I could do something about it.

I looked back at my father solemnly. The cost of fighting could be *very* high.

"I'll be okay," I replied.

I hoped I was telling the truth.

* * *

Costi had told me to meet him outside the hall where the Council met, but when I got there, I didn't see him. I leaned against the wall near the edge of the stone building, watching as way more people than just the councilors and delegates filed through the doors. That couldn't be good.

Suddenly, I was being hauled around the corner and pushed up against the wall. My already-nervous pulse skittered into what I was sure was medically dangerous territory as Costi held me in place with his hard body. Bracing one hand above my head, he leaned in close to my ear. "I can't take this."

My whole being responded to him—blood rushing, heart tumbling, thrumming with urgent, unmet need. Sucking in a shaking breath, I ran my hands up his chest and wound my arms around his neck.

"Layla," he grated out as he trailed his nose along my jawline, causing my breath to stutter. "I can't *stand* that asshole." He pressed his hips firmly into mine, and my head spun.

"What are you—" I gasped sharply as he bit my earlobe. "What are you talking—"

Costi made a frustrated sound against my skin. "*All morning*," he said, punctuating it with a nip to my neck. "He's been *bragging*. That you *took him out.*"

Loose pieces rattled through my mostly occupied mind, finally falling into place. Sliding my hands to his arms, I pushed gently and he rocked back, breathing hard and staring down at my open lips. His eyes were burning, and his hair looked disheveled, like he'd pushed his hands through it too many times.

"Are you talking about Cal—"

Costi roughly stopped me from saying the name with his fingers over my mouth.

"I didn't take him out," I mumbled around his hand, which he dragged along my cheek and pushed into my hair. My heightened emotions tipped into anger. "Does he think *everything* is a date?"

Costi looked down at me through lowered eyelids as he ran his fingers along my scalp.

"What are we doing, Costi?" I whispered, my head tilting without my permission into his massaging hand.

"Mm. I'm pushing you up against a wall. You're not dating Grey. I'm not dating Holly."

My eyes popped open as rage seized me. "So, she *did* go after you."

Costi lowered his head and hit me with a smirk that was downright *wicked*. "A lotta witches go after me."

"Are you trying to… to make me jealous?" I said breathlessly.

"*Yes,*" he whispered darkly. "You get it now?"

I got it. But my heart shattered. "We can't."

Costi pushed away from the wall. My legs wobbled like jelly, and I leaned heavily to keep myself upright.

"*No one,*" he bit out, rising to his full height. "*No one* tells you and me what we can't do."

I was already shaking my head. "The second anyone finds out, they'll kick you out of the Circle. But I… I don't think they'll let *me* go. Not now."

Costi's throat worked around a swallow. I could see he knew I was right. I might have been able to run away from the Northern Sea Circle to be with him. But after the coordinated attack on the eastern witch communities? There was no way the Mountain Circle was going to let a spell caster go, even a broken one. If they caught me with Costi, I didn't think Cedar Grey and his friends would hesitate to physically restrain me so I couldn't follow.

His face had gone blank, but his gray eyes churned with something desperate. "They don't have to find out. We can keep it quiet."

"No. I won't do that to you."

Costi froze.

"You deserve—" My breath hitched around my despair. "You deserve someone who can love you openly. You aren't a dirty secret to be hidden away. I won't treat you like that."

He stared at me, his lips open around words he couldn't form. A single tear tracked from his startled gray eye, and he quickly smeared it with his palm, looking away from me.

I couldn't stand his pain. I surged forward and wrapped my arms around his middle, hugging him close.

He shuddered against me. "I won't have anyone else." His fierce voice was raw. "I *can't*."

"I won't either," I murmured into his shoulder.

He pushed me to arm's length, and I stumbled back into the wall. He quickly followed, putting us back in the same position we'd started in. "One kiss," he demanded. "Just one."

Sharp longing pulsed through me. "We definitely can't." It would never be just one.

"Then for fate's sake, distract me." His eyes tracked hotly over my parted mouth. "I'm Troubled. I don't have any impulse control. Layla, you've got three seconds."

My mind ticked uselessly.

"Three," Costi said. "Two—"

"I saw my dad," I blurted.

He released me suddenly and blew out a breath, shoving his fingers through his hair.

"Okay. Good. How is he?" Costi asked, pacing away. He'd been with me for the story's unfolding. My dad's slow decline in health over my childhood. How I missed someone I never really knew but wanted to honor the good man he was now.

"My mother left him. She's living with Cedar Grey."

"*What?*" His lips twisted in a sneer. "What's with Junior, then, some kind of twisted stepsister thing? That's fucked up."

My guts flipped over. I hadn't actually considered that Mother might be *involved* with the councilor, even though that was the most logical explanation. "She was the one pushing me at him in the first place."

"Doesn't matter," Costi said gruffly, throwing his arms across his chest. "He's not getting you, and she's not getting anywhere near you."

I warmed with his protectiveness.

"Is he okay? Your dad?"

I considered. "I think so. He's sad, though. He still loves my mother. And… he's convinced we can't win."

"Win the war, you mean? Why's that?"

"I don't know. He can't tell me. It almost seems like he knows something important, but…"

Costi nodded, looking off into the woods in consideration. He knew my dad couldn't distinguish reality very well these days, that details got muddled in his mind.

"If we're going to the meeting, we should go," I said.

He made a noise that might have been agreement but didn't move. "Layla." His voice stopped me as I turned to go. "*Thank you.*"

* * *

No one noticed us slipping in late—the chamber was in chaos. Costi used his intimidating body to make way for us through the crowd.

Quince shouted from the dais, "We were elected to discuss these matters. *Please* let us do our jobs."

I moved in front of Costi so I could see. He stayed behind me, not touching, but close enough to haul me out of harm's way.

"I didn't elect *you!*" a witch shouted back, straining toward the platform. He was being restrained by two others. "You think you're gonna dissolve the Saltmarsh Council like you did Northern Sea? *Think again.*"

Quince held up his hands, stepping back. "I know you're angry. You've lost people—"

"He's angry because we're sitting ducks, and you Arcaenum people aren't doing a *fated thing!*" a robed spell caster I didn't know yelled above the clamor of voices.

"We are doing all we can—"

"Like Hell you are!"

Cedar Grey stepped up on the dais, clasping Quince's arm and saying something to him. The gathered witches moved restlessly, hurling questions at the councilors.

"If I could have everyone's attention," Grey boomed. The crowd shifted slightly, some settling down. "I am Cedar Grey, councilor for the Mountain Circle Arcaenum. Due to the extraordinary situation we find ourselves in, we haven't had adequate time to address concerns. We will do so now, in an orderly manner." He stressed the word *orderly*, glaring out at the witches. "I'll thank you to allow the assembly leader to continue."

"Thank you, Councilor." Quince straightened his black robes. "We will proceed as if this *were* a public meeting, with concerns being voiced one by one, giving the councilors the option to provide additional information. Since this wasn't a planned meeting, we will hold on any decisions, but we will make official note of all concerns and go through the voting process next time."

"If the Mountain Council could join us on the dais," Grey said. "Again, I ask for order," he called out, as sharp protests accompanied the councilors stepping forward. I counted a dozen members, including Rhodes. Someone brought her a folding chair to sit in front of the others, who remained standing.

It was already getting overly warm and humid in the room, witches fanning themselves.

"This is gonna be brutal," Costi said, echoing my thoughts.

When the Arcaenum was in place, Quince invited the first person to speak. It was the angry witch, now calmed down a bit. His companions had released him, and he settled into the familiar pattern of speaking at a public meeting.

"I'm Branch Lowri," he growled through gritted teeth. "Water engineer and councilor for the Saltmarsh Circle. My *concern* is that our elected Council will be dissolved, leaving us without representation."

One of the robed Mountain Circle councilors on the dais stepped forward. "We understand the concern, but the counterpoint is that we are in the midst of a crisis situation and do not have time to work out a process with new members." The witch brought her hands together in front of her. "I propose the solution of appointing two delegates from each of the refugee Circles' former Councils until our spring election."

"Your concern and a proposed solution are recorded," a familiar voice called out.

A complicated reaction fizzled through me. Holly looked professional in a knee-length dress with a jacket, her hair styled in an elegant updo. With her experience doing administration for the Northern Sea Circle's Council, she must have been a natural choice to help the Arcaenum.

The meeting dragged on through a dozen speakers—everything from a concern over dwindling funds for supplies from the outside to an idea for circlewrights to darken the sky as they had during the Northern Sea evacuation.

"Great idea," muttered Costi behind me. "Mark exactly where the Circle is with a nice big black dot."

"They have to know where we are already," I said, voicing my fear.

My heart lifted when I saw the next speaker. "My name is Jenny Luna, *formerly* elected councilor, and my concern is that the Mountain Circle sold us out."

Gasps and muttering erupted as Grey glowered at the caster. "And what evidence do you have of this? What's our supposed motivation for cramming in thousands more witches than we can hold?" he demanded, breaking protocol.

A few laughs followed his response.

Luna crossed her arms over her chest and glared back. "We're supposed to believe that every Circle in the eastern part of the continent was accidentally discovered at once *except* this one? Then all the survivors fled here, and no one followed them? Give me a break. Someone sold out our locations. I want to know what *you* paid for safety."

"We won't entertain this kind of nonsense," Grey said with finality. "Have her removed."

Removed? I didn't understand what he was talking about until the two guardians stepped forward.

"The *fuck?*" Costi spat, and I saw what he'd been reacting to. One of the pair was Ewan—Datura's assigned guardian and our roommate. His normal easy grin had been replaced with a nasty version that made me cold.

Luna backed away as Grey's guardians advanced. "*What?* You can't—"

On either side, they hooked under her shoulders and pushed her through the crush of stunned witches.

What is going on? The guardians didn't drag witches out of public meetings. I looked up at Costi. His eyes were narrowed. He gave me a slight shake of the head.

"Next speaker, please," Quince said to the absolutely silent chamber, gesturing at me. Grey's eyes swung angrily toward me and pinned me.

My heart beat rapidly as nervousness washed through me. Would he have me thrown out too? Every eye trained itself on me.

"Just stick to the facts," Costi said quietly. I could feel him behind me, supporting me.

In the crowd, I suddenly felt young and small. I wished I had a stool to stand on. I cleared my throat and tried to project my shaking voice. "I'm Layla Rosen, Mountain Circle delegate." I still wasn't sure what exactly I was the delegate for, so I didn't clarify. "My concern is that our patrolling teams are under tree cover, making it impossible for spell casters to see into the sky, and if they cast, they risk causing a fire. I don't have a proposal for a solution at this time."

The councilors on the dais looked at each other. Hadn't they known about this already?

Quince scratched his head. "I propose the solution of clearing a perimeter around the Circle."

"Excuse me!" called a voice from the back. "I'm the forestry delegate. Please consider the *extremely* negative impact of clearing that much land."

Quince let the interruption go. His forehead was shiny with sweat in the overhead lights, and exhaustion lined his face, deep circles blooming around his eyes.

Artemesia Rhodes got to her feet slowly, one of her fellow councilors assisting her. "I propose the alternative solution of forming a security advisory committee and allowing them full decision-making in these matters." The elderly former guardian looked directly at me and Costi, and I swore her eyes held a glint of mischief. "Our current situation is far more dangerous and complicated than we are set up for. We are negligent in expecting Security Coordinator Daire to handle all of it without assistance."

"Your concern and two proposed solutions are recorded," Holly recited solemnly.

"Next speaker, please," Quince said tiredly.

They were still at it when we finally ducked out hours later, with barely an hour for Costi to get ready before his evening patrol. It was amazing how quickly people could adjust to routines. An attack hadn't come immediately, so the prospect seemed much more distant. We were getting on with our lives.

I'd missed a text from Calamus while we were in the meeting. He had found us a space to work the new circle spell the next day.

"Oh, I have another date with Calamus tomorrow," I told Costi coyly as he made efficient work of his dinner, standing at the kitchen counter while I leaned against it.

None of our roommates were home. We weren't sure what to do about Ewan. This business with Grey was *wrong*. Costi had told me to stay clear of him until they had a chat. I needed to talk to Datura about him, too.

He gave a menacing laugh. "The Hell you do." He was freshly showered and shaved, his damp hair curling appealingly.

"He's going to try another circle spell for me tomorrow," I said.

"I'm coming with you. Last time, he pulled a demon. He's gonna accidentally summon a nest of angels."

"Yeah, knowing my luck. This one is supposed to trap my familiar."

"Good. Let's catch the little bastard." Costi picked up a brush to scrub his empty plate, but I took it from him.

"I'll do it. You have to go." I looked down and bit back a smile. We were being domestic, and I liked it. Eating together in the kitchen was innocent enough. We were friends. Just… really good friends who didn't date anyone else.

Costi brushed his fingers over my hand. "See you later."

* * *

I didn't think this circle spell was going to work. Nothing else had so far, and I couldn't imagine anything changing. But I wasn't upset anymore. I felt as though a huge weight had been lifted from me.

It was time to give it up and do something else. I wanted to protect my Circle, but that didn't mean I had to be a spell caster.

I could pull magic, so maybe a circlewright? Maybe I could try some of the old spells Hazel had dug up. I didn't have a lot of patience for tracing, though, especially after working the summoning circle so many times. Lately I had found I really enjoyed feeding people—I was sure I could find a place in the kitchens to try it out. I wondered if I had what it took to become a guardian. Fate, I could try *anything*.

I could have Costi.

If I weren't a spell caster, no one would care. The knowledge sparkled inside me, and for the first time in a long time, I stopped dreading the future.

When I got to the circle casting room Calamus had reserved, the door was open, and he had already gotten started with the tracing. "This one doesn't take much effort to hold," he said.

"Thanks again for trying," I said. I wiggled my hands around. My limbs felt full of nervous energy. I could see the circle taking shape—Calamus traced the runic form of my name into place, personalizing the spell to me.

Costi joined us moments later, and Calamus sighed without glancing up. "What are you doing here?"

"Making sure you don't screw up. Is there a fire extinguisher?"

Calamus didn't dignify that with a response. Calamus was the more mature man, but Costi was hilarious, so I mentally handed him the point, biting my lip to keep from laughing.

I watched quietly while Calamus traced. Costi had pulled out his phone and was scrolling without comment, being good for my sake. Magic brushed my senses as the circle rose. "It's working," I whispered.

"Get ready," Calamus said.

Several things happened at once. Calamus stepped back from the circle as it caught, swirling with loops and whorls of bright magic. I felt a sharp, alarming *tug* deep inside me and gasped out loud, clasping my chest.

Costi reached for me.

"What the f—" he started, then vanished.

Chapter 16

LAYLA

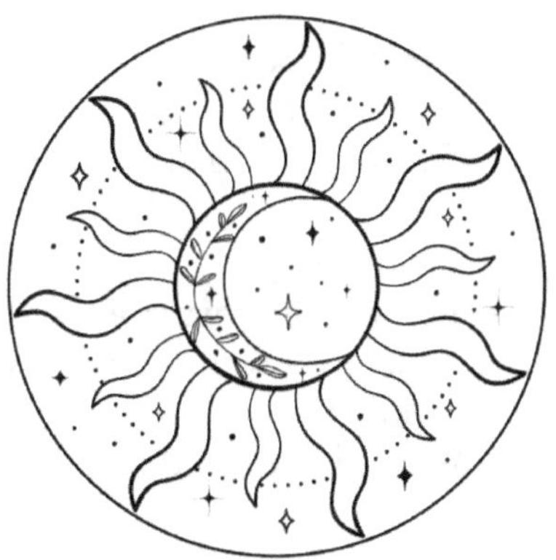

My ears were ringing. I couldn't form words as Calamus strode over to the place where Costi had been standing.

"Did you see that?" His words were like ice picks, too loud. I felt raw and strange.

"Wh-What did you do?" I forced out through numb lips.

Calamus looked back at the circle, now a stable, glowing ring in the center of the burned-out tracing. "The spell is working," he said with a frown.

"What did you *do*, Calamus? Bring him back!" I cried, my breath coming too fast.

He placed his hands on my shoulders and shook me. "Layla, calm down. We have to think. I didn't do anything. The spell is working."

I wrenched myself away from him. "You have to bring him back."

Calamus paced, examining the circle and the floor.

Oh fate, what if Costi is gone? What if he's dead?

He paused. "Invoke," he said.

"What? We have to—"

"The spell is *working*, Layla," he repeated, turning toward me. "Invoke your familiar."

"How is that going to—"

"Layla, invoke!"

With nothing else to hold on to, I did as he suggested. It took me a few times to concentrate, but I finally made it through the mental sequence I had tried a hundred times without effect—

And I felt it catch. The enormity of it scoured my soul before my conscious mind could process it.

"What the *fuck* was that?" Costi's voice was venomous.

I cried out and rushed toward him, but Calamus clamped a hand around my wrist with a bruising grip that forced me to jerk to a halt.

"Let go!"

"Layla, don't," he said urgently.

Costi stepped toward me, and it was then I realized he was *inside* the circle. A barrier flashed as it shocked him with energy, and he swore viciously, jumping backward. He was trapped in the spell.

I looked at him and jolted as if *I* had been shocked.

"You better take your hand off her," Costi said in a low voice that promised immediate violence. He whirled and delivered a volley of lethal kicks to the barrier. Light crashed over it and cracked in sparkling waves, showing the cylindrical shape of the spell, but it held. The magic resettled, leaving him inside, clenching his fists and breathing heavily. "Drop the spell, Grey. *Now.*"

I felt Calamus shaking. He'd been holding on to me to keep me in place, but now I thought he was holding on for dear life. He drew in a shuddering breath. "Are you a demon?"

"Do I *look* like a fucking demon?" Costi snarled.

Calamus and I were silent. Because… he *did* look like a fucking demon. More precisely, he kind of looked like the demon we had contacted in Hell.

I stared at my best friend and almost-lover. His eyes were too silver, his ears tipped with wicked points that framed a sharp face.

Costi, but not.

Oh fate, he was *not human.*

Costi stared at us in confusion, then glanced down at his hands, as if checking that he was himself. As if that jarred something back into place, his face returned to normal.

Unsettled, I took a step back, colliding with Calamus.

Costi's human-gray eyes tracked the movement. "What exactly is going on here?"

"I'm calling my father. The Arcaenum. Daire," Calamus announced. He pulled his phone out of a pocket in his robes and nearly fumbled it. He backed to the door, obviously unnerved.

"*Grey,*" Costi hissed. "Drop the spell. I'm not gonna do anything to you, just chill."

Calamus slammed the door closed.

Costi barked a laugh. "He thinks I'm *that* dangerous, and he just shut you in here with me?"

I felt tears begin to track down my cheeks.

"*Layla,*" he said in alarm, pushing his hands into the barrier with a flash. He stalked around the confines of the spell, unable to get closer. "Fate, you know I'd *never* hurt you. I was pissed, but I'm calm now. *Please* don't be scared of me."

I shook my head, unable to speak.

"Talk to me," the demon creature with Costi's voice begged. "Tell me what's wrong. Do you know how to break this thing? Let me out."

I trembled. I knew exactly how to get him out.

"*Not mine,*" the demon Adriel had said. Because I was someone else's.

I banished my familiar, then invoked him again.

Costi appeared by my side.

* * *

"Oh," I breathed. The tears came harder, but Costi made no move to touch me. When I looked up at him, his face was frozen in a shocked expression—he had just put the terrible puzzle together as well.

"How…?" He swallowed. "How's this even possible? How could I not have known?" He wrapped his arms around himself.

I scrubbed my eyes with my sleeve. "You were only seven—"

"Natural summoning," he murmured.

It fit. "From… from Hell?"

"Fucking fate!" Costi slammed a hand over the top of his head, feeling around.

"You don't have horns," I said hoarsely. "But… the ears…"

He clamped his fingers over the side of his face, then yanked his phone out of a pocket, using the camera to peer at himself through the cracked screen.

"You look normal now," I said. My voice sounded distant.

"What kind of magic…?"

The sounds of people walking up the stairway came from the hall. "We have to get out of here."

Costi swore. "There's no other exit."

"What are we going to do?"

"Tell them it's not your fault. You didn't know about this."

"What about *you?*"

He pushed his hand through his hair. "I'm *screwed.* They're never gonna let me—" He straightened as the door opened.

Calamus took us in coldly. Cedar Grey, looking less intimidating without his council robes, stood with Daire, who was glaring angrily. Behind them strode Ewan and the other guardian Grey seemed to be using as personal security.

"You let him out?" Calamus accused me with a pointed finger. "You *invoked* him out."

Calamus tried to fall back, but his father and Daire advanced into the room. Costi and I stepped back in one motion. There wasn't any question whose side I was on.

The security coordinator was in her black guardian uniform, her hair bound in a tight braid around her head. "All right, Blackthorn, your spell caster insisted we get here as fast as possible and is hurling some frankly wild accusations," Daire said, cutting her gaze to Cedar Grey and then back to Costi. "You wanna tell us what's going on?"

"Layla had nothing to do with this," Costi said, standing at attention and looking into Daire's eyes fearlessly.

"Care to elaborate?" Councilor Grey raised an open palm with exaggerated patience.

"*I* will explain," said Calamus, shouldering past his father. "I traced a circle spell to retrieve Layla's missing familiar, and I caught *him* instead. Blackthorn is a demon."

Daire scoffed. "He's a pain in the ass, but I wouldn't go that far."

"I witnessed Layla invoke him like a familiar. I saw him *change shape*," Calamus seethed.

"My son wouldn't make up fanciful stories." Councilor Grey gazed at Costi warily. "Did you find a way through, demon? Are you here as a spy?"

I knew what he was talking about—the mirror Calamus had opened to communicate with Hell. I glanced at Daire, who looked confused. He'd kept her in the dark.

Costi was uncharacteristically quiet. Whether it was the shock of the situation or a strategy to avoid the normal kind of escalation he liked to cause, I didn't know.

"He's not a spy." I was suddenly the new center of attention in the room. My face heated. "I think… I think it was a natural summoning."

Grey glowered at me. "And you didn't think anything of it? Your Circle didn't notice a grown man appearing next to you suddenly?"

No, but they *had* noticed a young boy who couldn't speak our language and who they couldn't keep away from me. "We were children. I was three," I said.

"That's ridiculous," said Daire. "No one summons that young."

Grey put a hand to his chin. "The more likely scenario is that at some point your childhood friend was… *replaced*."

I shook my head, wrapping my arms around myself. "No. I know him. He's the same."

"What are you gonna do with me?" Costi interrupted.

Our guests looked at each other.

"I suppose we should call an emergency meeting of the Arcaenum and get this straightened out," said Daire, scratching her chin uncomfortably.

"Let's not be hasty," said Grey. "Some of our councilors are… easily influenced. They don't think strategically," he hinted, looking at Daire intently.

I took in an uneven breath. "You *have* to call the Arcaenum. You can't keep secrets like—"

Grey interrupted me, glaring down his nose. "We needn't bother them for every little thing."

Daire looked to Grey. "Perhaps we should discuss it privately." She turned to Costi. "In the meantime, I think you should come with me to headquarters and hang out there tonight."

"You're *arresting* him?" I blurted.

"It's all right, Layla," Costi said, his head bowed. "I expected it."

"Her too." Calamus looked at me sadly. "She can invoke him. She'll let him out."

Daire raised an eyebrow at me. "If that's true, I would consider that a breach of security."

Calamus's casual betrayal felt like a slap. "I'll come."

"Keep them separated," Councilor Grey told Daire. She gave him a tight nod.

Grey motioned the guardians in, and they each took one of Costi's arms. Ewan snatched Costi's phone.

Even though the guardians were both tall and physically fit, I was certain Costi could take them out easily if he wanted to. But he allowed them to restrain him. He was cooperating.

Costi looked back at me over his shoulder. His eyes were like a bank of storm clouds, sad and distant. It wasn't any threat from the guardians that was keeping him in line. They had *me*. Calamus's circle wasn't nearly as good a trap.

Daire turned to me. "Walk with me, please, Layla."

The guardians escorted Costi through the Circle, with Daire and me following, creating a spectacle that made me want to turn inside out. We'd done nothing wrong. Witches who committed *actual crimes* weren't even treated like this.

Daire led us to a smaller building next to the barracks. A hasty sign had been affixed to the bricks—Security Headquarters. Down a short hallway, she paused in front of a door.

"Take him to the holding cell," she told the two guardians.

Costi locked eyes with me. "Call Diana," he said. Diana Blackthorn—the woman who fostered him for ten years after he'd… *arrived*. I nodded, my eyes filling with tears. "Be good, Layla," he told me as they pulled him away.

I forced my head up and clamped down my feelings. I wouldn't break in front of Daire.

The room she ushered me into seemed to be her personal quarters. She showed me to a guest bedroom with an attached bathroom.

"You'll stay in here," she told me. "I'll be working out there. The windows are secured. I'll know if you get up to any shenanigans."

"I won't," I promised. I guessed she didn't consider me much of a threat.

"Your mom doesn't deserve this. I'll talk to her and Councilor Grey, see if we can get you out of here."

When I said nothing, Daire sighed. "I don't know what to think about this demon nonsense." She turned a shrewd eye on me. "Blackthorn's a terror, but *you* are a good kid. This is why you're supposed to keep away from the Troubled." She nodded to me and closed the door. I heard something rattle into place on the other side—she'd locked me in.

I stared numbly at where she'd disappeared from. The feelings I'd been suppressing slammed back into me with a vengeance. I started to shake violently, holding my hands desperately over my mouth to stifle the sounds of my uncontrolled sobbing.

How? How could this happen? He hadn't known. *No one* had known. And I *loved*—

I took a shuddering breath, stopping myself. That line of thought had to end immediately. We'd just gone from *absolutely not allowed* to *astronomically complicated.* I wished I could talk to Costi about it, but his advice would probably amount to *"Shut up and kiss me,"* so…

I had to get a hold of myself and help my… my friend. I dragged myself to the bathroom and washed my face. They'd taken Costi's phone but not mine. The battery was languishing at half empty since I'd been out most of the day, and I didn't have a charger, but it was better than nothing.

I pulled up Diana's contact info and hit Call, hoping she hadn't changed her number.

"Layla, sweetie!" Her rough voice came through the speaker. "Everything okay?"

"Not really. Are you at the Mountain Circle?"

"Yeah, I'm… Hang on, I gotta get somewhere where I can hear you better." There was a rustle, voices in the background. "I'm here. What's wrong, baby? How's the boy? I haven't heard from him in a while."

"I'm calling about him," I said.

"Fate, what's he done now?"

I blew out a breath. "This is hard to know how to tell you."

"He get you pregnant? Always knew he had a thing for you—"

"*What?* No!" Fate, how long had Costi had a *thing* for me? "It's… How much do you know about where he came from?"

Diana made a humming sound. "Unfortunately, not much, honey. They found him on the playground right after that bad attack in Greece. Couldn't speak a word of English, but they were afraid to bring in a translator from outside in case he talked about witch stuff. We just put him in school, and he picked it up well enough."

"Did he say anything later? Remember anything?"

"He remembers quite a bit from… before. You should ask him. What's this all about, Layla?"

"You know he's different," I said.

"He's had his challenges," Diana said defensively. I warmed at her protectiveness toward him.

"Not like that." I picked at a loose thread on my skirt. "He's *really* different."

She was quiet while I hesitated, listening to the phone's light static. "Wherever he… came from," she said carefully, "he's one of us now."

"You knew."

"I *don't* know. But I had my ideas. Especially when he first came to me…" Her sigh rushed through the speaker. "What's going on? You best put him on the phone, Layla."

"Something happened." I swallowed thickly.

Diana's voice was grim. "All right. Tell me."

Chapter 17

COSTI

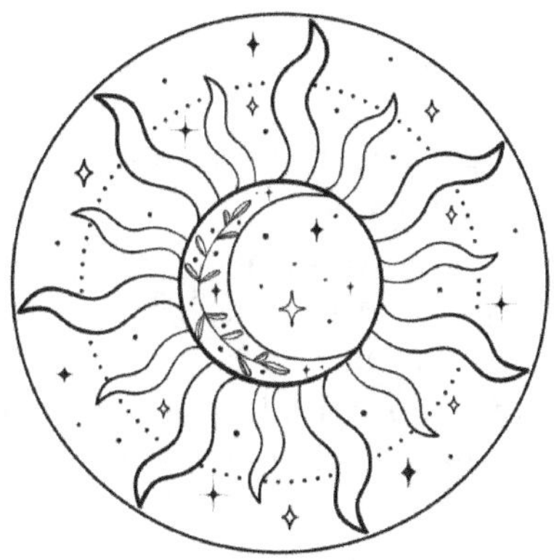

It was cold in here now that I wasn't burning angry, but I wasn't about to let anyone know it bothered me. I'd seen this holding cell in the barracks—a brightly lit white room with nothing but a metal toilet—but I never figured I'd be sitting on the floor of it for hours.

Plenty of time to start second-guessing every weird feeling I ever had, trying to figure out if I was a demon. What kind of magic could stick to someone's face for seventeen years? What kind of self-delusion made me not realize what *species* I was? How the *fuck* could I be bonded to Layla as a familiar and not even know? I'd felt different from other witches growing up, but wasn't it just the kind of different that came from being adopted? From being Troubled?

Not human…

Resting my elbows on my knees, I pushed both hands into my hair. This was a fucking mess. There was no way they'd let me stay a guardian.

I should just bail. Go pretend to be human somewhere else. I bet I could get a job outside kicking troublemakers out of bars or something.

I'd take Layla with me. I didn't care what these assholes thought. I'd get her out of here. Nothing mattered more than her.

I ignored the booted footsteps echoing in the hall, the opening of the locked door, and the shadow that fell over me.

"Well, well," an obnoxious voice said.

I raised my head and tried to project the eye-rolling annoyance I was feeling. Cedar Grey, the shit who thought he was a ruler and not an elected official. His dogs flanked him—Ewan and a spell caster. He was amassing quite the little collection.

"Hello, demon," said Grey Senior. Fate, I hated this whole fucking family.

"Gonna be like that, huh?" My voice sounded gravelly from disuse. I didn't bother standing up.

"I'll admit, I was surprised by this. You Northern Sea witches are typically such pushovers." He sneered down at me. "But then, you're not a Northern Sea witch at all, are you?"

"You believe all the weird shit Calamus tells you?"

"I could replicate his… *experiment* easily," Grey said, unbothered. "But it's plain to see there's something wrong about you, and it's not just that you're Troubled. Now tell me why you were sent here."

"Can't help you with that," I said. Yeah, it was insolent. But it wasn't like he was going to listen to a word I said anyway. Witches like him were all the same. Once they made up their minds about someone, they never changed.

Grey nodded at his spell caster flunky, and he invoked his familiar. The small pale demon narrowed its black eyes at me and hissed viciously, showing its little fangs.

Am I seriously related to these things?

"Do you care to answer me now?" Grey smirked as if I couldn't take him and his little entourage out in thirty seconds.

"Why bother?"

"Convince him," Grey said to his pets.

The caster flicked a finger at my torso. A bloom of fiery light slammed into my chest, and the breath was knocked from my lungs as pain seared through me. The blow forced me to the floor.

My training kicked in automatically. I rolled onto my back and leaped to my feet, leveling a devastating head punch to the asshole who'd dared cast at me. He collapsed in a heap and his familiar disappeared with a tiny, satisfying pop.

My ruined shirt smoked, and I slapped out the smoldering fiber. I pulled my lip back in a snarl and whirled to face Grey. "I'll show you a *fucking demon*," I growled, swallowing up the space between us. I was a full head taller and a lot broader than him and pissed that he didn't look intimidated.

"Try it," he said, holding up a hand, "and I'll make sure your little spell caster never sees daylight again."

That stopped me cold. Ewan twisted my arm behind me to control me, and I let him.

Trembling with rage, I stilled. "What do you *want*?" I bit out. My burned skin pulsed with agony in time with my heartbeat.

"Tell me *why you were sent here*," he seethed.

"Why do you think?" I spit back through clenched teeth. There was no reasoning with this witch.

Grey jabbed a finger into my burned chest and twisted. I forced back a grimace. I wasn't giving him anything. "Tell your *prince* to back off. He may be in charge of things in Hell, but *I'm* in charge here. He thinks he can sneak around behind my back and send his spies? Remind him that it's only by my goodwill that his demons are allowed out of the pit. Tell him I can make things *very unpleasant* for our little familiars."

I couldn't help it. I laughed—a dark, horrible sound. "Next time I see him, I'll be sure to let him know."

Grey glared up at me. "You can stay in this prison or go back to that one," he said before sweeping out of the cell.

Ewan shoved me back and hesitated, glancing at the unconscious caster on the floor. I took a menacing step toward him and he backed up, feeling for the door.

"You know what this is, right? Grey telling you to do stuff, and you doing it? There's a name for it. Starts with *I*."

He held his hands up. "Hey, man, I'm not looking for trouble."

"You just landed yourself in a whole heap of it if you're gonna help the angels."

The guardian grinned weakly. "Come on, Blackthorn. It's not like *that*."

"What's it like, then? 'Cause from where I'm standing, you look like a traitor."

"Shut up, asshole. *I'm* doing my job. You're the one selling secrets and fucking around with that spell caster."

I was fast, but he was already slamming the barred door in my face.

"Damnit, take your *guy* with you!" I yelled after him, kicking the metal and regretting it as pain shot through my body. With a grimace, I carefully lowered myself back to the hard floor next to my new friend, wishing I had been knocked out too.

A demon prince, huh? Every time I thought we'd gotten all of Grey's dirt, he shoveled up more. What *else* was he hiding?

I hissed in pain as I brought a hand to my sternum. The caster had hit the opposite side from my heart, thank fate. My owl tattoo was ruined, a three-inch circle seared into my chest where the intricate wing stretched out. Insult to injury.

Injury to injury, if I was being honest. This wasn't good. My leg and arm were still messed up from the *last* two times I'd been mauled. This demon thing was a shit deal—all the hate but no handy benefits like instant magical healing.

At least the wound had self-cauterized. It wasn't bleeding.

Time passed in burning agony, and I was nowhere close to figuring any of this out. My memories before Northern Sea were fuzzy. Blue water. Sun. Love. Nothing that made me think *Hell prison full of demons*. I tried to remember my mother's face—any details from my previous life—but it was lost to time.

The caster I'd punched unconscious groaned pathetically. I kicked him viciously awake as he grabbed his head dramatically, curling into a pile of red fabric.

"Took me a minute, but I know who you are." Ash's assigned Mountain Circle caster—the one who'd been giving them so much trouble. I hadn't bothered to learn his name.

"You *hit* me," he rasped.

"You *cast* at me, you bastard. You could've killed me."

He pushed himself gingerly to a seated position, leaning next to me against the white wall. "You're fine. My control is excellent."

"Yeah? Well, mine isn't."

"Is that a *threat*?" The caster's eyes screwed up momentarily and he let out a wail of dismay, scrambling away from me. "What did you do to my familiar? Is this some sort of demon trick? Let me invoke!"

I chuckled. "Having a problem? It probably hates you. I know I do. Does Ash know you take orders from Grey, angel-lover?"

"How dare you! Stay away from me! The Councilor will have you punished for hurting me." The caster huddled miserably in the corner.

I rolled my eyes. I was too tired for this shit. "He doesn't care about you, little suck-up. He left you in here, with me."

Footsteps in the hall turned out to be Ewan and some other guardian. *How many of us has Grey roped into this?*

He frowned at the witch trying to hide from me. "All right, Blackthorn. The Arcaenum is meeting, so come along like a good boy."

"Or else what? Your buddy here is tapped out."

"I don't know, *Constantine*, but The Councilor's got your spell caster. It's not too hard to imagine what kind of security threat she poses, and what he might have to do to stop her from letting you go free."

My rage was doused with cold terror.

I suddenly found myself feeling very cooperative.

Chapter 18

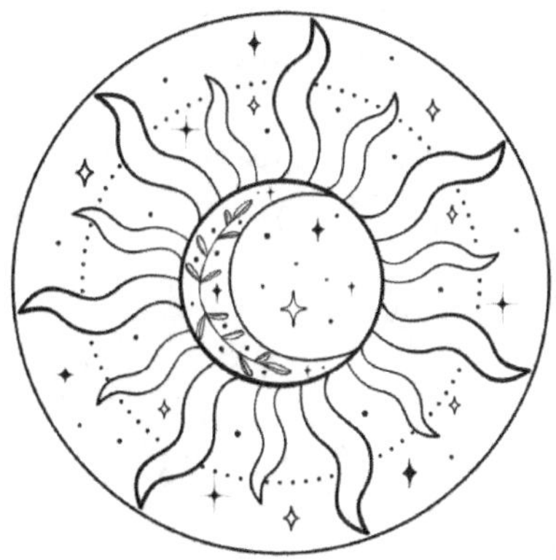

A firm knock on the door had me hiding my phone under a pillow. I sat up straight and quickly smoothed out my hair, thinking it would be Daire with my mother.

Without waiting for me to answer, Calamus strode in. His red spell caster robes swished around him as he crossed the room to where I was sitting on the bed.

"What do you want, Calamus?" My voice came out more snappish than I'd expected.

The spell caster blinked in genuine shock as if he hadn't just turned Costi in to his meddling dad and then gotten me locked up in a room. "I came to see how you're doing," he said.

"How I'm *doing*? How do you *think* I'm doing?"

"There's no need to take things out on me, Layla," Calamus said acerbically.

There was *every* need to take things out on him, but I decided to be the bigger person. "Yes, well, as you can see, I'm still being detained, and I'm upset. Can I help you with anything else?"

Calamus sighed and sat on the bed next to me. "I'm sorry you're upset."

He was sorry because I was *upset*. That was *it*?

"Let me make things better for you," he said.

"How?"

He placed one cold hand over mine on the bedspread. "If we got engaged…"

My body reacted viscerally before my mind could catch up, and I snatched my hand away, feeling acid hit my throat. Emotions warred for dominance—shock, disgust, confusion, anger. "How… how could you think—"

Calamus gave a wry smile. "I realize it's sudden, but is it so unexpected? You need this—need *me*. We have a good regard. We can grow to love each other."

I choked. "I don't think so."

He frowned. "I've been nothing but nice to you."

"That's not…"

He cleared his throat. "I'll be frank with you. You're the most beautiful woman I've ever seen, but there aren't a lot of spell casters our age, and you're not likely to make a match with all of these problems. The Arcaenum is on the verge of declaring you Troubled. I'm willing to help you. To protect you. If you'll just let me."

It was so ugly, the shame that rose in me. Was that how he saw me—a consolation prize and a problem to be solved? Was that all I was worth?

Calamus leaned in, taking my numb hand in his with a small smile. "We'll be good together, Layla."

It didn't matter. I was so tired of trying to earn approval from people who didn't care about me. Let them revile me.

I drew in a shaking breath, pulling my hand away. "We won't be anything together. Ever."

I expected cold rage, but Calamus hesitated. "This is because of Blackthorn. I have eyes, Layla."

"It's because you aren't listening to a single thing I tell you," I said tersely.

"I know you're… attached to him, but surely you can see now that he tricked you. We can find a way to unbind you. You can summon a new familiar, a normal one."

Unbind? A knife slicing through my chest wouldn't have been as painful. I hadn't had time to consider the bond between Costi and me, but my heart told me it was precious. "N-No. No, I can't do that. Where would he end up? In Hell? Or *worse*—"

"Him parasitizing you like this isn't right. When you unbind, he'll go back where he came from. Where he should be. You have to admit, he doesn't belong here."

"He *does* belong here. He belongs with *me*," I said, wrapping my arms around myself.

Dark emotion bled into Calamus's usually even voice. "Fate, Layla, it's unnatural. Even if he wasn't a *demon*, he's a guardian. He can't *have* you."

I tilted my head up at him and looked him in the eye. "And you think you can?"

He sighed softly, standing. "You're upset right now, and you're not thinking straight. Consider what I'm offering." He left in a wash of red, closing the door with infuriating restraint. The lock clicked into place.

I wished I was the kind of woman who would yell after him or break something, but a lifetime of being a good little witch and pushing down negative feelings left me with only numb confusion. I pulled out my phone, but the battery was drained. My hand clutched uselessly at the coverlet.

Another knock came at the door, and Daire strode through. "Layla? The Arcaenum is meeting after all," she said. "I don't know how they found out about—" She stopped, glancing down at my hand. I shoved my dead phone behind my back guiltily. Daire grunted. "You've got ten minutes."

I took the world's fastest shower and swished with mouthwash, nervous energy pinging through my body. Diana Blackthorn had come through and alerted the councilors. A tiny bud of hope blossomed.

I looked as good as I could manage and was calm when Daire returned. Cedar Grey wouldn't be able to keep secrets this time. I was about to tell the Arcaenum *everything.*

* * *

"You mean to tell me—"

"I don't *mean* to tell you *anything.* I *am* telling you—"

"I should have expected someone like *you* to be aggressive—"

The sounds of muffled shouting became louder when Daire opened the door to the meeting hall. Heads turned. We'd walked into the middle of an argument.

My eyes sought Costi immediately, and my heart resumed beating when I found him. He looked worn, and his uniform was damaged. He straightened when he saw me. The two other guardians had a firm grip on his arms, but he wasn't the one fighting.

"As if we needed more problems," one of the councilors spat. I had seen her at the previous meeting—Linnea. She was toe to toe with an angry-looking Artemesia Rhodes. The elderly ex-guardian was small but determined next to her.

Costi's friend and fellow guardian Ash was leaning against the wall nearby with Diana Blackthorn.

Calamus was watching me with an unreadable expression from where he stood next to his father. *He* was impeccably dressed and looking fresh despite the late hour. I guessed the failed marriage proposal wasn't weighing on him.

Councilor Grey didn't look nearly as worried as I thought he should be, and that was… concerning.

The rest of the Arcaenum was gathered, their faces in various states of alarm and careful neutrality. My mother perched elegantly on a metal folding chair at the center of it all. She didn't bother to greet me.

Great, the gang's all here.

Councilor Quince, the assembly leader, dragged a hand down his face as Daire escorted me to a chair. "If everyone could take a seat, we'll try to figure out exactly what is going on here," he said.

"This is a waste of time. I suggest we adjourn," Grey said smoothly. "This is an argument between individuals. We needn't involve a formal meeting. It's late, and I remind everyone that we're all very busy and under threat of imminent attack."

Councilor Rhodes thumped her carved walking stick on the floor to draw attention. "It was I who called this meeting, and I insist that we proceed. It is far more than a personal argument."

Quince looked to Grey, who said, "Very well."

Rhodes straightened, using her stick for balance. Her white hair puffed out around her head like smoke. "I called this emergency meeting because I received an unexpected visitor." She stared down the councilors like she was scolding them. "Diana Blackthorn, a clothing maker and foster mother to the guardian Constantine Blackthorn." Rhodes indicated the younger woman, who was standing against the wall. "As I mentioned before we began, our conversation revealed some… very strange and convoluted reports, some of which implicate members of the Arcaenum."

Grey's face remained impassive, but Quince seemed like he was about to be sick, a flush darkening his skin. "We're far too busy for some seamstress's strange reports. We have refugees to deal with—"

No way was I letting the Council out of here without hearing the truth and fixing this. I opened my mouth to tell them what Councilor Grey was hiding—

"She told us, among other things," Rhodes interrupted, "that her foster son and Layla Rosen were being detained unlawfully and without the Arcaenum's knowledge."

Daire sat up straight next to me. "Now you just hold on. It's my job to keep the guardians in line."

"It's *not* your job to lock up our spell casters," Rhodes countered.

"The… nature of the complaint was…" Daire floundered, turning to Cedar Grey and Calamus.

Councilor Grey stood and smoothed his beard. "What Daire is trying to say is that it was discovered that Constantine Blackthorn is a traitor."

The room went silent.

"I already told you I'm not a spy, you—" Costi broke off with a choked sound, grimacing in pain as if the only thing keeping him upright were the two guardians holding on to him.

"Costi!" I was dashing toward him before I knew what I was doing. When I took his face in my hands, his skin was clammy and feverish. "You *are* hurt! Oh fate, you're *burned*!" Up close, I could see that the marks I had noticed were the charred edges of his uniform. An angry, untreated wound marred the skin of his chest.

I spun to face Grey. "What did you do to him?"

"This young spell caster is determined to think the worst of me." Grey's voice lifted to the assembly. "I didn't touch Blackthorn."

Behind me, Costi huffed out a bitter laugh.

"I hope you have some evidence for the serious claims you are making, Councilor," Rhodes said to Grey. "In the meantime, this young witch needs medical assistance."

"Therein lies the problem. He's not a *witch* at all," Grey declared, raising his voice to address the room. *He's admitting his secrets?* No, he was taking control, preparing to twist the story to his own advantage. Just like Costi had surmised. "This is a demon who escaped from Hell by bonding to Layla Rosen as a familiar."

Whatever the councilors were expecting, it wasn't that. Their expressions ranged from confused to amused. Daire looked embarrassed, rubbing the back of her neck. Rhodes frowned seriously—she must have already heard part of this from Diana.

"I knew that boy was trouble," my mother said, her face alight with vindication.

Councilor Linnea chuckled, breaking the tension. "A bit tall for a demon, isn't he?"

"Tell them about the other demon," I said loudly. If we were doing this, the *whole* truth was coming out.

The scattering of nervous laughter halted.

Councilor Grey's eyes glittered with anger, and I fought the urge to shrink away. "As Layla was so kind to bring up, we've made a startling discovery. After no communication from our *allies* for generations, my son was able to make contact with Hell. We have discovered it is a prison, ruled by a monarchy of demons who look quite similar to humans."

The councilors looked back and forth between one another, whispering. I regarded Cedar Grey cautiously. He had accused Costi of being a spy, but it seemed he'd been doing some spying of his own.

Ash crept near me and pushed something into my hand—two pills that looked like pain relievers. I locked eyes with the beautiful guardian and nodded my thanks. Costi was still being restrained but let me give him the medicine without complaint and swallowed it dry. I had to get him out of here soon.

Rhodes said, "And you think Constantine Blackthorn is one of these demons. That he somehow made himself Layla's familiar."

"He is," Calamus interrupted. "Both a demon and her familiar. I witnessed his transformation, and Layla was able to invoke him."

My body flashed hot with anger. Calamus Grey had some nerve to think he'd ever be able to call himself my friend, let alone my spouse. He was so full of himself, so ready to throw anyone off a cliff. Telling on us to his dad and the Arcaenum like a child.

"Councilor Grey and his son are hiding things," I said. *Two can play tattletale.* "Calamus did a circle spell that created a permanent video call to Hell, and then The Councilor threatened me not to tell anyone about it."

"You're being very dramatic," Cedar Grey spoke up before anyone else had the chance. "I asked you to keep the circle spell to yourself until we had a chance to investigate it. That kind of announcement shouldn't be done in a panic."

"It's been weeks! You weren't going to tell the Arcaenum!"

Quince held up his hands in what was supposed to be a calming gesture. "Let's settle down a bit. Some of the councilors did know about this, but we've all been occupied with other important matters."

"What would it serve me to keep this kind of knowledge to myself?" Grey spread his hands out widely. "I apologize to the Arcaenum for not bringing this forward more quickly."

Councilor Rhodes had retaken her seat, looking fatigued. "You blocked my agenda item at the last meeting. And now I hear you're representing us to our allies. That's a matter for the full Arcaenum."

"What about the demons? What do they want? You said there's a *monarchy.* Are they lost to Inperium?" Linnea's eyes looked wide and serious.

"Our familiars are loyal," Daire said. "The spell casters have had nothing but cooperation from what I've seen."

"That is what I've been trying to ascertain." Councilor Grey clasped his hands behind his back. "The presence of one of them in our realm raises the odds that they're playing both sides somehow."

"Would you stop with that? Costi isn't a *spy*. He's been with Northern Sea since he was little." The frustration in my voice probably wasn't helping my case.

"But he is… what they say he is?" Rhodes's ancient blue eyes flickered with something sad. Pity, maybe. "You haven't denied that."

My ears rang. "Yes," I admitted, barely hearing myself.

All the attention in the room was now focused on Costi and me.

"This is some sort of trick," Daire said. "A mistake, maybe. The Northern Sea guardians have known this witch his whole life."

"Show them," Costi murmured.

"What?" I turned to face him. "No! You're barely upright," I hissed.

The corner of his lips turned up a tiny fraction. He murmured for my ears only, "I'm fine, baby. Sick and tired of all these secrets. Give these bastards a show."

This was a gamble. There was a world of difference between them hearing about something and seeing it with their own eyes. But if they could accept that this was a natural summoning and beyond our control, they might be sympathetic. If we showed them, there would be no turning back.

"Are you sure?"

With a grim nod from Costi, I… *banished* him. My stomach swooped in fear as he disappeared.

The guardians who'd been holding him jumped back in surprise. Gasps punctuated the small blip in reality, and a shocked chatter rose from the assembled witches. Quince surged forward and ran his hand through the space where Costi had been.

My body trembled, and I tried to slow my breathing and remember how to call him back.

Oh fate, what if I can't do it?

I stumbled through the internal invocation sequence and felt it catch. Barely a moment later, Costi reappeared beside me. He looked as human as ever.

"Trippy as fuck," he declared, then slumped over me heavily with a grunt. Why did this man, twice my size, keep thinking I could hold him up when he was injured? The two guardians grabbed him and pulled him upright again before we collapsed into a heap.

"How is this possible?" Rhodes's voice was like thunder.

"It was a natural summoning," I said faintly. "I was three, he was seven. We don't remember what happened. They found him playing with me and assumed he was a survivor of the attack in Greece. But I must have… pulled him out of wherever he was before. No one thought he wasn't an ordinary kid. Neither of us had any idea until now."

"Layla's magical ability has always been advanced, even as a child," my mother chimed in. She was looking at Costi and me speculatively. "It makes sense that she attracted a more powerful familiar than usual."

Something so obvious dawned on me that I barked out a laugh, drawing confused gazes. Costi *was* my familiar. It wasn't just some kind of strange bond, we were… *functional*. We had cast a spell the night Northern Sea was attacked. A *huge* spell.

"You weren't aware of what you are? You don't remember your life before coming here?" Rhodes addressed Costi.

"I remember some," he rumbled, glancing down. "Didn't seem like anything strange."

"This story is very convenient," Cedar Grey said. "Even if it is true, we can't be sure where his sympathies lie. With us or… his people."

Costi scoffed. "What *people*? I was raised by witches. I'm a witch. A guardian." He looked directly at me. "My loyalty is here."

"I'd like to remind everyone that Hell is our ally. Unless Councilor Grey's recent discoveries have turned up anything to the contrary, I'm inclined to take their demons fighting beside our spell casters as continued cooperation on their part," Rhodes said.

"It doesn't matter anyway," I said with a tight grin that was probably horrifying. I finally had a sword in this fight, and I intended to use it. "You need us."

Costi's mouth popped open beside me. He'd just figured out the same thing I had. "Son of a—" he said in a low growl. "How'd we do it, though?"

"I'm sorry to interrupt your private conversation," Cedar Grey said snidely. "Is it anything you'd like to share with the rest of us?"

I smiled. "We killed half a dozen angels with one spell and saved the Northern Sea Circle from destruction."

Grey's eyes narrowed angrily. "Is that a threat?"

"The threat is to the angels if they try to attack the Mountain Circle," I shot back. "We're on your side." Maybe not *his* side, but the witches' side. "I'm taking Costi to the infirmary," I said with finality.

Ash strode forward and locked eyes with me as we came to a silent agreement. The two of us wrestled Costi away from the guardians.

"You're just… okay with all this?" he said to Ash, who hooked their shoulder under his arm and hoisted him upright.

Ash scoffed. "Don't be foolish. This isn't even the weirdest thing about you."

Chapter 19

LAYLA

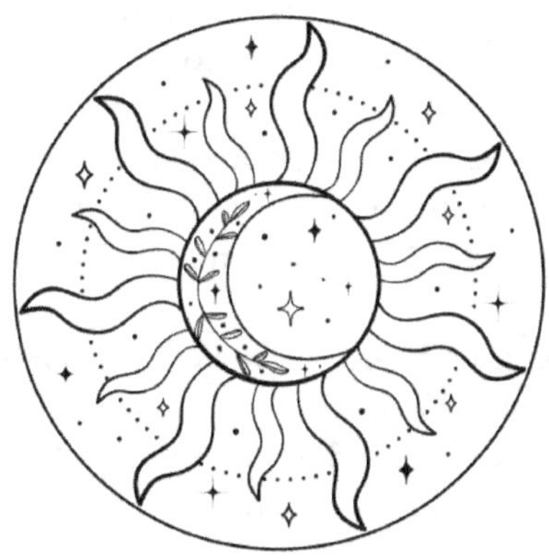

The Mountain Circle medical center was swathed in white and blue. A light sheet separating the beds fluttered in the fall breeze from an open window, late-afternoon sun turning the light golden. It should have been comforting and relaxing, but I was strung tight.

I perched on the edge of a wooden chair, watching over Costi as he slept off a high fever. The medical staff had treated and bandaged the burn wound on his chest, gotten him started on antibiotics, and hooked him up to an IV for hydration. Already, his normal color was returning. I'd tucked a blanket over him, and his rest looked peaceful.

It was the opposite of how I felt.

When the nurse had asked what caused his injury, he told them—a *spell caster*. Casters could incinerate an angel with one shot. Grey could have *killed* him with a stunt like that if the caster wasn't precise. I was livid, demanding to know why he didn't tell the Arcaenum that Grey had not only *commanded* a caster to hurt a guardian, but that they had gone through with it.

Costi's only reply was "He threatened you."

Cedar Grey was using our friendship to try to control us. He was up to something, and I was going to find out what it was.

"You look ready to end someone," Costi said. His stormy gray eyes were watching me, black hair a delicious mess. "I kinda like it."

I wanted to say something playful back, but I couldn't get past the question pooled miserably on my tongue. "What are we supposed to do?"

He turned his head, looking up toward the ceiling. "No idea," he said. "This is so fucked up. Layla, what *am* I?"

My heart twisted with the desolation in his voice. "You're Costi," I said, swallowing back tears.

He closed his eyes. "They're gonna make me leave."

"No. I won't *let* them. Besides, they *need* us."

He shook his head. "Grey will make sure I'm gone to save his own ass."

"Then I'm going with you." I twisted my hands together, fighting the need to reach out to him.

"I'd get you out of here. I don't give a fuck about the Arcaenum or what they want. But…" His throat bobbed. When he spoke again, his voice scraped out of his throat. "What if I'm… something dangerous? What if I hurt you?"

I bristled. "Constantine Blackthorn! I've known you my whole life, and that's the most *ridiculous* thing I've ever heard you say."

He turned back to me then, his gaze shining with something complicated.

Booted footsteps alerted us to someone approaching.

"We're not done," I told Costi.

"Oh good, you're both in here. Saves me some time," Daire said, appearing at the gap in the curtain. The security coordinator wore the uniform of the guardians, her silver-streaked hair pulled back in a neat bun as usual.

I pushed my chair back, ready to defend Costi. He'd worked hard to become a guardian, and I wasn't about to let Daire kick him out for something that wasn't his fault.

She glanced behind her. Another set of footsteps approached, this one with a marked thump between each step.

"Councilor Rhodes!" I started to pull the wooden chair around for the elderly witch to have a seat, but she waved me off, leaning on her walking stick with both hands.

"The Arcaenum adjourned just an hour ago," she said, looking exhausted. "That meeting was *far* too long."

I cringed. "I'm so sorry."

"We did learn some interesting things," Rhodes said. She didn't seem inclined to elaborate.

"And me?" Costi's voice was a rasp.

Daire cleared her throat. "One week medical leave. If you could quit getting injured, Blackthorn, I'd really appreciate it. You get more days off than days on. If I didn't need every team I can get right now, I'd have them throw you out of the Circle for your antics."

I blinked.

"I want you on rotation with Rosen as soon as possible. Are you going to need a second guardian while you cast? Because we're already short."

"I got her," Costi said without skipping a beat. "I can do both."

My heart panged with emotion.

"Weirdest damn thing I've ever heard of," Daire muttered as she left.

That makes two of us.

"It looks like everything is all settled." Councilor Rhodes gave us a rare smile, her face crinkling.

Everything was… *settled*? What exactly—

"It would be very helpful," the elder witch said with a twinkle in her eye, "if you two could figure out how to cast spells."

* * *

Layla and Costi's story continues in The Demon Familiar!
Get it at: mybook.to/demon-familiar

Also by Tamsin Hawthorn

Spell Caster's Familiar Series
The Spell Caster
The Demon Familiar
The Angel Siege

Inperium War Novella
The Captive Dreamer (March, 2026)

Regency Romantasy
Court of Fiends (June, 2026)

Short Stories
A Ghostly Canticle (Paranormal Playground Anthology)

Acknowledgments

Thank you for reading, your support means the world to me!

My eternal gratitude goes to my husband—you are the catalyst that makes my magic work.

Thank you, Shanna and Stephen, my best friends in this life (listed in order by meeting date). You have been waiting patiently for years, wondering when I would finally publish something. I hope you won't read this book, but if you do, I hope you hate it so I can tell you I told you so.

A special thanks to my beta readers! Without your enthusiasm, I would never have published this book. Amber, Brittany, Soren Storm, Caitlin Regencia, Ashley G, Ellie, Beth Throlson, KatalystV2, Roxanne GL, Emma, B Isobel, Avery Bridge, and other anonymous readers.

Thank you to Mandy at Hot Tree Editing for final-eyes reading.

Glossary

Angel: A vicious harpy-like winged creature, looking like a monstrous human with talons. Angels tend to infest abandoned buildings in remote locations and will start to menace the local human population if they become too numerous. They are impossible to kill, except by a spell caster.

Arcaenum: The elected council of the Mountain Circle, responsible for organizing the witches to make collective decisions.

Circle: A witch community, hidden from the modern world.

Circle Spell or Circlework: A witch spell created by drawing a circle of magic symbols from a diagram and infusing it with magic. This process can take hours.

Circlewright: A witch who can use magic through circle spells, without the need for a demon familiar.

Delegate: A witch nominated by an elected member of the Arcaenum to serve as an expert who advises the councilmembers in an area of special interest.

Demon Familiar: A spell caster's ally from Hell that enables them to cast magic with their hands.

Guardian: A witch who is trained to defend spell casters in a fight, often one of the Troubled.

Inperium: The rigid Angelic system of hierarchy that arbitrarily assigns rulers and followers. In witch mythology, the angels enforced this hierarchy aggressively.

Spell Caster: A powerful witch able to pull enough magic to summon a familiar. They are then able to cast, using their hands to fling magical energy.

Troubled: Witches who are considered violent or antisocial.

Witch: A human capable of sensing, and possibly using, magic.

About the Author

Tamsin Hawthorn is an author of swoony paranormal and fantasy romance living in the marshlands of coastal South Carolina. She spins stories about magic and perseverance in the face of impossible odds. Her favorite trope is star-crossed love.

When not writing, Tamsin can be found outside or hiding in bed with an e-reader glued to her face.

Sign up for Tamsin's newsletter, the Hawthorn Branch, on her website at www.tamsinhawthorn.com/newsletter for sneak peeks at upcoming releases, or join her on Instagram @authortamsinhawthorn.